8/22

D0880914

WHITECAPS

Captain Danny Wadsworth

Captain Danny Wadsworth

Sterling House Publishing
Pittsburgh, PA

Sterling House Fiction Paperback
1-56315-048-4

© 1997 Captain Danny Wadsworth
All rights reserved
First Printing—1997

Cover design & typesetting: Drawing Board Studios
Request for information should be addressed to:

Sterling House Publishers
The Sterling Building
440 Friday Road
Department T-101
Pittsburgh, PA 15209

Printed in the United States of America

Acknowledgments

Thanks to my friend Barbara Nannery who encouraged me to put these ideas in book form and for her assistance in editing. Special appreciation goes to my wife, Marsha, for her invaluable assistance, patience, and for allowing me to go fishing so often.

Dedicated to the memory of
Captain Sidney Hilton,
who sparked my interest in
deep-sea fishing.
It's a 'crying shame' he left so soon.

The wooden hull of the 'Lady B' glided gently across the mirror calm surface of the deep blue water. The commercial fishing boat was forty miles from shore and seemed to have the whole ocean to itself. No other vessels were in sight except for a southbound freighter in the distance, making its way down the Carolina coastline. Being early March, the recreational and charter fishing season had not yet started. Only the commercial guys were out, and most of them were fishing for king mackerel farther south, below Diamond Shoals Light. Gene Davis, captain of the 'Lady B', wanted to test the waters a little closer to Nags Head. Instead of running south to Hatteras like the others, he had held a more easterly heading and intersected the Gulf Stream at one of his favorite ledges, hoping to find tuna there. It would save him from having to make another two-day trip south. The overnight fishing trips were hindering his social life. Since returning from Vietnam, and starting his own commercial fishing business, the ex-Marine had rekindled an old high school romance with Barbara Ethridge and was considering marriage.

The boat's old diesel engine purred steadily. Most of her 47-foot length was open deck to accommodate nets, long-lines and other gear. But today, Captain Gene was using the fishing method he was raised on . . . trolling for tuna the way he had done hundreds of times, working as mate on his father's charter boat.

He slapped the old ship-to-shore radio which was hanging from the ceiling of his cluttered cabin. Whistling into the microphone, he said, "Hey . . . Ray! Ray Crabbe on the 'Southern Belle', you still on this channel? Come back to 'Lady B'." Gene was trying to contact the captain of the other boat who left Wanchese the same time he did that morning. Hearing no reply, he adjusted the squelch and slapped it again, "Damn it!" Gene had reason to be aggravated. He had picked the radio up from the repair shop yesterday, paying ninety-three dollars to have it fixed.

His mate and friend, Stormy Pruitt, came running forward to the small wheel house, pointing off their starboard beam, "About two hundred yards, under those birds! I know it was tuna I saw busting that time!" The captain brought the boat about, but again the fish disappeared before they could get to them.

"Were you able to contact Ray on the radio?" Stormy asked.

"Hell, no, this piece of shit is acting squirrelly again."

"I'll bet those guys down south are smokin' 'em. These fish up here must have lockjaw. If you asked me, I'd say let's steam on down there."

"Well, I didn't ask you. Beside's, my daddy taught me to never leave fish to look for fish. We know they're here. We just gotta wait 'em out, that's all." A wave slapped against the hull sending salty spray across the windshield.

"A breeze is making up," said Stormy looking across the expanse of ocean which was becoming choppy.

"That ought to help us," replied Gene, "my daddy says it's easier to fool the fish when there are whitecaps on the water."

"I swear, Gene, you wouldn't know shit about fishing if it weren't for Cap'n Willie. . . my daddy this and my daddy that!"

All of a sudden, two of their reels started singing. As line was being stripped away, they knew instantly it was tuna. "Must be dinner time!" Gene grinned at Stormy, who ran for the arching rods. Then another, and yet a fourth line was hooked up! Gene turned the rudder slightly and engaged the trolling valve to keep the boat creeping ahead in lazy circles. He hurried back to help Stormy bring in the fish. They had a whole school of hungry yellowfin tuna all to themselves. By sunset they had filled the box with fish averaging twenty-five pounds each, but decided to continue as long as fish were biting. There was plenty of light under the rising full moon. Before long, tuna were stacked on the deck like cordwood. The two men were becoming exhausted, but were excited about all the money they would make. The market for tuna was high. All the while they fished, the wind grew stronger and before long the sea was ugly. So, they took up their lines and started for home.

They both knew the 'Lady B' was overloaded, from the way she wallowed between the swells. At times, Gene could hardly stay in his chair. Stormy sat on the floor of the small cabin, bracing his feet against the bulkhead. The compass was swinging wildly as the old boat was being pounded by waves coming from three directions. It was a struggle for Gene to hold her on a steady course. It seemed they could hear the boat's aging joints groan in pain. Stormy was not one to scare easily, but he quickly donned a life jacket and tossed one to Gene, who said, "That's not gonna do you much good. If something happened out here, you'd die of hypothermia in less than an hour."

"Well, at least I'd live an hour longer than you," retorted the crusty mate.

When they caught a glimpse of Bodie Island Lighthouse, they were still a long way out. Gene found his radio was working on low power and got through to the Coast Guard. They told him the warning flag had been raised at Oregon Inlet and advised him to consider going south to Hatteras instead, but Gene was determined to make it to his home port. Once he made his mind up to do something, it was hard to make him change.

As the 'Lady B' drew closer to the inlet, facing a solid wall of breakers, the two fishermen realized trouble loomed ahead. A strong ebb current was pushing hard against the nor'east wind creating high rollers . . . the kind that can move old shoals and form new ones. Gene had traveled through Oregon Inlet all his life, and knew the bar was subject to shift under these conditions. He should have turned the 'Lady B' around and waited for flood tide to carry them safely through. No one will ever know why he didn't. Perhaps it was his strong desire to get home. On the way in, he had told Stormy he had made up his mind to ask Barbara to marry him.

The captain shouted, "Stormy, we're too heavy! We're gonna hit bottom if we don't lighten the load!" The mate wasted no time chunking over the tuna as fast as he could. He heard Gene tell the Coast Guard they were coming through. About that time, the 'Lady B' fell off the steep face of a fifteen-foot wave and struck a sand bar, hard! Stormy felt the planks twisting and cracking beneath his feet. The remaining fish slid across the deck to the port side, spinning the boat around like a top. White water crashed through the windshield knocking Gene out of his chair. Stormy was swept overboard! Seconds later, his life jacket lifted him to the crest of a wave. He could see the 'Lady B's propeller and red copper bottom paint . . . the old gal had capsized. He did not see any sign of his captain.

Stormy survived the chilly waters for two hours before the changing tide washed him ashore on the northern tip of Hatteras Island. He trudged across the sandy dunes to the Coast Guard station where he learned they had been earnestly searching for them. The 'Lady B' had come to rest on the shoal and was being pounded apart by the savage surf.

Planks from her wreckage washed ashore for months after that fateful night. Captain Gene Davis' body was never recovered. His brokenhearted mother wrote a poem in his memory. She called it "Whitecaps".

> The sea is like a person,
> emotions can run high.
> Whitecaps upon an angry sea,
> waved my darling son goodbye.
>
> The storm that brought his whitecaps,
> held secrets 'neath the foam.
> What started as a gentle breeze,
> was calling his soul home.
> We all encounter whitecaps,
> but the sea of life goes on.
> It's when our way gets choppy,
> that we cherish days becalm.

TWENTY-ONE YEARS LATER

A trio of playful dolphin greeted the morning's first charter boat as it approached the edge of the Gulf Stream. The sea was teeming with life, thrilling the six anglers who had booked the 'Grand Slam' for a day of deep-sea fishing. An occasional flying fish skimmed across the water while overhead, sea gulls circled and dove in search of their morning meal. One of the anglers spotted a giant stingray with a ten-foot wingspan prowling inches below the surface. Moments later, another passenger . . . a pretty young woman, who was wearing a purple and gold college sweatshirt with an embroidered pirate, pointed thirty yards off their starboard beam and shouted, "There's a shark!" Watching the ominous dorsal fin slice through the water, she said, "It's like another world out here."

Placing his arm around her shoulder, her boyfriend, who was wearing a seasickness patch behind his ear, added, "I never imagined the Atlantic Ocean could be so calm."

"You folks sure picked a nice day," commented Captain Sid to the couple riding beside him on the flying bridge. "It's not often we get such a smooth ride this time of year." An hour earlier, when the first golden rays of sunlight emerged from the endless horizon, it became evident the sun gods would smile on them today. Having been first to depart the dock this morning, Sid's sleek sportfishing boat was cutting a path across the shimmering sea for the fleet to follow. Except for the gentle ocean swell, the only turbulence was the foamy v-shaped wake left behind them, which attested his course was straight as an arrow.

"Here's the color change," Sid said as they crossed a tide-line, identified by a narrow band of drifting sargassum weed. The ocean changed tone abruptly from aquamarine to vivid blue. "Did you notice a few minutes ago we were in 68 degree waters?" Sid said while pointing to a gauge in the instrument panel. "It jumped to 75 when we crossed into blue water."

Thirty-nine year old Captain Sidney Hilton, a towering, mild-mannered man with dark hair and hazel eyes, had navigated to the

5

edge of the continental shelf about forty miles southeast of Oregon Inlet on North Carolina's Outer Banks. Identified on the nautical chart as *The Point*, it's known to be one of the hottest spots for big game fishing on the east coast. The topography of the ocean floor, about three hundred feet below, is rugged lumps and gullies dropping off steeply to well over a mile deep just a little farther to the east. Several oceanic currents converge at *The Point*, often bringing great congregations of squid and fishes. Sometimes massive schools of tiny baitfish are suspended in the water column like cumulus clouds in the sky. Swimming fin to fin they somehow know, by nature's design, there is safety in numbers.

Most of the other boats stopped to troll along the weed line Sid's boat crossed a few minutes earlier. Through the small speaker on the 'Grand Slam's' marine radio, Captain Paul Edwards on the 'Ranger' could be heard calling his dock neighbor, Captain Stormy Pruitt on the 'Bushwhacker', "Come on over here Stormy, we just got ambushed by gaffers. Looks like there's enough for both of us."

Paul was referring to dolphin, a popular game and food fish known as mahi mahi on many restaurant menus. He called them *gaffers* because the fish in this school weighed ten pounds or more, requiring the use of a gaff to lift them into the boat. As Paul talked, cheers in the background demonstrated how thrilling it was to see these aggressive fish in action. Indeed it was an ambush. Darting from beneath the cover of flotsam they attacked the baits from the side. Once hooked, the dolphin would flip and dance atop the water. Sometimes their spectacular aerobatics resulted in their freedom.

Ordinarily, Sid would have stopped to fish on the color change as well, but today's party had asked him to target tuna. Knowing he could always go back to the tide-line later if he had no luck out here, Sid had run a few miles beyond the fleet to one of his favorite deep holes where there had been a good tuna bite yesterday. Captain Sid pointed out a glassy sheen caused by fish oil rising to the surface, evidence that predators were feeding on bait fish below. He slowed the 'Grand Slam' to trolling speed and dropped the outriggers into place while Tommy Wilson, his mate, put out a spread of eight baits to be trolled at the surface.

"Do you think there's tuna here, Captain?" asked a member of the party.

Over the drone of the diesel engines and the chatter on the marine radio, Sid answered, "There's something feeding down there for sure. Could be tuna, could be something else." Sid paused for a moment while he tossed over a teaser lure and adjusted it to ride on the face of the second wave behind the boat. Then he continued,

"Captain Paul Edwards saw a blue marlin out here yesterday big enough to swallow a fifty-pound tuna." Within minutes, Sid located a school of baitfish on his fathometer and said to Tommy, "Watch your baits, we just went over a good mark back there."

A sinewy young man in his late twenties, who usually had a cigarette hanging from his lips, Tommy seldom used sunscreen on his overly-tanned bare back. His full head of curly black hair was his most recognizable feature; that, and the dark-rimmed polarized sunglasses he wore which had leather blinders fashioned on the sides to block the glare. It seemed as if his entire wardrobe consisted of tattered cut off jeans and deck shoes so old and worn, they were molded into the shape of his feet. Even though Tommy was one of the most experienced mates on the dock, he was not particularly well-liked by many of his counterparts. Tommy could be argumentative; so, the other mates had little to do with him. Although his personality was often hostile toward other men, Tommy seemed to have a way with women. He had no difficulty finding female companionship, though usually no more than a one night stand. Sid had told Tommy numerous times if he were friendlier with the fishing parties, they would give him bigger tips. After all, tips accounted for the greater part of a mate's income.

Nevertheless, Tommy had another spat with a customer that morning. It started when they departed the dock. As Tommy took several frozen packages of ballyhoo from the freezer, a novice angler in the party picked up one to examine it. He was intrigued with the distinctive skull and crossbones logo on the vacuum sealed package which contained several of the slender, eight-inch long, needle-nose fish. He asked, "What's a ballyhoo?"

"Bait," Tommy replied tersely, never lifting his eyes from the leader he was tying. Unlike most other mates, he had little patience with inexperienced anglers who asked a lot of dumb questions. Tommy went about his duties hoping to avoid further inquisition, but there was no ignoring this guy. He was relentless . . . giving Tommy the third degree all the way out. "How fast are we going?" "How much fuel does the boat carry?" "What makes the water so blue?" "Why do boaters call the toilet the head?"

On this trip, Tommy was more tolerant than usual. Maybe he was trying not to lose his cool because there was a woman in the group, a good-looking blond, and he didn't want her to see his irritable side.

Once fishing lines were in the water, Tommy was all business. After all, he wanted to live up to his reputation and throw a limit of tuna on the dock that afternoon. He picked up several ballyhoo from the bait cooler and started removing their eyeballs. "Ooh, that's gross! Why are you taking out their eyes?", asked the inquisitive fella.

"The blindfolds keep falling off!" Tommy blurted his usual sarcastic answer to that particular inquiry. Noticing the others were genuinely interested, he explained truthfully, "It makes the bait swim better. If you don't remove 'em, the eyes will bulge out and cause it to swim funny."

"You never said exactly what a ballyhoo is," said the insistent angler.

Now annoyed, Tommy thought, this guy's gonna worry the shit out of me all day long. Dangling one of the ballyhoo by its tail in the guy's face, he teased, "It's a goddamned baby marlin! Man, give me a break! You've asked me fifty questions already!"

The scorned man was perplexed by Tommy's rude outburst. Trying to smooth things over, one of the other fishermen started laughing and said, "Tommy, don't mind my pal, Barney, he gets on my nerves at work sometimes, too."

Realizing how harsh his words must have sounded, Tommy apologized, "Sorry, Barney. I lost it there, man. I guess I'm a little testy today . . . didn't get much sleep last night." He fished a cigarette out of his pocket, flicked his Bic, then picked up a package of ballyhoo and said, "These are not baby marlin, Barney. Ballyhoo are caught in nets off the Florida Keys. They make excellent trolling baits, and you can bet every charter boat out here is dragging 'em."

"Marked another school of bait; tuna ought to be close by!" Sid announced from the bridge.

Tommy scanned the boat wake to make sure his spread looked good, then started rigging another bait while holding his cigarette with his lips. The anglers watched as he skillfully manipulated the ballyhoo onto a tuna hook, broke off its long nose, and with amazing quickness secured the fish's head to the leader with a small rubber band. To complete the presentation, he held up the line allowing a colorful sea witch lure to slide down over the ballyhoo's head.

The man who booked the party said, "You really know your stuff, Tommy. If I were a fish, I would bite it myself."

Tommy said, "I don't use hair on all my rigs," referring to the colorful nylon threads hanging like a skirt around the sea witch. As he held up another rig without a sea witch, he said, "At least half the baits I pull are natural, like this. We call this *fishing naked.*" Glancing toward the blond babe, who was descending from the bridge, Tommy remarked, "I don't know about the other boats, but sometimes I catch more . . . *fishing naked.*" While watching for her reaction to his suggestive comment, Tommy did not see the splash of their first strike.

Snap! One of the flat-line clips popped open and a fishing rod bent sharply. The gold-finished reel attached to it screamed rapid clicks as line peeled off the spool. Tommy shouted, "Fish on! Tuna on the flat-line!". He reached for the arching rod and bellowed to the party, "Get someone in the chair!"

There was so much pressure on the rod Tommy had to loosen the drag setting before he could manage to lift it out of the rod holder. "This is a hot fish!" Tommy shouted up to Captain Sid.

For an instant, Tommy wondered if it could be a blue marlin, even though they had not seen one in the baits. He gazed into the wake hoping a "big blue" would break the surface. Like every other mate in the fleet, Tommy wanted to get a shot at that monster marlin Captain Paul Edwards had seen yesterday.

There's an undercurrent of competitiveness among the professional mates at Pirate's Cove Yacht Club. To catch the first blue marlin of the year, especially one so large, would give Tommy bragging rights for the season. An awesome vision had stuck itself forever in his memory. It happened one day last fall when the biggest fish he had ever seen exploded out of the water only a few yards behind the transom. Tommy vividly remembered the way one of his favorite lures, a blue 'n white Hawaiian Eye, had been knocked up the leader line like a bullet when the powerful fish attacked the Spanish mackerel rigged behind it. On that particular day, following a two-hour struggle, the giant marlin was finally brought to the gaff, much to the relief of an exhausted angler. Once Tommy and Sid saw the subdued fish lying on the deck, they both speculated the twelve-foot marlin might be a "*grander*," weighing a thousand pounds or more, but the scales at Pirate's Cove stopped short . . . at 989 pounds.

Sid noticed Tommy was still gazing into the boat wake and called down to him, "Tommy, did you see something back there?"

"No, just wishful thinking."

When Tommy turned around to plant the rod butt into the gimbal on the fighting chair, all he could see were long tan legs and above them, cleavage! The blond babe was first in the chair. Tommy had hardly been able to take his eyes off her all morning as she moved about the boat. The sun's tanning rays combined with the warm Gulf Stream air had prompted her to shed her sweatshirt, revealing a hot pink bikini barely big enough to cover her ample breasts.

She laughed with excitement when she first gripped the fishing rod, but her expression quickly changed to surprise when she felt the strong tug of the powerful fish. Her boyfriend, who was standing by the chair, shouted up to the bridge, "Slow down, Captain! She can't turn him!"

Captain Sid vigilantly continued trolling at seven knots for several seconds longer, hoping to hook up with another tuna before altering his speed. The woman's muscular legs strained as she pushed her feet hard against the footrest on the fighting chair. With all her strength, she pulled the rod with her left arm and cranked the handle on the reel with her right, but the loud clicker persisted to cry as the fish robbed more line. During all this, Tommy was getting an eyeful. He just knew the clasp on the bombshell's skimpy bikini top would break any second under the strain of her heaving chest. Then, came another loud *Snap! ,* but to Tommy's disappointment, the sound was the other flat-line clip springing open. Instinctively, he yelled, "Fish on!"

Up on the bridge, Captain Sid jigged the shotgun line, the one farthest back, trying to attract another hungry tuna. He shouted, "Both short riggers are hooked up, Tommy!"

Then almost simultaneously . . . Wham! Wham! Wham! Three more hookups! Both long riggers and the shotgun were being stripped of line. It seemed the tuna had been waiting for someone to come out and feed them!

Finally, Captain Sid slowed the 'Grand Slam' to a crawl. He looked down into the cockpit and laughed with satisfaction at the sight of the anglers scrambling like they were in a Chinese fire drill. Even after his twenty-five years of professional fishing, the first fifteen working as a mate for Cap'n Willie, he still thrilled at moments like this. All six anglers were hooked up with yellowfin tuna in the 40 to 60 pound class.

When Sid keyed the microphone on his marine radio, the other captains recognized his familiar voice, "We are covered up with tuna down here on the five-hundred line," referring to his position on the loran plotter.

A fellow captain responded, "Pretty work, Sid, I figured you'd track 'em down for us."

Another captain spoke up, "Welcome back, Sid." It was Craig Brooks, one of the captains from the Oregon Inlet Fishing Center fleet, "I thought you were still in Mexico."

"Got back Monday, Craig. You'd better steam on over here and get some of these tuna before the boys from Pirate's Cove catch 'em all," Sid kidded.

"I don't expect that to be a problem. Those fellows are pretty good about abiding by the limit." Most captains on the Carolina coast practice a self-imposed limit of three tuna per fisherman which amounts to plenty of tasty table fare for everyone to take home.

It was an hour before sunrise on a cool Saturday morning in mid May. Twenty-one year old Bradley "Bull" Sullivan, III leaned against his Toyota pickup sipping on a hot cup of 7-11 coffee while watching captains and mates prepare the charter boats for the parties of optimistic fishermen who were already arriving at Pirate's Cove Yacht Club near Nags Head. He had heard the yellowfin tuna catch had been excellent yesterday.

This morning, Bull enjoyed a sense of freedom. For the first time in his life, he was on his own, free to follow his dreams. Bull couldn't help recalling his fondest childhood memory . . . the time he went with his dad and uncle on a deep sea fishing trip off Cape Hatteras. Cap'n Willie had located a school of dolphin under a drifting piece of plywood, and the aqua blue ocean was so clear dozens of brightly colored fish could be seen darting all around the boat.

To attract fish, the mate, a tall and friendly young man, threw over small chunks of the bonito Bull's uncle had caught earlier. Bull's dad hooked the first fish; instead of lifting it into the boat, the mate told him to leave the fish in the water as a decoy until someone got another one on. Sure enough, using this tactic for the next hour, the group bailed dolphin until their arms grew tired.

When the young Bull brought his first dolphin into the boat, he took a moment to admire its brilliant colors. The fins were radiant blue and green. The dolphin had a bluish head and back merging with golden yellow and dark flecks along its sides that reflected the sunlight. Sadly, the colors faded rapidly after the fish died.

Cap'n Willie kept track of the number of fish caught and told the anglers when they had reached the self-imposed limit of ten per person. Ten year old Bull glowed with pride because he had caught the biggest fish of the day, a thirty-six-pound *bull* dolphin for which he received a state citation certificate. That was the day young Bradley Sullivan picked up his nickname, "Bull," and caught sea fever.

Bull's thoughts were interrupted by the thundering sound of a pair of turbo-charged diesel engines roaring to life from one of the charter boats. What an impressive display, he thought, more than two dozen 50-footer's docked side-by-side at Pirate's Cove Yacht Club. Bull noticed lights being switched on in the condominiums across the harbor. Many private boat owners would also take advantage of today's calm weather. The offshore waters forecast called for southwest winds ten to fifteen miles per hour with waves less than three feet. Perfect conditions for cruising to blue water, although many seasoned captains insisted choppy seas with a few whitecaps made for better fishing.

Bull admired Captain Sid Hilton's world-class sport fishing boat, the famous 'Grand Slam', with her outriggers and antennas reaching skyward. The 54-footer, built by Ricky Scarborough boatworks at Wanchese, had distinctive Carolina lines and a proud flared bow. On the seat of Bull's pickup lay a recent issue of a saltwater fishing magazine featuring an article about Sid Hilton, one of the top captains in the fleet. The article told about his running from Carolina all the way to Cancun, Mexico, where Sid booked sailfishing parties in March, April and early May.

Bull had seen the 'Grand Slam' refueling at a marina in Fort Lauderdale last winter. He recollected seeing several 55-gallon drums cradled in the boat's cockpit and now realized they held the extra fuel needed for the Gulf of Mexico crossing. At the time, Bull thought to himself how much he would like to be making the trip with them. It was around the first of March, and Bull was in Fort Lauderdale with some of his college friends on spring break. They were staying at his parents' condominium. Ever since they bought the condo in Florida eight years ago, Bull's obsession with boating and fishing had increased. Every time the Sullivans vacationed there, which was usually two or three times a year, his father chartered a boat to take them fishing.

Now, on this fine Carolina morning, Bull watched Captain Sid climb to his bridge to turn on his running lights, radar, and check his spotlight. These are crucial accessories for charter boats getting underway before daylight. Even in predawn darkness, these seasoned helmsmen could run at full cruising speed through the narrow and tricky ten-mile channel to the inlet. The only slowing down was to accommodate other boat traffic or to make the elbow turn at Hell's Gate.

As Sid inspected the line on one of his two teaser reels, he noticed Bull in the parking lot leaning against his pickup and thought perhaps the young man was a member of his charter for today. They both heard the sound of tires suddenly skidding as a red Dodge pickup slid recklessly into an empty parking space. It was Captain Sid's mate, Tommy Wilson, arriving late. The magazine article Bull read also mentioned Tommy as one of the top mates in the business.

Tommy hopped out of the truck and ran toward the 'Grand Slam'. Bull was just out of earshot to hear their conversation, but it was evident the captain was none too happy. As the tardy mate stepped aboard, Sid reprimanded, "Tommy, you've got to get your act together." The tone Sid used was not characteristic of his usual mild manner. "You used to be the first mate to get to the dock every morning. Now, most of the time, our parties arrive before you do! What's with you lately?"

"Chill out boss man, I don't see the party here yet." Tommy retorted.

Sid did not appreciate his insolence and continued to lecture, "What did you do? Stay out all night with those pot-head friends you've been hanging around with?"

"No, Cap'n, I've got a new girlfriend," Tommy answered. "Met her at the Raw Bar last night and ended up at her place. Didn't realize till this morning her cottage was all the way up at mile post three."

"I swear, Tommy," Sid said in a more kidding tone, "if you ever get a boat of your own, you ought'a name it 'Skirt Chaser'."

Tommy laughed, "That would be a good name, all right."

Sid said, "I've already loaded the ice. Check our bait situation. Might need to run up to the store and pick up a case of ballyhoo from Cap'n Willie."

"OK, I'll go up there in a minute. Do we have any Tylenol on board?" Tommy asked as he walked into the salon.

Sid got the final word, "If you're gonna be stupid, you gotta be tough. You can't expect to stay up partying all night and not have a headache the next morning."

Bull's attention had been diverted to several other boats, as their parties boarded. He looked on with envy as many of them started getting underway. This was the life he wanted. Walking to the end of the dock, he watched the fleet pass by. On the last boat to depart, the 'Lucky Duck', stood a young woman who caught his eye. Something about her looked familiar. Then, Bull recognized her. It was Kelly Edwards, from his biology class at college. He knew she was working on a degree in nursing. The first time Bull laid eyes on her as she entered his classroom last fall, she became the object of his desire. Kelly was a natural beauty, 5'8" tall with a lovely tan complexion, big brown eyes, arched eyebrows, and soft, flowing shoulder length auburn hair. Bull caught himself staring at her all during the instructor's lecture. At one point, their eyes met and she smiled. After class, he made it a point to introduce himself, but noticed she was wearing a wedding ring. After politely telling each other their names, Kelly said she must hurry to catch her ride. After he found out she was married, Bull considered Kelly off limits and had not tried to get to know her. Now that he knew they shared a common interest in offshore fishing, he wished he had talked with her more.

Bull noticed Kelly was wearing yellow oilskins like many of the mates had on. Then it dawned on him. She *was* a mate! It appeared she was giving the passengers instructions about where the life jackets were stowed. He observed Kelly's movements until the 'Lucky Duck' disappeared 'round the bend.

Silence fell upon the marina, except for the sound made by a flock of mallards landing in the nearby marsh. Bull looked toward the ship's store, noticed the dockmaster was checking the fuel pumps, and walked in that direction.

Following his unpopular decision to drop out of college, Bull had arrived at the Outer Banks only yesterday. No longer could he ignore the yearning that had drawn him to the sea. Since recovering from the surgery, his goal, his dream in life, was to captain his own world-class sportfishing boat, just like Sid Hilton. Bull knew before this could ever happen, he must first find a way to learn the ropes. He was hoping to find a captain willing to take him on as mate.

Bull was an athletically built, clean-cut, and handsome young man at 6' 1" with light brown hair and blue eyes. About three years ago, his life took a turn on the field of a high school football game. It had come down to the district championship between arch rivals, the Tar River Raiders and the Pike County Red Devils.

As quarterback, Bull had just used his team's last time-out, after completing a long pass into the end zone rallying them to within one point. The score was 21 to 20, with only seconds remaining on the game clock. Bull conferred with his coach. Would they go for the extra point to send the game into overtime; or, be gutsy and try for the two point conversion, which would clinch an undefeated season for the Raiders.

It was a tense moment. The kicker was pacing the sidelines, waiting for the coach to send him in. Up in the stands, Bull's parents, Brad and Diane Sullivan were surrounded by fans chanting, "Go, go, go, go . . . " Seated next to Mrs. Sullivan was a scout from Notre Dame. Scouts from Florida State and Michigan were already after their son. Bull was being called the next Joe Montana. He had made the All State team twice and had been mentioned by a well-known sports writer as having the makings of a Heisman Trophy candidate.

The home crowd cheered as Bull trotted onto the field and his team lined up in the shotgun formation. Bull had confidence his team could make this crucial play happen. "Twenty-five, sixty-four, hutt!" The pivotal play started to sour as the center's snap was low. Bull bobbled and nearly dropped the ball, but managed to hang on to it. He scrambled out of the pocket avoiding the rush. Seeing an open receiver, he drew back to fire a bullet into the end zone. Just as the pass was released . . . Wham! . . .Bull was blind sided by a 285-pound All-State tackle who was also intent on impressing the scouts. As Bull was driven into the turf, he heard the crowd cheer and knew the pass must have been completed. But, he also knew something was terribly wrong. While others cheered, Mrs. Sullivan had risen to her feet, screaming "Bradley!" A mother's intuition told her this was serious.

That play dashed the hopes of a young athlete to someday play pro football. Bull had suffered permanent damage to his rotator cuff and was forced to give up the sport he loved. He would never again throw a pass.

Bull was not your typical spoiled rich kid. In fact, to talk to him, you would never suspect he came from such a prestigious family. In Greenville, his father and mother were both doctors. His grandfather had help establish the medical school at East Carolina University.

With hope erased of ever playing professional football, Bull reluctantly did what his parents expected of him. Upon graduation, he enrolled in the pre-med curriculum at the same college they had attended. The Sullivans were counting on him to carry on the family tradition. Needless to say, they were very disappointed with his poor performance in medical school. Unfortunately, Bull had been unable to channel the energy he found for football into his studies. Although he was a star on the gridiron, as a college student, he was average at best. This was surprising since all through high school he had earned academic honors. Somehow, the sports injury had changed his outlook on things.

The only other sport Bull enjoyed nearly as much as football was fishing and boating. His father had introduced him to blue water at an early age. On his very first deep-sea trip, an ember had been sparked. And now the spark was maturing into a burning passion. He must find his future on the sea.

After much discussion, the Sullivans realized becoming a doctor was the last thing on their son's mind right now, and finally agreed to allow him a respite from his studies. They believed his obsession with becoming a boat captain would be short-lived. They made it clear, however, their financial support would be cut off if he did not return to college in the fall.

As Bull approached the ship's store, he thought about Kelly again. Maybe she knew of a captain who needed a mate.

Kelly was right at home on the 'Lucky Duck'. While her husband, Captain Jimmy Edwards, carefully guided the vessel through the inlet, she got acquainted with the members of today's fishing party and shared with them a bit of history about their boat.

"The hull of the 'Lucky Duck' was built thirty-five years ago by a legendary offshore fisherman who was also one of the Outer Bank's most capable boat builders. The 'Lucky Duck' was his prototype, designed to take rough seas in the sometimes treacherous inlet."

When the young couple found this boat abandoned, it was in a sad state of disrepair. During their first year of marriage, they struck a deal with the owner of the boat yard and spent all their free time restoring it. Many bottom planks were replaced, and the hull was fiberglassed.

Kelly and Jimmy lived in a modest house in Wanchese willed to Kelly by her late grandmother. The bank agreed to take a mortgage on their home so the young couple could borrow enough money to repower and rig the boat with the equipment and marine electronics required for offshore charter fishing.

Kelly went on to say, "Although the 'Lucky Duck' may not be the largest or fastest boat in the fleet, 'she' is a proven fish raiser." She explained that pelagic species such as tuna and marlin seem to be attracted to certain boats more than others. "It has something to do with the sound of the engine and underwater appearance of the boat's wake at trolling speed. We were one of the first boats to catch a limit of tuna yesterday," she said.

Both Jimmy and Kelly had been practically raised on the water. Jimmy always said he could swim before he could walk. By the time he was twelve, he was working as the mate on his uncle Paul's charter boat; and as a little girl, Kelly spent many days on her father's crab boat. He was a waterman and earned his living by crabbing and working fish nets in the sound.

The 'Lucky Duck' was Jimmy and Kelly's pride and joy. They made a terrific team, and their parties usually tipped her very well. That was the money she used to pay her college tuition.

As the sky gradually brightened, the horizon glowed a reddish hue. Captain Jimmy told one of the passengers, "This would make a nice picture." Jimmy was a photography buff himself and encouraged parties to bring a camera. In the boat's cabin, he kept a photo album of notable catches for all to enjoy. His passenger snapped the shutter capturing the perfect picture . . . a parade of boats silhouetted by the fiery orb making its ascent. "I'd like to see that after you get it developed. In fact," said Jimmy, "if you leave me your roll of film, I'll develop the pictures and mail them to you."

As the fishing party settled in the cabin, Kelly joined her husband on the bridge. It would be two hours before the boat slowed down to trolling speed. This was her favorite part of the trip . . . watching the dawn of a new day. Then her thoughts turned to the guy she had noticed standing at the end of the dock . . . he looked so familiar . . .

A bell rang as Bull opened the door. The ship's store seemed empty of people, yet voices could be heard clearly. The voices were charter boat captains, coming through the marine radio on a shelf behind the cash register, discussing where the school of tuna might be found today.

"Where you headin' for this morning, Stormy?"

"I'm gonna start out at the 500 line where Sid hit 'em yesterday."

Then, Bull heard a friendly welcome from across the store, "Hello there, young fella. Can I help you?"

If the man's vaguely familiar face was not enough, the name embroidered above his shirt pocket removed all doubt of his identity. "Hey, I know you!" Bull said with a smile spreading across his face. "Cap'n Willie! I fished with you a few years ago."

In his late sixties, with a weathered face and receding white hair streaked with bits of brown, the salty old gentleman cracked a smile and joked, "A few years ago? You must have been in diapers."

"Well, I was only a kid about ten years old," Bull laughed, "I was with my dad and uncle. You were in Hatteras."

"Who's your dad?", asked the friendly gentleman.

"Sullivan. Dr. Bradley Sullivan Jr. from Greenville."

5

"Oh, yes. He used to fish with me quite often before he opened that big clinic of his. What's he up to these days?"

"Well, he doesn't fish as much as he used to. His practice keeps him very busy. Most of the fishing we've done in the last few years has been down in Florida where my folks own a condominium."

While Bull spoke, Cap'n Willie pulled an old photo album from under the counter and started turning pages. "Well, tell your father he ought to come look at our condo's here at Pirate's Cove." Then, he paused and tapped on one of the pictures with his index finger, "Unm, yes, this could be it." Cap'n Willie pulled the faded picture out of its plastic cover and looked at the name and date on the back. "Yep, you ought to recognize these folks." The picture was of two men and a boy. The youngster was struggling to hold up a big bull dolphin. Captain Willie had kept a photo journal of notable catches aboard his boat.

"That's me! That's me all right, with my dad and uncle!" Bull confirmed with a broad smile, then asked, "Is your boat here at Pirates Cove, Cap'n Willie?"

"No, I'm a semi-retired dry-lander now. Several years ago, not long after you caught this nice fish, I sold my boat and business to my mate, Sid Hilton."

"Was Sid your mate on the day I caught this fish?"

"Indeed, he was, but he has since sold my old rig and moved up to that yacht 'Grand Slam' you were admiring a little while ago."

Bull mentioned he was hoping to find work and a place to stay through the summer.

The bell on the door rang as a couple of private boat owners came into the ship's store to get ice and bait. After Cap'n Willie had waited on them, he said to Bull, "The wife and I have an efficiency apartment attached to our house. We've been thinking about renting it since my wife's mother passed away a few months ago."

"Sorry to hear about that," Bull sympathized

"Don't be, she lived to be a hundred," Willie chuckled.

Almost simultaneously the telephone and the doorbell rang as other customers entered the store. Captain Willie walked toward the phone telling Bull, "Be back here at two o'clock, and I'll take you to see the apartment if you want."

To pass the time, Bull drove down the beach road eight miles to check out the Oregon Inlet Fishing Center. Of course, the offshore charter fleet based there had already departed for the fishing grounds, but a friendly waitress at the restaurant mentioned a bluefish blitz in the surf nearby.

After a hasty breakfast, Bull put his truck into four-wheel drive and plowed through the deep sand on the access trail to the beach where he found himself in the company of more than a hundred other four-wheel drive vehicles. Most carried several long surf rods attached to their front bumper. Dozens of fishermen and women were scattered for miles along the seashore, each laying claim to a small portion of the beach. Some wore chest waders and walked into the rolling surf heaving long casts. Suddenly a flock of sea gulls appeared and started dive-bombing over a school of feeding fish about fifty yards beyond the breakers. Several fishermen rushed in and managed to cast far enough to get a strike. Bull watched one of them drag a fifteen-pound bluefish out of the foamy surf onto the golden colored sand. "I've got to get rigged up for this," he said to himself. Then, his thoughts and eyes swept across the sea, past the frenzied sea gulls and far beyond the line of buoys marking the entrance to the inlet. Knowing blue water lay just beyond the distant horizon, Bull longed to be out there.

The next few hours, he spent exploring the eastern-most section of the Carolina Coast where the Outer Banks arc into the Atlantic. The high rise bridge spanning Oregon Inlet offers a breathtaking view of where the ocean meets the sound. From this elevated vantage, Bull could see the shoals and sandbars concealed by shallow water, and appreciate just how tricky navigating the narrow channel could be. The entrance lay between whitecapping breakers, continually rolling across the numerous sandbars extending out into the sea on both the north and south sides of the inlet. Like Neptune's fingers, reaching up to snag any unsuspecting vessel, these ever-shifting sands have plagued mariners since the inlet was formed during the great hurricane of 1846. In the days ahead, Bull would cross this bridge frequently to judge sea conditions and admire the panorama of the ocean and sound, separated only by a fragile barrier of sand.

The drive toward Cape Hatteras took him through some desolate sections, with nothing in view but windswept sand dunes. The only vegetation were patches of wild sea oats and stands of stubby coastal trees and bushes. There are places along this brief stretch, one might think he were in a desert, if not for the occasional glimpse of the rolling surf on one side and quiet Pamlico Sound on the other. At times, the narrow island seemed barely wide enough to accommodate the two lane highway which was flanked by an endless row of utility poles strung together with wires. Bull was surprised to see so many birdwatchers along the way. A car or two was parked by every observation platform with someone armed with binoculars gazing at waterfowl. Paying closer attention, he saw ducks and geese feeding in the ponds and tidal flats by the sound. He spotted a pure white, stork-like bird, with long legs, standing like a sentry against a backdrop of brown marsh grass. On the ocean side, a line of pelicans came into view, playing follow-the-leader, scaling very close to the water, almost touching it. One might think these huge, bulky birds would have difficulty flying, but they made it look effortless, flapping their wings only a few times between each long glide.

He passed through the villages of Rodanthe and Avon where clusters of beach cottages were built on stilts. Residents and shopkeepers were busily preparing for the upcoming tourist season. At Buxton, he took the road leading to Cape Hatteras and toured the tall lighthouse, which is precariously close to the edge of the continent, after more than a century of beach erosion.

Returning to Nags Head, Bull scanned his radio for local stations and listened with interest to messages about businesses and attractions on the Outer Banks. On one station he heard the operator of a fishing pier giving a report, "We've had a nice run on trout and bluefish here at the Kitty Hawk pier this morning on the first of ebb tide."

Bull noticed a sign for *The Lost Colony*, the nation's first and longest-running outdoor drama. His parents had taken him to see the pageant the year he studied about Sir Walter Raleigh and the mysterious disappearance of the first colonists to settle in the New World. Bull recalled his dad laughing and saying, "I know what happened to the lost colony; the mosquitoes carried them away."

It was easy to see why the stretch of beach from Nags Head to

Kitty Hawk attracted so many tourists. There are modern resort hotels, hundreds of rental beach cottages, waterfront condominiums and opulent beach houses four stories tall, golf courses, amusement parks, go-cart tracks, shopping malls, outlet stores, and quaint shops selling sea shells and unique gifts. As he drove, Bull passed the Wright Brothers Monument where Wilbur and Orville made their first flight in 1903. Later, he saw a sign for a restaurant called "Kelly's." Of course, it made him think of her. He was envious that she was in the Gulf Stream while he remained on shore . . . where his greatest challenge was trying to decide where to have lunch.

Bull pulled into the parking lot of a rustic two-level shopping complex across the road from a giant sand dune known as Jockey's Ridge. He was lulled there by all the colorful kites and hang-gliders. On the second level, he found a friendly deli shop that made fresh sandwiches and homemade ice cream. While he was eating lunch on the breezeway, he watched the hang-gliders and decided someday he'd have to give it a try.

At two o'clock, Bull returned to Pirate's Cove Yacht Club to see Captain Willie concerning the apartment for rent. At the entrance to the complex, he stopped his pickup to admire an icon of what had drawn him to these shores. In the center of a small elongated pond, surrounded by a meticulously manicured floral garden, a huge blue marlin seemed to be leaping high above a gushing fountain. Bull later learned the mount was indeed a *grander* that had weighed 1021 pounds and had been caught by a boat based here.

As Bull entered the ship's store, he saw Cap'n Willie answer the telephone. Unbeknownst to Bull, it was his own father's secretary saying, "Dr. Sullivan is returning Captain Willie Davis' call."

"That's me," said Cap'n Willie.

"Please hold for Dr. Sullivan," she said.

Willie had seen Bull come in, and did not want the young man to know he had placed a call to his father. Covering the phone with his hand, he said, "Hello, young fellow, id you want to see that apartment?"

"Yes sir."

"I'll be with you as soon as I get off the phone. Why don't you wait for me out on the observation deck. You'll see some of the boats coming in from fishing."

Part of the fleet had returned early with their limit of tuna. Across the harbor, he saw Tommy washing down the 'Grand Slam'. In the fish cleaning station, several men were busily cutting fillets and packaging the catch of the day for the happy anglers.

Down the dock, Kelly was posing for photographs with fishermen proudly exhibiting the many tuna they had caught aboard the 'Lucky Duck'. Bull wanted to walk around and say hello, but Cap'n Willie came out the door saying, "Follow me, young man. I live just off the bypass at Nags Head."

The cozy little apartment was clean as a whistle, fully furnished, and even had cable TV. Cap'n Willie introduced his wife, Bitsy. She was a petite woman with chubby features and silver hair she wore in a bun. Willie had already told her he knew Bull's father and thought the young man would make a good tenant. After greeting him and learning a little about his background, she walked to a picture hanging on the wall. It was of a handsome young man wearing a Marine's uniform. Touching it with gentle fingertips, she said, "This was my son." There was a noticeable moment of silence, seeming to be in tribute to the young man in the picture. Bull thought perhaps he had been killed in action while serving in Vietnam. "You remind me a little of him," she continued, "it's not often I see such a clean cut young man now'a days." Removing the picture and holding it to her bosom, she smiled and said, "It's a pleasure meeting you. We look forward to having you as our new neighbor." Then she added, "and please call me Miz Bitsy, everybody does."

With a feeling of satisfaction, Bull spent the rest of the day settling into his new home on the Outer Banks.

Next morning at four-fifteen, there came three quick knocks on Bull's door. Glancing at the clock and still in his underwear, he sleepily walked to the door and cracked it open. There stood Cap'n Willie, "Sorry to wake you, son. You can go back to sleep if you want, but I got to thinking you might want to go down to the dock again this morning."

"Yes sir!" Bull became alert. "As a matter of fact, my alarm clock should be going off any minute."

"You're welcome to ride with me", said Cap'n Willie. "I'll be coming home at lunch time. You can get *your* truck, then."

"Sure, just give me a couple of minutes to get ready. Come on in." As Bull closed his bathroom door, he noticed Willie starring at the empty space on the wall from which his wife had removed their son's picture yesterday. It had obviously been there for some time as the paint was darker where the picture had been hanging.

Naturally, Bull was curious and thought, I'll ask; after all, Vietnam happened a long time ago. So, as they rode together in Willie's old pickup, he asked, "Your son, the Marine in the picture . . . did he ah, . . . not make it back from Vietnam?" As soon as the question was asked, Bull felt as if he were imposing into the kindly old captain's private affairs and quickly retracted, "I'm sorry, I had no right to ask."

Keeping his eyes on the road ahead, the old captain replied, "My son made it through Vietman without a scratch. It was Oregon Inlet that killed him."

7

Bull had heard, of all the inlets on the Carolina coast, Oregon inlet, south of Nags Head, held the reputation of being the most treacherous; and, even though Bull's interest was peaked, he said, "I'm sorry to have brought up such a painful memory."

"It's all right . . . I don't mind talking about him. In fact, it's been too long since I *have* talked about him." Cap'n Willie sipped coffee from his mug and lifted his eyebrows as if collecting his thoughts to tell the story. "His mother named him Gene Kelly Davis, after the actor who danced in the movies. *Singing In The Rain* was the first movie she and I saw together. Of course, Gene grew up fishing with me. He worked as my mate from the time he was twelve years old 'till he got his draft notice. That's when he decided to join the Marines. His mother and I worried about him everyday he was over there. But he made it through. Came home with honors and big plans for getting into commercial fishing; so, naturally I helped him get started. We found a solid old work boat, and fixed her up. He named her 'Lady B', to honor his mother, Bitsy. I painted the name across the stern myself. Gene didn't mind hard work and was doing very well. In fact, he was about to marry his old high school sweetheart, Barbara Ethridge." Willie hesitated. "She left town right after Gene died. Came back a few years later married to a fellow named Fisher, Charlie Fisher. She has a daughter about your age."

"What's her name?" Bull asked with interest. "Maybe I could meet her. I'm sort of in between girlfriends."

"Don't get any ideas about this girl." Willie sounded almost protective, "She's already married . . . to a charter boat captain."

Bull wondered if the old captain could possibly be talking about Kelly, the girl he had seen on the 'Lucky Duck' yesterday.

"Anyway, it was twenty-one years ago, March, when we lost Gene. His mate, Stormy Pruitt, survived to tell about the ordeal." Approaching the stop light at Whalebone Junction, Cap'n Willie placed his well used mug into a cupholder on the dash, down-shifted his old pickup, and rolled to a stop. Bull was spellbound as the old man told of his son's harrowing experience. And when the light turned green, he continued the story, "I don't know why he didn't lay off until flood tide. Like I said, he had a stubborn streak about him, and he wasn't afraid to do anything. From the time he was a little boy, Bitsy would often say 'Gene Kelly has no fear!'."

Bull sympathized, "I can imagine how hard his death must have been on you and Miz Bitsy."

"You're right about that. It took me the longest time before I could pass through the inlet without shedding a tear. I don't think Bitsy ever has gotten over it."

Bull sat in silence, imagining how frightening the whole ordeal must have been. The sage old captain concluded, "Ours was not the first Outer Bank's son lost in the brine. I reckon, as long as sons and daughters are called to a life at sea, there will be mothers and fathers grieving for the few who never return."

As the pickup crossed the bridge to Roanoke Island, Cap'n Willie said, "But, enough about the past, we'll be getting to the marina in a minute. Tell me what kind of work are you looking for?"

"Well, I'm hoping to find something related to boats."

"Like maybe being a mate?"

"Is it that obvious?"

Willie remarked, "You know, being a mate on a charter fishing boat is hard work. It's long hours, washing the boat after every trip . . . and every day is no cakewalk out there. Some days are mighty rough, and folks get seasick. You know, it's the mate who's gotta clean up the puke. And when the head gets clogged . . . it's the mate who gets crap up to his elbows taking the toilet apart . . . not many are cut out for mate'n."

"If I didn't know better," said Bull, "I'd say you've been talking to my Dad. He told me almost the same thing."

Cap'n Willie was quick to answer, "Oh, no, I'm just saying I've seen lots of young fellows show up at the docks want'n to be a mate, but they don't last long, because they're not willing to do the work."

"How about that girl on the 'Lucky Duck', is she a mate?" Bull asked hoping to learn more about her.

"You mean Kelly Edwards? Yes, and she has recently passed the Coast Guard exam for her captain's license. That's a little different situation; y'see her husband, Jimmy, is captain. They run their boat together."

Bull felt somewhat disheartened to learn Kelly was married to a captain and they had their own boat. As Willie's old chevy pickup squeaked to a stop in the parking lot at Pirate's Cove, Bull said, "Cap'n Willie, I'd appreciate any advice you could give me on how to get hooked up with a charter boat."

"Well, it ain't gonna be easy, but I'll tell you what you do, son. You go on down to the dock this morning and observe what's going on. Offer to lend a hand if you see the opportunity to help a mate load ice or bait. Then, when the boats start pulling out, walk down to the end of the dock like you did yesterday and watch them leave. After that, come back up to the store for some hot coffee and a donut."

At the time, Bull did not understand Cap'n Willie's methods, but obediently followed his instructions. To Bull's delight, when the 'Lucky Duck' passed by, Kelly waved as if she may have recognized him.

Afterwards, Bull went to the ship's store and asked Cap'n Willie what was the purpose of his being on the charter dock this morning? The store was not busy at the time, and Willie was glad to explain, "Young fellow, I don't know of a single captain looking for a new mate right now . . . but I do know this. The first thing a captain looks for in a mate is dependability. The mate's got to get his butt out of bed before the rooster crows. Offshore trips can't be run without a mate. If the mate don't show up, the captain's gonna be none too happy. It's a pain in the ass at five o'clock in the morning trying to find a substitute. If you want one of these guys to hire you, you gotta prove to 'em you can get to the boat on time. You need to be on the dock again tomorrow morning . . . and the morning after that . . . and so on. That's the way Sid got his job as mate on my old boat. He was on the dock, ready to go when Gene decided to take off and join the Marines."

A few minutes later, a private yacht owner came into the store and asked Cap'n Willie if he knew anyone who would clean his teak and wax his boat today.

Willie said, "Ask that young man right over there, he's looking for some work."

Bull spoke up, "Yes sir, I'll be glad to help. Just show me what you want done, and I'll take care of it."

8 All day long Bull worked diligently on the boat. He was putting the finishing touches on the teak when the charters started returning from the day's fishing. The 'Lucky Duck' happened to be docked along the same pier as the boat Bull was working on. As Captain Jimmy backed the boat into its slip, Bull obligingly handed the dock lines to Kelly. She recognized him right away as Brad, a boy from school.

"Thanks," she said. "I thought that was you on the dock this morning."

"Yeah, I saw you going out. How'd you guys do today?"

"Pretty well," Kelly smiled.

"We caught the limit," reveled one of the anglers in her party.

As Kelly attended to her duties securing the lines, Bull said, "I know you're busy....I'll catch'ya later," and returned to his project.

Bull tried not to be obvious, but couldn't help watching the couple unload the party's fine catch of tuna and dolphin. Her husband was a young man about Bull's age, of average height and build, with a ruddy complexion, reddish brown hair, and neatly trimmed mustache. The fishermen were obviously very pleased; there was much esprit de corps as they posed for pictures holding the largest of the fish.

As the group departed, one of them said, "Captain Jimmy, we want to come back in the fall, do you have any open dates?"

Jimmy retrieved his booking calendar from the salon, then walked to the parking lot with the party to schedule another trip. His dutiful mate, and wife, climbed the ladder to the bridge with water hose and bucket in hand to begin the wash down. When she sprayed the outrigger poles, she accidentally turned the hose onto Bull, who was still working on the nearby boat. She soaked him good.

"Hey! Watch it!" he shouted in a shocked yet friendly tone.

"Sorry! I didn't realize you were on that boat."

"You're a pretty good shot with the water hose," Bull joked as he shook water off his arms.

Kelly climbed down off the 'Lucky Duck' and walked over to speak with Bull, who was holding a can of teak oil in one hand and a paint brush in the other. She said, "I'm really sorry about that. You're the first person I've seen on this boat in weeks."

"I can believe it; this teak has really been neglected."

"You've got it looking a lot better. Is this your boat?" Kelly asked.

" I wish!" Bull laughed as Jimmy came walking down the dock.

Kelly introduced them, "Brad, this is my husband, Jimmy. Honey, this is Brad, he's in one of my classes at school."

"*Was* in one of your classes . . . afraid I'm a dropout," said Bull.

"No! What happened?", asked Kelly.

"It's a long story. I may return in the fall; but, till then, I'm staying right here at Nags Head."

Kelly said, "I'm sorry, I don't remember your last name Brad."

"Sullivan. But, please, lose the 'Brad'. My friends call me Bull."

"Bull? How did you get a nickname like that?" asked Kelly.

"Believe it or not, my Dad started calling me Bull when I caught a citation size bull dolphin when I was just a kid."

"Nice meeting you, Bull," said Jimmy. He stepped over to their boat, and said," Sugar, I noticed a vibration on the way in. Think maybe I'll go overboard to check if anything's around the shaft."

"Hey Jimmy, I'd be glad to do it for you. Your mate has already soaked me with the hose anyway," said Bull, pulling at his wet T-shirt.

"Sure, why not?" Jimmy was not crazy about getting into the cool water anyway.

Without hesitation, Bull slid off the swim platform of the yacht he was working on and swam toward the 'Lucky Duck'. Looking up to Jimmy, he asked, "Which side?"

"Port . . . I think maybe I picked up a crab pot line. Isn't the water cold, Bull?"

"Not too bad, once you get used to it." Bull took a deep breath and went under the boat. After about thirty seconds, Jimmy and Kelly looked at each other wondering how much longer Bull could hold his breath. After another ten or fifteen seconds he emerged, "You're right. You got a crab pot rope around the port shaft. I tried to get it off, but it's too tight. I'll need a sharp knife."

Jimmy handed Bull a knife with a serrated blade. "Here, use this. It'll cut through rope better than a fillet knife."

Bull disappeared underneath the boat again. After nearly a minute, Kelly was getting a little anxious and asked her husband, "Think we better check on him?"

Just then, Bull surfaced with a hand full of rope. He took a breath and said, "I checked the other side while I was down there and got a piece of heavy monofilament fishing line off it. You've got a few barnacles on the shafts, but otherwise, the bottom is quite clean."

Jimmy gave Bull a hand getting out of the water and said, "You can hold your breath a lot longer than I can."

"I've done a lot of snorkeling and free-diving on the reefs down in the Keys."

"Thanks a lot," said Jimmy.

"Happy to do it for you."

Handing Bull a towel, Kelly said, "Your watch! You forgot to take it off. I hope you didn't ruin it."

"Water can't hurt this watch. It's a diver's watch. My mother gave it to me when I graduated from high school."

For the next three weeks, Bull was at the dock every morning at five o'clock. Captain Willie's advice was paying off. He had met a few of the captains and had even become friends with a couple of the mates. After their morning preparation was done, Jason and Larry would often shoot the breeze with him while they waited for their parties to arrive. Even though it was now obvious Bull was looking for a job as mate, Jason and Larry did not feel threatened by his presence. In fact, they encouraged him. Larry even arranged with his captain for Bull to go along with them as an observer one day.

Not every mate was happy to have Bull around. One morning, Bull noticed Captain Sid had walked up to the ship's store, leaving a load of things for Tommy to carry from his truck to the 'Grand Slam'. To be helpful, Bull went over to the truck and picked up a 48-quart cooler, heavy with ice, from the tailgate intending to carry it to the boat as a favor. When Tommy turned around and saw Bull carrying the cooler, he went into a rage . . . accusing Bull of trying to steal it. "Keep your god-damn thieving hands off my stuff!" Tommy shouted as he jerked the cooler from Bull's hands.

To say the least, Bull was surprised by Tommy's irrational reaction. "I was only trying to help you," he said in his own defense.

"Well, I don't need your damn help! Stay away from the 'Grand Slam'. You got that?"

Bull had never been one to lose his temper, but he felt like tackling Tommy right then and there. Most likely, he would have, if Jason and Larry had not intervened.

Larry said, "Leave him alone, Tommy. He was only trying to help you, for Christ's sake!"

Tommy said, "Well, now he knows, I don't want his help."

As the three boys walked down the dock to friendlier territory, Jason said to Bull, "Don't worry about Tommy, everybody knows he's the biggest asshole on the dock."

Larry added, "I don't know why Captain Sid puts up with Tommy's shit."

Jason said, "I'll tell you why. He's a damn good fisherman. Tommy's probably the best in the business when it comes to hooking a billfish."

Jason quipped, "Hey Bull, I'll tell you a good way to get even. After we all leave, you can push Tommy's pickup over the dock into the harbor."

The three of them laughed at the idea. Truth is, not too many people knew Tommy's background. He was the illegitimate son of a stripper, raised solely by his widowed grandmother. He never had the benefit of a father's guidance, which could explain his difficulty in getting along with other men. In and out of trouble as a youth, he had quit school at the age of sixteen and started working for tips on a head boat at Virginia Beach.

Each day, after the charter boats had departed, Bull earned money doing odd jobs around the marina for private boat owners. He was gaining a fine reputation for his meticulous workmanship cleaning teak and bright work. He received frequent invitations from many of these grateful boat owners to join them on a fishing trip, and he gladly accepted whenever he didn't have other work to do.

Bull had volunteered to do a few springtime chores around the house for Cap'n Willie and Miz Bitsy. After he painted their shutters, they rewarded him with a month's free rent and some good down home cookin'. He couldn't get enough of Miz Bitsy's chicken 'n pastry with banana pudding for dessert.

Cap'n Willie also took time to show Bull the basics of rigging baits. There is an art to properly rigging a ballyhoo, Spanish mackerel or squid so it will swim and appear natural enough to fool a marlin. Bull listened closely to every word . . . considering himself fortunate to have an old master like Cap'n Willie as a tutor.

During this period, Bull also had a chance to get acquainted with Kelly and her husband. In fact, Jimmy had become Bull's closest friend on the Outer Banks, except of course, for Cap'n Willie. On the days Kelly took nursing classes at ECU, Jimmy ran half-day inshore parties, usually bottom fishing on nearby wrecks or trolling along the beach for bluefish and mackerel. Many tourists to the outer banks prefer this type of fishing over spending ten hours on an offshore boat.

Jimmy usually arranged for one of the dock boys to go along as mate on these nearby excursions. Recently, to Bull's delight, Jimmy had asked him to serve as mate. Bull loved it! Just the chance to have a charter boat rocking under his feet was reward enough. And, as for inshore fishing . . . it was a lot of fun! Sometimes, they caught spot and croaker two at a time; other days, they had good luck with trout and flounder. Bull learned the technique to trolling for blue-fish and king mackerel.

On one particular outing, they were on their way to an inshore wreck to fish for sea bass when Jimmy sighted a cobia swimming near the sea buoy. He told Bull the fish might be enticed to take a yellow bucktail sweetened with a strip of mullet. Their party includ-ed a fourteen-year-old girl and her parents. On her second attempt at casting, she hooked the cobia on twenty pound spinning tackle. Her parents were proud and excited when the thirty-one pound fish was landed. Of course, Jimmy came down from the bridge and took a photograph of the happy angler with Bull holding up the fish for her. The photo would surely find its way into the boat's album.

When the 'Lucky Duck' came in that day, Kelly had already re-turned from class and was waiting at the dock. She made a fuss over the big cobia and congratulated the young angler on her outstand-ing catch. Afterwards Kelly, Jimmy, and Bull made plans to have dinner together at RB's Seafood and Steak House.

That evening, as the three of them climbed into Jimmy's compact pickup and rode north on the beach road toward the restaurant, Bull took the opportunity to quiz his friends about how they met. He learned Kelly and Jimmy had been childhood sweethearts. Kelly asked Bull why he dropped out of college. He admitted his grades were slipping, and he had just split up with a girl he had dated for over a year. Then, Bull teased, "Do you have a sister? I'm available."

"No, sorry. I'm an only child, but I do have a cute girlfriend I can introduce you to." Turning to her husband, she asked, "Don't you think he'd like Heather?"

"Oh yeah! You'll like Heather, Bull," said Jimmy with a grin. "She's a foxy redhead!"

"She sounds dangerous," laughed Bull.

"Not at all," Kelly replied, "she's a great girl and I don't think you'd be disappointed."

Soon the guys got onto the subject of fishing and were talking about running out to the twenty-mile tower to see if the amberjack had moved in yet. While the guys chatted, Kelly's mind wandered to her own dating days. Then she thought, "I've never been on a date . . . not a real date. It's always been me and Jimmy since I was five years old."

Kelly's mother, Barbara, had been raised in Manteo, a quaint

Elizabethan village on the waterfront. However, she left with a broken heart following the sudden death of her fiance, Gene Davis,
who was Cap'n Willie's son. For the next five years, she lived at
Reedville, a small fishing community on the Chesapeake Bay where
she met and married a waterman, Charlie Fisher. Before Kelly started school, they moved back to Dare County, and had been living
next door to Jimmy's parents for sixteen years.

Kelly was now twenty-one. Most locals considered her to be one
of the prettiest girls on Roanoke Island. In the twelfth grade, she
was selected homecoming queen. Although Jimmy was almost a
year older, they had gone through twelve years of school in the
same classrooms. Their families were not only neighbors, they were
close friends who played cards on Friday nights and often took vacations together. Somewhere along the way, Jimmy and Kelly's relationship started changing from being pals to becoming
romantically involved.

As she sat sandwiched between Bull and Jimmy, she felt very uncomfortable: not because of the cramped seating, but because of her
thoughts. This was the first time she had allowed these emotions to
surface . . . Jimmy pressured her into marriage when he learned of
her plans to go to nursing school. Most of the people Kelly met in
college were single. She was always being approached by good-
looking college guys not suspecting she was married. In fact, that
was how she first met Bull.

She was not quite sure of her feelings when Jimmy asked her to
marry him during their senior year of high school. She knew she
cared deeply for him, but something was missing. "Aren't I supposed to be delirious with bliss," she had thought, "or is that only
in the movies." After pressure from both families, she suppressed
her doubts and agreed on a wedding date. When Kelly married Jimmy on the first Sunday in August following their graduation, she
was only eighteen years old. Their honeymoon was a three-day trip
to Virginia Beach.

Secretly, Kelly was jealous of her girlfriends who were still single. And now, for the first time, she resented never dating any other
guys. "How can I know what love is?" she wondered.

Her thoughts were interrupted by Jimmy putting his hand on her
knee and asking "Did you bring the checkbook, Sugar?"

"Yes, dear," she answered quickly. Kelly felt a wave of guilt pass
over her for having thoughts doubting their relationship. She told
herself, "I'm a married woman, for God sakes."

Early the next morning, a Saturday, several captains were gathered on the dock discussing an impending Nor'easter. Waves at Diamond Shoals light, already running four to five feet, were expected to increase to eight feet by evening. The small craft advisory, in all likelihood, would be upgraded to a warning later today.

Knowing this might be their last chance to fish for several days, the captains evaluated the situation. Most felt sure they could make their day early, and get back through the Inlet, before the seas built too high.

Across the harbor, Sid saw most of the private yachts were also preparing to fish today. He said to Stormy, "I hope they know what they're in for today."

"Sid, you know damn well they're going, 'cause the weekend's the only time most of 'em get a chance to fish anyway." Stormy lit a cigarette and went on to say, "Hell, they'll be all right; look at all that money they're ridin' on." He was referring to the fleet of privately owned high-dollar yachts . . . all seaworthy vessels, built to take the rigorous demands of offshore fishing. Even the charter crews acknowledged many of the private captains were excellent boat handlers and their mates were accomplished fishermen. As the charter fleet departed, the private boats fell into formation with them.

10

Bull was on his way to blue water again, too. Since the party of anglers on the 'Lucky Duck' numbered only three, Jimmy and Kelly had invited him to go along with them.

It was after the fleet passed through the inlet, about three miles into the ocean, Captain Stormy on the 'Bushwhacker' noticed a small center console boat with a single outboard engine running parallel to the fleet. He said on his radio, "I hope to God that outboard ain't thinking 'bout going all the way to the stream today."

Another of Stormy's captain friends answered, "Well, you know damned well he is! Anybody'd even bring a boat like that through the inlet on a day like this has got to have shit for brains."

"You're right about that. I 'magine when he gets out another mile or two, he'll turn that tub around and go put it back on the trailer."

Due to the rough sea conditions, it took longer than usual for the fleet to reach the fishing grounds. Once there, they spread out along the edge and searched for a school of tuna or dolphin. Seas in the Gulf Stream were rougher than expected this early in the day. Bull was not about to admit it, but he was feeling queasy. He watched a fifty-foot boat near them completely disappear from sight behind a giant swell.

To make matters worse, fishing was slow. Not a single strike had been reported on the radio during the first hour. Captain Stormy, who had a rich eastern Carolina accent, a knack for telling a story, and was not the least bit shy about talking on the marine radio, said, "I know where my party ate breakfast this morning . . . It looks like somebody spilled the buffet from Sue & Ollie's Restaurant right here on my deck. Hell, it don't look like that man chewed up his sausage very well. I swear there's one or two o'those little sausage links down there that look like he must have swallowed 'em whole."

Finally, a tuna hookup was reported. The 'Carolina Pirate' had a double. Sure enough, other boats soon had action also. It appeared there would be a tuna bite today, after all.

A while later, Stormy called Jimmy on the 'Lucky Duck', "Do you see what's on your starboard side over there, Jim? That damned outboard!"

"Yeah, he made the trip out here, Stormy. Looks like there's a woman on board hooked up with a tuna right now."

Sid said, "We better keep an eye on them. We don't want to leave such a small boat out here with this big front coming through later."

As soon as the woman's fish was landed, the small boat operator revved up his outboard and sped away toward the west. Stormy said, "Well, I reckon they've had enough. 'Least they got a tuna to take home with 'em."

Most of the charter boats had four or five fish in their boxes by eleven o'clock. That's when an unfamiliar voice was heard on their radios calling the 'Ranger'. It was Cap'n Ray Crabbe, a commercial fisherman on the 'Southern Belle' who was working about ten miles north of the fleet. He seldom spoke on the working channel for the charter boats unless he had something that needed to be said.

Ray called his old friend Cap'n Paul Edwards on the 'Ranger' and told him in his distinctive southern drawl, "Paul, I thought I better warn you boys down there you gotta good forty-mile-an-hour blow coming your way. It's right rank up here now."

Hearing those words, every captain's eyes turned to the northeast. In the distance, a windswept wall of water could be seen where the ever flowing Gulf Stream collided with cool air rushing down from the opposite direction. Within moments, the sea disappeared beneath a blanket of foam. Crews sprang into action, pulling up outriggers and zipping curtains, while captains turned bows into the whistling wind. The front had arrived much sooner than predicted.

Waves were already running eight to ten feet. The captains maneuvered their vessels toward the compass heading of 310 degrees and began the grueling ride to the inlet hoping they would be able to make it through. The fleet normally traveled at better than twenty knots, but making only half that speed they were still taking a pounding. It was almost three hours before, in the distance, they saw the familiar high-rise of the bridge that crosses Oregon Inlet.

The first two captains to reach the inlet reported although it was very rough, the inlet was passable thanks to an incoming tide. One by one, the captains used their years of experience to calculate the best moment to ride a rolling wave across the bar. By four o'clock, all captains, crew and anglers were happy to be back at the dock. Someone in the 'Lucky Duck's' party suggested Kelly have T-shirts printed up saying, "I survived 10-foot seas while fishing off the Carolina coast," kidding that they would be big sellers on a day like this. Bull walked to the bow of the 'Lucky Duck' with water hose in hand and began washing down the boat, grateful he had not gotten seasick.

Like all the other boats, the 'Grand Slam' was covered with a layer of salt after running through such rough seas. Tommy was busy washing the clear plastic curtains on the flying bridge when his roving eye caught sight of a striking young brunette, standing on the dock with an older couple and talking with Captain Sid.

Tommy ogled her shapely long legs, beneath a short black skirt. He imagined she must be wearing a *wonder bra* under her skimpy top as no girl could possibly be built like that. She had rings on every finger, even her thumbs, and a tattoo of a butterfly on her right ankle. Showing an equal interest in Tommy, she teased him with a sexy wink. Tommy rinsed off the curtains and worked his way closer to her.

Pointing toward the 'Grand Slam', she asked Captain Sid, "Is this your boat?"

"Yes, and this is my mate, Tommy."

It was just the introduction she wanted. As Sid resumed his conversation with the couple, she lifted an eyebrow at Tommy in a flirting manner and said, "Hi! My name is Suzette, need some help?" Dazzled, Tommy was momentarily speechless. Moving like a tigress, she stepped aboard the boat and climbed into the fighting chair. Even though his mind was clouded with lustful thoughts, he managed to ask, "Hi, ah . . . are you and your parents here to go fishing?"

"They're talking about it, but my mother would die of seasickness if she got on a boat. She got carsick on the way down here!"

Tommy laughed and said, "What about your dad?"

"You mean Richard?" looking toward them, "he's my mom's latest husband. He's Captain Sid's brother."

"Brother?" Tommy glanced at him, but his eyes quickly returned to Suzette's curvaceous figure, "Oh, yes, I see the resemblance."

Suzette continued, "Well, anyway, they got married in Vegas about a month ago, and they're considering buying a condo here at Pirate's Cove. Mom invited me to come down with them for the weekend to check it out. I didn't have a gig, so here I am!"

"Gig? What do you do?"

"I sing in a band."

"Cool. I'd like to hear you sometime. So, where do you live?"

"Ooh, I like a guy that gets right to the point."

"What I meant was where are you from."

Suzette laughed and said, "I have my own apartment in Richmond; I'd be glad to give you my number . . . if you want it. Do you ever get to Richmond?"

Tommy smiled, "Oh sure, I have some friends who live in the Fan." Tommy looked up at the way the flag was flapping in the wind, "I don't think anyone will be fishing tomorrow."

"That's what Captain Sid was saying. Mom and Richard are making plans for us to have dinner with him and his wife tonight. Sounds like a blast, huh?" Suzette said sarcastically.

"Bummer!", Tommy interjected.

"Are there any good places to go dancing around here?"

"Oh Sure!", Tommy answered with anticipation, "I can show you a couple of places where they really get wild."

Suzette noticed her mother and stepfather seemed to be wrapping up their conversation with Captain Sid. She jumped onto the dock and asked, "Mom, why don't you and Dad enjoy dinner with Captain and Mrs. Hilton without me being in the way. Tommy's invited me to have dinner with him and go dancing afterwards. That'll be OK with you, won't it, Mom?"

Suzette's skill at manipulating situations to her satisfaction was obvious. Her mother replied, "Why, certainly, dear, if it won't be an inconvenience for anyone," she said looking toward Tommy. Who quickly responded, "No problem ma'am, I'll take good care of her."

"Great!" said Suzette, as she told Tommy to pick her up around seven at unit number six in Buccaneer Village condominiums.

Suzette was watching for Tommy out her window. When his pickup stopped in front of the condo, she grabbed her purse and said "Bye, Mom; Bye, Richard. I'm leaving now, you have a nice dinner with the Hilton's."

Her stepfather said, "Don't be too late, your mother will worry."

Before Tommy could open his door, he saw Suzette walking down the sidewalk. It was a cool spring evening on the Outer Banks and even though she had a silk-look trench coat pulled snuggly around her, he thought she looked drop-dead gorgeous. When Tommy leaned across the seat to open the door for her, she very seductively allowed her coat fall open, and revealed she was wearing nothing but hi-heels and sheer black stockings held up by a lacy red and black teddy. Tommy's mouth dropped open wide and hung there as his testosterone level rose to his ears. His eyes quickly surveyed every delightful inch of her loveliness. He had never encountered anyone so provocative as Suzette. As she slid across the seat close to him, Tommy was nearly overcome by the sweet smell of her perfume. Suzette snuggled against him, while cinching the coat around her waist, and said in a sassy manner, "I want to make sure you never forget me. From now on, you'll compare every girl you're with to me."

As Tommy drove away, he exclaimed, "Hot damn! I've died and gone to heaven."

The next morning at three o'clock, the phone rang at Sid's home. It was his brother Richard calling, "Suzette has not come home yet and her mother is getting very concerned. After all, we don't even know this boy, Tommy, she went out with."

"Richard, tell Sharon not to worry. I'll go out right now and look for them."

Not seeing Tommy's pickup parked in front of the apartment he rented, Sid drove on to the marina. There it was, Tommy's red pickup, parked behind the 'Grand Slam'. Sid had mixed feelings---happy to have found the young couple; yet peeved, because Tommy knew better than to bring his girlfriends to the boat. With music blaring from the stereo system, Tommy and Suzette did not hear Sid enter the cabin. Empty beer cans cluttered the table, and the boat smelled of pot. Suzette's silk lavender coat lay open across the couch. The pathway to the forward stateroom was strewn with Tommy's clothes and shoes. Sid did not yet see anyone, but above the rhythm of alternative rock music pouring from the speakers, there were sounds emerging from the forward cabin . . . heated moans of a couple at the height of passion. Sid stepped down into the galley where he could see them through the open doorway. It was blatantly evident what was going on.

Shocked and embarrassed by the sight, Sid quietly crept out of the salon and climbed up to the flying bridge. He turned on the ignition switch and one of the big 8V92 diesel engines roared to life. "That ought'a flush 'em out!" he thought.

Tommy and Suzette quickly dressed and scurried off the boat to Tommy's pickup. Knowing he had been caught in the act and fully expecting the consequences, Tommy said to Sid, "I'll be back in a few minutes."

Sid used his cellular phone to call his brother, "I found the kids on the boat. They had been up talking all night and lost track of time. Tell Sharon everything's fine. Suzette is on her way home right now."

After finishing the conversation, Sid considered the situation. Even though it was obvious Suzette was promiscuous, Tommy still knew better than to bring girlfriends to the boat for sex. "I'm running a business here, not a sugar shack," he thought. When Tommy returned a few minutes later, Sid said, "Tommy, it is a crying shame I have to do this. You're a damned good mate, but I've had it with you. I'm gonna have to let you go. Get your gear off the boat right now."

Tommy replied, "Yeah, well, I've been thinking it's time for me to move on anyway."

It only took a few minutes for Tommy to gather his personal belongings . . . a couple of fillet knives, a tackle box, a fishing rod, a pair of old deck shoes, a bag of clothes, and half a carton of cigarettes. As Tommy walked toward his pickup, Sid had an urge to call him back and give him another chance, knowing such a knowledgeable mate would be hard to replace. Recalling all the problems he had endured with Tommy lately, Sid sat quietly and watched him drive away.

Daybreak found Captain Sid still on the 'Grand Slam', taking an inventory of it's fishing tackle. Now that Tommy was gone, Sid wondered where he might be able to find a mate for tomorrow's trip. If the low pressure system responsible for yesterday's rough seas moved through today, tomorrow could be fishable. As Sid tuned his marine radio to the weather channel, he was thinking he would walk up to the ship's store in a few minutes to get a cup of coffee and talk with Cap'n Willie about that boy "Bull" who had been hanging around the dock lately.

Sid scanned his radio across channel 22-Alpha and heard a Coast Guard broadcast for an overdue boat. There was a search and rescue effort underway. A Virginia woman, who was vacationing at a cottage in Nags Head with her family, had called the Coast Guard at ten o'clock last night. Her daughter and son-in-law did not return home from a fishing trip on their boat. She said they had just bought the boat and were eager to try it out.

12 The Coast Guard had checked the parking lot by the public boat ramp at Oregon Inlet and found an empty boat trailer attached to a vehicle matching the woman's description. They had initiated their search last night and made announcements on the marine radio about the missing vessel. The message described a 22-foot center-console open boat powered by a single outboard motor with two persons on board.

The message was repeated at about six o'clock, just when Captain Sid turned on his radio. Immediately, Sid realized who the search was for. He called the Coast Guard on his radio and told them he had information that might be helpful. The radio operator on duty replied, "Copy that 'Grand Slam', please switch and answer channel 26-Alpha."

Captain Sid reported to them, "Yesterday, a boat matching your description was fishing among the charter fleet about thirty-eight miles southeast of Oregon Inlet." Sid continued, "Around eleven o'clock, the boat was seen leaving the fleet, running alone, and heading toward the Inlet."

"Copy that sir, what were the sea conditions at the time, over?"

The coast guard interview continued until as much information as possible was collected and relayed to the two helicopters conducting the search. Up until the time Captain Sid contacted them, they had been concentrating within ten miles of the beach. The Coast Guard had not expected the small vessel to be so far out, especially considering a small craft advisory had been issued yesterday.

Based on this new information, the search was extended to an area about thirty miles offshore and an airplane was also sent up to search. Remarkably, just after eight o'clock, one of the chopper pilots, Lt. Commander Nancy Kidwell, reported the hull of a capsized vessel had been located with one survivor seen. A Coast Guard rescue swimmer was lowered to the water's surface with a cable suspended from the helicopter. A fatigued and emotionally drained woman was plucked from the rough seas and hoisted to the helicopter, hovering twenty-five feet overhead. Even before her rescue basket was pulled inside, she was pleading, "Did you find my husband? Did you find my husband?"

She told the crewmen how their boat was swamped yesterday when very strong winds came up suddenly. The first wave they took knocked out all of their electronics. The engine stalled and would not restart. They tried to call for help on their hand-held VHF radio. It, too, had gotten wet and no one answered. "It happened so quickly," the woman explained anxiously. "We put on our life jackets when a wave filled the boat with water. The next big wave flipped us over. I managed to grab hold of the propeller; but my husband, Linwood, could not get back to the boat. He was holding onto an Igloo cooler." She caught her breath, drank some more water and continued, "We saw the charter boats going by, but they were too far away to see us. I tried to keep an eye on Linwood, but we kept drifting farther apart and before long, I lost sight of him. Please find him!", she sobbed. The woman was taken to the medical clinic at the Coast Guard station at Elizabeth City and was found to be suffering mild hypothermia and dehydration.

Meanwhile, the other helicopter and a C-130 airplane searched the swollen sea for the woman's husband. Based on her story, the Coast Guard quickly calculated the most likely area he might be found taking wind, drift, and current into account. One pilot said to the other, "This is going to be like looking for a needle in a haystack . . . him hanging onto a white Igloo cooler when all we can see down there are whitecaps."

Much to their surprise, about sixty minutes into the new search pattern, a crewman on the plane miraculously spotted the man's orange colored life jacket. When the chopper lowered a rescue basket, the man made no attempt to grab it. He just continued hugging the Igloo cooler. It took two rescue swimmers to literally pry the man's fingers from the handles of the cooler before getting him into the basket. He told his rescuers, he had become so tired, he dosed off with his head resting on the cooler. He wasn't about to let it go, maintaining his grip even in sleep. Just before dawn he was startled awake by a terrifying experience . . . a ship nearly ran him over! "It sounded like a train. I could almost touch it!", he said.

It took three days in the hospital for him to recover from exhaustion and dehydration. Not all rescue missions have such a favorable outcome. It took a great deal of tenacity for this man and woman to survive in rough seas for twenty hours.

Word spread quickly around the dock that Tommy had been fired. Within hours, a couple of mates from other boats approached Captain Sid asking if he had found a replacement yet. Truth was, about half the mates at Pirates Cove would jump at the chance to work aboard the 'Grand Slam', but Sid Hilton was a man of high ethics who would not recruit a mate from a fellow captain and cause hard feelings.

While Sid was sorting out a box of tangled hooks and jigs, he heard someone say, "Hello, mate, you better get that boat ship shape."

Without looking up, Sid recognized the affable voice of his old boss. "How are you doing, Cap'n Willie?"

"Just fine! I want to tell you, Sid, you did a nice job helping the Coast Guard locate that missing man and his wife."

"Oh, I didn't do anything any other captain wouldn't have done. I just told 'em they were out there fishing around us yesterday."

"Yeah, but with it blowing a gale, no other captain had his radio on this morning at six o'clock. If you had not called the Coast Guard when you did, that man and woman would most likely be dead right now. You know, they couldn't have lasted much longer."

"Well, I guess they owe their lives to Tommy Wilson then."

"Why do you say that, Sid?"

"Because if Tommy hadn't been down here on my boat screwing my brother's stepdaughter at three o'clock this morning, they would have never called me in the first place!"

"Oh, I see. I already heard talk up at the store this morning that you had let Tommy go. Didn't come as a surprise though. What's gotten into that boy lately? I wonder if he was fooling with some of those drugs coming down here from up north," said Willie.

"That boy sure knew how to catch fish; he'll be hard to replace," said Sid.

"Oh, I don't know." Cap'n Willie stepped down from the dock

into the boat and leaned against the fighting chair saying, "Have you met Bull? He's staying in the apartment over at my place."

"Oh, sure, I've seen him around. Seems like a nice kid," said Sid.

"Well, you know why he's here, don't you?"

"I figure he wants to be a mate."

"I believe he's got the makings of a good one," said Willie.

"What makes you say that?"

"He's been bitten by the sea. Same as you were . . . you know how the water can get to a fellow." Sid stopped what he was doing and looked at the old captain who said, "I remember seeing you, Sid, as a young teenager . . . out there on the dock every morning begging me to take you fishin'. You were willing to work for nothing jus' so you could go along," said Willie.

Sid jokingly replied, "Well, now that you mention it, you know, I do remember working for nothing when you first took me on. I believe you still owe me, old man." They both laughed. Then Sid said, "Tell Bull to come by this morning. I'll talk to him, but no promises."

Since none of the boats went fishing that day because of the weather, Bull was sleeping in. Cap'n Willie called his apartment and told him the 'Grand Slam' needed a new mate.

"What happened to Tommy?" Bull asked.

"Never you mind that. If you want a chance at getting this job, you better get over there before some other mate decides to jump ship."

The interview went well, especially when their conversation revealed it was actually Sid who gave Bull his unusual nickname ten years ago when he was still mating for Cap'n Willie. Bull said, "You had trouble remembering my name, Bradley, and when I caught that citation size bull dolphin, you started calling me "Bull," and it stuck. My dad and uncle picked it up, and they've called me Bull ever since."

One reason Bull's father liked the nickname was because he envisioned his son playing college football. He thought a tough, memorable nickname like "Bull" might somehow give his son an advantage.

Sid agreed to hire Bull on a trial basis through the summer to see how things worked out. The elated Bull was then given the grand tour of the boat and a briefing on basic safety procedures. Sid said, "I'm hiring you to help me catch fish and keep this boat in shape, but your first obligation, of course, will be to the safety and comfort of our passengers."

"Understood, Captain," the new trainee replied eagerly.

Sid said, "I have to run a couple of errands. You grab some lunch and meet me back here at two o'clock, and we'll get ready to go fishing tomorrow."

Bull was so proud to have his new job! First, he stopped by the ship's store to thank Cap'n Willie for putting in a good word for him, then he drove to Jimmy and Kelly's house in Wanchese to share the good news with them. When Bull stepped onto the back porch, he could see Kelly through the screen door studying at the kitchen table. He walked right in and proudly announced his new position. Kelly jumped up and gave Bull a congratulatory hug as she shared his excitement.

"Where's Jimmy?" Bull asked, wanting to tell him too. "I saw his pickup outside."

Kelly explained that since no one went fishing Jimmy's Uncle Paul, who owned a rental cottage at Kill Devil Hills, had asked him to ride up there with him to fix a plumbing problem. Kelly invited Bull to join her for lunch. She was just about to make herself a sandwich anyway. While they ate, Kelly asked, "How's it going with you and Heather?".

"Oh yeah, Heather. She's nice. We're going to a movie Friday night. Of course, I can't stay out too late; Captain Sid has charters lined up for the next six days straight."

After a pleasant lunch, Kelly stood at the screen door and waved goodbye as she watched Bull drive away, wishing he could have visited longer.

As it turned out, the small craft warning remained in effect for another day. Captain Sid and Bull spent the day working on tackle and familiarizing Bull with where safety equipment and key fishing gear were stowed.

Sid watched Bull rig a few ballyhoo baits and was impressed with the knowledge he already possessed. It was evident Bull would be a quick learner, and Sid was feeling much better about his decision to hire him.

Around three o'clock, Sid said, "Bull, go on home and relax for the rest of the day. Get plenty of sleep and be back here about five o'clock tomorrow morning . . . we're gonna take some folks fishing."

Next morning, Bull was the first person at the dock; naturally he was excited and anxious about his first day working as a mate for hire. Being familiar with the morning preparation routine, he had most of the work already done by the time Captain Sid arrived. Bull asked, "Do you want me to check the oil in the engines and generator, Cap'n?"

"Sure, I'll go into the engine room with you and show you a couple of things we need to keep an eye on down there."

Right before their party arrived, Sid sensed Bull's anxiety and said in a calming voice, "Settle down Bull, I remember my first day, working for Cap'n Willie. I was nervous as a goldfish in a bass pond. But you can relax, this should be an easy trip. These folks come fishing with me two or three times a year. I think they mostly come for the boat ride."

Sid's soothing tone made Bull feel more at ease. The party soon arrived, and before they got underway, Sid introduced Bull to them as his new mate. Winds had diminished overnight to less than 10 mph, and the sea was mirror calm. It promised to be a good day for fishing. The fleet unexpectedly came upon a well-formed weedline only twenty-five miles from the inlet. The storm had pushed a body of pretty blue water close to shore. Sid instructed Bull to put out a six-bait spread, "Maybe we can find some dolphin if we troll along this weedline," he said.

No luck. Almost an hour passed without a strike. Bull shouted up to Sid, "Tell me what I'm doing wrong, Captain."

"It's not us, Bull. No one else is catching anything either."

A member of the party tried to cut the tension by saying, "You couldn't ask for a nicer day to be out here. If the fish decide to bite, that'll be a bonus." Then he joked, "Hey Bull, do you know the difference between a pregnant woman and a light bulb?"

Bull thought for a moment, "No, what's the difference?"

"You can unscrew a light bulb," the laughing angler answered.

After several other jokes were exchanged, Sid suggested Bull rig a ballyhoo behind a pink sea witch and put it on a planer to get it down deep. It did not take long for success to strike. "Fish on the planer!", shouted Bull.

Bull felt a strong sense of accomplishment as one of the delighted anglers pumped the rod to bring the fish close to the boat. It was putting up a respectable fight. "What do you think it is, Captain Sid?" Bull asked excitedly.

"Well, I haven't seen it jump, so it's probably not a dolphin. Acts like it could be a small tuna or maybe a wahoo."

A member of the party quickly spoke up, "I hope so, they are good eatin'. Grilled wahoo was the special at the Seaside Restaurant last night, and it was some kind of good."

When the snap swivel was almost within Bull's reach, Sid stopped the boat completely. It was now Bull's job to pull in the leader line and gaff the fish. It is during this critical period many fish are lost. Bull took two wraps on the leader and shouted, "It *is* a wahoo!"

Captain Sid also got a look at the fish and said, "A nice one, probably forty pounds!"

Bull's adrenalin soared. For a split second he thought to himself, "Wouldn't you know it, my first fish is a dang wahoo!" Bull had heard other mates talk about these feisty fish with razor sharp teeth. He tried not to let anyone see how nervous he was. He said to the angler, "I wish this were a wire leader instead of monofilament. If those sharp teeth touch the line, this wahoo will be history."

Sid helped prevent it from happening by engaging the props to move the 'Grand Slam' forward just fast enough to keep the fish from swimming in circles and cutting the line. As Bull pulled the fish within gaff reach, Sid shouted a reminder, "Gaff him just behind the head!" But being inexperienced, the sight of such a nice fish gave Bull a case of wahoo fever. He was scared to death he would lose the fish. Much the same as when an unseasoned deer hunter gets buck fever at the sight of a trophy rack coming within gun-range, and he misses the shot. Bull's first swing with the gaff missed entirely. On his next attempt, Bull was less particular about where the gaff landed and caught the big wahoo in its mid-section. The party cheered as Bull heaved the forty-pound wahoo up over the side. Before Bull could get the feisty fish's head into the fish box, the wahoo jerked suddenly and plopped out of control onto the deck. This would not have happened if the gaff had been properly placed just behind the fish's head.

Nothing will make a group of anglers scatter faster than the chaos caused by a big wahoo flopping wildly in the cockpit. Three people sought safety in the cabin while two others scurried up the ladder to the bridge with Captain Sid. The angler who caught the fish stayed in the fighting chair but lifted his feet up and out of the way.

Bull grabbed the fish bat to subdue the beast. As he knelt to administer a calming blow to the wahoo's head, the fish's powerful tail knocked the gaff across the floor. The sharp point grazed Bull's knee. Luckily, the cut was barely deep enough to draw blood. This was a sobering experience and opened Bull's eyes to the possibilities of some dangerous things happening if proper safety procedures were not followed.

By the end of fishing time, Sid and Bull had scrapped out a decent catch for their party. They caught another wahoo, four king mackerel, about twenty dolphin, and they released one small sailfish. What great luck! Bull got to display a billfish flag on his first trip!

On the ride home, most of the talk on the marine radio was about the big blue marlin raised behind the 'Bushwhacker'. Captain Stormy Pruitt gave a colorful description of what he had seen, "The big son of a gun came up on a teaser just as pretty as you please. Bryan pitched a horse ballyhoo right in front of his nose, but he wouldn't take it! He swiped at it a couple of times and left. We thought he was gone. Then, 'bout a minute later, the big rascal was eye balling the teaser again! This time, we pulled up a naked ballyhoo on the short rigger to him, and sure enough, that big ole monster jumped on it like stink on shit! He was smoking a *fifty*! For a minute there, it was all I could do to keep up with him." Stormy paused and the radio went silent.

Sid asked, "What happened then, Stormy? Tell us the rest of the story."

"Well, then, he hunkered down deep, and we had about a fifteen minute stand off. 'Next thing you know, the line went slack! He was charging toward the boat! He went airborne right off our stern. Damn! What a sight! He was a real flyer! That big rascal grey-hounded all the way around to my starboard beam. He aired himself out good. The last time he jumped, I saw him whip his big tail all the way around to his head and got it wrapped in the leader. When he straightened out, 'twas all she wrote. That bad boy snapped a two hundred-pound tuna leader like it was a piece of kite string."

"How big was he, Stormy?"

"He was every bit as big as the one in the fountain there at the entrance to Pirate's Cove. I'm sure that marlin would go better than a thousand pounds. One of the members of my party got a really good video of him when he was greyhounding."

"I'd like to see it when we get to the dock," said Sid.

Later that afternoon, after he had finished washing down the boat, Bull felt pleased with his first day as a professional mate. He earned eighty dollars mate's pay from Captain Sid and one hundred dollars tip from the party of fishermen. He celebrated by treating Kelly and Jimmy to dinner at RB's Seafood and Steak House.

During dinner conversation, Kelly mentioned an upcoming banquet and dance honoring Jimmy's Uncle Paul who was retiring from the charter fishing business after this season.

She said, "It's the last Saturday night this month. Bull, why don't you ask Heather to go. We can all sit together."

"Sure, I'll ask her." Bull said.

It was now the last week of June. During the six short weeks Bull had been at Nags Head, he had become one of the guys. He blended in nicely, usually wearing a screen-printed T-shirt reflecting his interest in off-shore fishing, a pair of shorts, topsider shoes, a favorite cap, and, of course, polarized sunglasses. Since going out on his own, Bull had talked with his parents only twice, by phone. He was unaware, however, Cap'n Willie had been in regular contact with the Sullivans. Bull's father usually called Willie every week under the pretense of getting a 'fishing report', but he always ended up hearing a progress report on his son as well.

Dr. Sullivan was pleased with how quickly Bull had learned the ropes and had found work with one of the top captains in the fleet. He was very amused the day Willie told him about Bull's experience with bananas. Cap'n Willie said, "If there's one thing the majority of captains on the Outer Banks agree on, it's that you can't catch fish with bananas on the boat."

No one knows for sure where this superstition started, but true fishermen around the world live by this aphorism. Many charter boat captains possess an uncanny ability to smell bananas. If a captain catches a whiff of a banana among his party's provisions, it is written somewhere, he has the right to inspect every bag of groceries to verify his suspicions. Then, once bananas are found, the captain will tactfully suggest it would be prudent to leave them on shore.

"I remember a few years ago," said Willie, "during a benefit billfish tournament for women anglers only, I couldn't figure out why we had not hooked a single white marlin when fish were in my baits all day. Practically every boat returned to the marina flying marlin flags, except for us. I wanted to crawl into a hole. In fact, I did. I lifted the engine room hatch, planning to check the stuffing boxes on the propeller shafts, and that's when I found the culprit. A bunch of bananas! Some SOB had placed a bunch of bananas in there. To this day, I don't know who!"

Dr. Sullivan laughed, but Willie continued, "Doc, that's nothing compared to what your son did. It was his third or forth day matin' on the 'Grand Slam.' About the time they reached Hell's Gate, Sid smelled bananas. He thought maybe the scent was coming from the boat up ahead; he hadn't detected bananas when the party boarded. Then, the smell of bananas became much stronger and Sid stomped his foot to get Bull's attention, below in the cabin. He scurried up the ladder to see what his captain wanted. Sid said in a solemn voice, "Bull, someone brought bananas on this boat, and I want you to find them."

The rookie replied innocently, "No problem, Captain Sid, they're mine. I just ate one. Want me to bring *you* up a banana?"

The following week, Dr. Sullivan learned his son had been initiated into the Blue Marlin Club. Several of Bull's friends, who were mates on other boats, tossed him off the dock into the harbor after 'Grand Slam' brought in a blue marlin weighing 425 pounds. Captain Sid would have insisted on releasing the fish had it not gotten tail wrapped and died during the fight. Cap'n Willie also mentioned to Dr. Sullivan, a thousand-pound blue marlin had been spotted by several boats lately. "If your son lands *that* fish, he'll become famous overnight."

Bull's father seemed to be warming up to the idea of his son's dream to become a charter boat captain someday. On those occasional days Dr. Sullivan went to the country club to hit the links, he would sometimes think how beautiful the ocean must be today and wonder how Bull was doing. He had even told his golfing friends about his son's ambition to become a charter boat captain.

That morning, when Bull arrived at the marina for work, he stopped by the ship store and said hello to Cap'n Willie as usual.

Willie told Bull, "It's official. The 'Grand Slam' is signed up for the Outer Banks Big Game Fishing Tournament in August."

"So, Sid's sponsor came through?", Bull asked.

"Sure did. The check came yesterday from the car dealer friend of his up in Virginia. Everything is all set. The 'Grand Slam' is registered in all levels of competition. That fellow sent an eighty-five hundred dollar check down here to cover entry fees."

"Holy shit! Eighty-five hundred dollars?" Bull exclaimed.

"That's a pile of greenbacks, ain't it, boy." Willie went on to explain the minimum entry fee was one thousand dollars per boat for the first level. Boats participating on all eight levels had a chance at winning more than $400,000 in prize money.

"Sid told me it was a big money tournament, but I had no idea it was that big," said Bull as he noticed a pickup truck drive past the store. "Sid's here. Catch you later Cap'n Willie."

"Here, take this and read it when you get the chance." Cap'n Willie handed Bull a copy of the tournament rules.

Later that morning, Dr. Sullivan telephoned Cap'n Willie and said, "I saw an article in the local paper about the marlin caught on the 'Grand Slam' the other day. The paper had a nice picture of the angler standing beside the big fish hanging by its tail. I'm quite sure I see Bull's leg and elbow, but dammit, they cut him out of the picture. The sportswriter mentioned Sid Hilton as the captain, but I'm very disappointed he didn't say a thing about Bull being the mate."

Willie responded, "I noticed the same thing myself, Doc. As Sid would say, it's a crying shame. Some of those writers just don't realize how important a good mate is to offshore fishing. I wish I knew how to make them give the mates more credit."

Later in their conversation, Willie told Dr. Sullivan about the upcoming billfish tournament.

"It sounds like all the top guns will be there," Dr. Sullivan said with interest, "I'm sure Bull is looking forward to it; he's always been very competitive. Do you think Sid and Bull have a chance at winning, Cap'n Willie?"

"Well, you never know what's gonna happen in a tournament. Few years ago, a couple of fellows on a 22-foot outboard won the whole thing with a grander. Let me tell you, seeing such a big marlin coming in on such a small boat was a sight to behold."

"Willie, do you think it will take a thousand-pounder to win this year?"

"Probably not, but I'll tell you what, Doc. If anybody's gonna catch that ole grander they've been seeing out there lately, I'll put my money on Sid Hilton. He has a natural instinct for finding big fish."

Dr. Sullivan asked Cap'n Willie to mail him a copy of the tournament brochure, adding he and Mrs. Sullivan might surprise their son by driving down for the festivities.

There was a healthy spirit of camaraderie and competition among the mates at Pirates Cove. They enjoyed getting together at the end of the day to swap stories. On Saturdays, there was a standing invitation for mates to drop by the 'Carolina Pirate' for a little get-together after their work was done. The 'Carolina Pirate', a private charter boat, ran parties on weekends and participated in several annual billfishing tournaments along the east coast. Captain Dan Parker, owner of a radio station in a small Virginia town, was a mate himself for a couple of summers during his younger years. He kept plenty of cold beverages on board and enjoyed sharing refreshments with the mates.

Today, Jason, mate on the 'Blue Mist', was sitting on the dock box complaining about getting stiffed by his party. "I worked my ass off for those jerks today. We caught sixteen tuna . . . I put sixteen nice tuna to the dock! Those cheap sons of bitches tipped me a lousy thirty bucks. Shit! I felt like throwing it right back in their faces."

Carey, mate on the 'Carolina Pirate', spoke up and said, "Damn, Jason, that's too bad; I got a hundred and fifty-dollar tip today."

"You lucky dog, Carey."

"I would have gotten a whole lot more if we had caught that monster marlin we saw today." Carey commenced telling the others about his close encounter with old 'Bubba'.

"Did you get a good look at him?" asked Larry.

"Oh yeah! We got a really good look at him," injected Captain Dan, as he opened the cooler and popped a brew. "I'd like to catch a marlin like that during the tournament!"

Carey took over the story, "You would not believe how big that marlin was! And wouldn't you know, the monster didn't even look at the mackerel I had rigged on my big 'one-thirty'. He went straight to a naked ballyhoo on a dink rig."

Nate, from the 'Morning Star', said, "I swear! Doesn't it happen every damn time? The biggest fish always go after the lightest line you're pulling."

Carey picked up the light-tackle rod 'n reel the marlin had attacked to illustrate his story, "I hate he ruined this rig; we had just caught a little white on it. I tightened the drag as much as it would stand." Shaking the reel so the others could hear it rattle, he said, "Old 'Bubba' smoked these washers. This little reel started making grinding noises, and that's all she wrote; the line snapped like a banjo string breaking."

"Shit!" said Larry, "Everybody's seen this monster but me. I'll tell you one damn thing, if the big rascal *bills* us, the 'Sea Dragon' is gonna collect! His ass is coming to this dock!"

Bull said, "Don't feel like the lone ranger, Larry. I haven't seen him either, but I'm looking for him every day.

"Hey, you guys!" Their conversation was interrupted by Jimmy calling from the parking lot, "Don't forget Uncle Paul's retirement party tonight." Bull watched as Kelly walked toward their pickup. She looked back at him and waved goodbye.

As their little gathering was breaking up, Cap'n Willie came walking down the dock toward Dan's boat and said to the mates, "Make sure you fellows are there tonight."

Captain Paul Edwards, Jimmy's uncle, was a living legend among anglers on the Outer Banks. His reputation for finding fish even prompted a few of the commercial fishermen to keep track of his whereabouts. Paul always displayed the American flag on his charter boat. He named it after the USS Ranger which was the first ship to carry the Stars and Stripes to a foreign port in 1778. At seventy-three years of age, Paul was still running offshore parties every day except Sundays. His Sundays had always been dedicated to church and family.

Down in eastern North Carolina, a special occasion like this called for a 'Pig Picking'. Sawyers Bar-B-Que had been slow-cooking three pigs since 4 o'clock that morning, and the smoked tender pork was now ready to be pulled and served. The feast took place on the festival grounds at Pirate's Cove Yacht Club under a large tent with mesh side-curtains to keep mosquitos out. The dance floor and stage for the band were at one end of the tent.

Bull and his date, Heather, were saving a table near the dance floor while watching for Kelly and Jimmy to enter the tent. At first glance, Bull did not recognize the girl who walked in right ahead of Jimmy. Doing a double take, he realized it was Kelly and was instantly mesmerized by her stunning appearance. He was overcome by the same captivating feeling he had on the first day their eyes met in class, only now she was even more beautiful. Her lovely tan shoulders and long shapely legs were revealed by a short red sundress, while auburn hair fell around her shoulders in loose sexy curls. When Kelly's luminous eyes turned toward Bull, he did not try to hide his enchantment. To be honest, she felt flattered by Bull's romantic gaze. As she walked to the table, Kelly thought to herself, "No one has ever looked at me like that, not even Jimmy."

Jimmy was so busy speaking with friends, he didn't even notice the way Bull was looking at his wife. However, Heather did, and when Bull said, "Kelly, you look fabulous," Heather spoke up, teasingly, "You didn't mention how fabulous I look."

It was obvious Bull had put his foot in his mouth as he stumbled for words, "Uh . . ."

Trying to help, Kelly laughed and said, "Oh Heather, you always look fabulous, doesn't she Bull?"

He stuttered, "Oh, oh sure! Sure Heather, you always look terrific." He clumsily tried talking his way out of the embarrassing situation, "It's just that I never see Kelly wearing anything except old fishing clothes!" His face turned red, "Sorry, I don't think that came out right either." They all laughed and sat down at the table. Jimmy joined them a few minutes later.

After dinner, the band performed a couple of ballads, then stopped to allow the president of the North Carolina Charter Boat Association to present Captain Paul Edwards with an engraved plaque. Paul was honored for his many years of service to the tourism and charter fishing industries of North Carolina. He was also given a beautiful *Steve Goione* painting of a marlin crashing a school of tuna.

The crowd applauded as Captain Paul accepted the award. Being the photographer in the family, Jimmy was busy capturing the occasion on film. A couple of fellow captains went forward to honor their old friend Paul with a few kind words. Just when the program was concluding, Captain Stormy Pruitt, known for his antics, and seemingly permanent smile, came forward and said, "If you don't mind, I would like to make a couple of comments on behalf of my close friend, Paul."

"Uh oh," said Paul, knowing there was no telling what his crusty friend might say.

"Seriously, Paul, we are all mighty proud of you for getting this much deserved award." Stormy paused, looked across the crowd, devilishly snickered, and said, "Paul has been fishing for so long, even if he misses a fish he can smell the hook and tell you what kind it was," he laughed. "I've been Paul's dock buddy for more than ten years, and I can tell you he's very tight-lipped about his fishing secrets. Up until last year, he would hide his best baits from me. I'm not lying . . . if there was a particular rig or color seawitch catching a lot of fish, he'd have his mate hide it away before they returned to the dock. My mate and I would be glancing over at his rigs, always hanging on the arms of the fighting chair, thinking, "Hell, we're pulling the same stuff as old Paul, and here he is throwing a jag of tuna on the dock, and we didn't catch but three! That Paul, he can be sneaky!" When the audience slowed their laughter and applause, Paul said, "But, if you watch him close, you can learn a whole lot from Paul. I know I have." Stormy was on a roll. The audience was enchanted by his down home charisma.

"I remember the time he was trying to untangle a backlash on an old Senator reel." Stormy looked over toward Paul, "You remember the day I'm talking 'bout, don't you?"

"Yeah," Paul laughed, "but you don't have to tell everybody about it."

"Oh, yes, I do. I told you I would never let you live it down."

The audience laughed as Stormy continued, "It was the dangest 'rat's nest' of fishing line you ever did see . . . was on a big old reel. Paul asked me if I could untangle it for 'em. I said, 'Hell, Paul, don't be so tight with your money. That line's probably four or five years old anyhow. Why don't you just cut if off and buy some new line, for heaven's sake?" Stormy paused for a moment, laughed a little and continued, "Well, most of you know 'Ole Paul is not one to give up on a spool of expensive fishing line, jus' cause it's gotta little age on it. Paul tied the end of it onto a piling. Then, he commenced to untangle the rat's nest as he walked backward down the dock. I was busy doing something on my own boat and wasn't watching him too close. Next thing I know, Paul screamed! 'AAAAOOOH!' I looked down the dock and all I could see was Paul's old hat flying up in the air, and splash! He had backed right off the end of the dock!" The crowd burst into laughter.

At that point, Cap'n Willie walked up onto the stage accompanied by a man carrying a large marlin trophy and an envelope. Willie took the microphone and said, "I'm glad Stormy didn't know any secrets to tell on me when I decided to retire," he laughed. "Like the time I fell asleep at the helm. Y'see, I never have mastered the art of sleeping with one eye open like some people I know. I had been fishing for twenty-eight days straight. My loran said the inlet was forty-five miles away. It was a long ride home; I was so tired; I must have nodded off. What woke me up was the boat jumping across my own wake; she had turned completely around! A couple of passengers came out of the cabin and hollered up to me, 'What's going on, captain?'" Willie paused for a moment, then chuckled saying, "I told 'em I spotted a box floating back there and wanted to check it out for dolphin." The audience exploded into laughter.

After they became quiet, Willie cleared his throat and turned to the honoree saying, "Again, Paul, congratulations from all your friends here at Pirate's Cove." He paused and turned to the crowd. Looking in the direction of a group of tables where many of the mates were seated, Willie said, "I'm sure the younger folks here would like to see us old fella's get off the stage so the band can start playing some of that music they're listening to nowadays. But first, we have been asked to make a very important announcement about the fishing tournament coming up in a few weeks." Turning to the man on stage with him, "Most of you already know this gentleman . . . let's welcome Mr. Bob Erickson, the director for the Outer Banks Big Game Fishing Tournament."

As the audience applauded, Bob said, "Thank you. This announcement Cap'n Willie and I are about to make will be of particular interest to all you professional mates."

Cap'n Willie held up the handsome trophy while Bob opened the envelope revealing the slip of paper inside. Bob said, "I have here a check in the amount of fifty thousand dollars!"

Willie spoke with enthusiasm, "This check, and you heard right, it's for fifty thousand dollars, along with this trophy is the Top Mate Grander Prize!"

The audience started buzzing with conversations . . . especially among the mates. Willie continued his enthusiastic tone, "This is a bonus category being offered only to mates working on charter boats entered in the tournament." He paused to let it sink in, "Of course, I know you mates already have financial arrangements with your captains and fishing parties. You know what you're going to be paid, and you have an idea of how much a bonus you can expect if your boat places in the money. But, this is additional money only mates can win. The entire fifty thousand dollars, and this beautiful trophy, will be awarded to the mate who brings in the heaviest blue marlin weighing one-thousand pounds or more! You gotta catch a grander to win it."

"Is this for real?" asked Jason from the audience.

Another mate asked, "How much is the entry fee?"

"There will be no additional entry fee required," answered Bob.

Still skeptical, Larry asked, "Who is the sponsor, and why is he doing this?"

Bob said, "Larry, we can only answer part of your question. The benefactor of this award has asked for his identity to remain secret, or he will withdraw the offer. I don't even know who he is myself. His only contact with the committee has been through Cap'n Willie."

Willie spoke up, "This generous prize is being offered to give you mates the recognition you deserve for all your efforts in making a fishing trip successful. And, even if no one wins, the publicity surrounding this prize will raise the level of awareness about how important a good mate is on a charter boat. So, in the spirit of friendly competition, the sponsor is offering this new category. May the Top Mate win!" The audience began applauding before Cap'n Willie finished. He got closer to the microphone and talked louder, "And by golly, we want to see that thousand pounder, 'Old Bubba', hanging right here on the dock at Pirate's Cove!"

The crowd cheered with excitement as the band started playing upbeat music. The first ones dancing were Kelly 'n Jimmy and Bull 'n Heather. The dance floor filled with captains and wives, mates and dates.

Later that evening, Bull's friend Jason came over to their table and asked Heather for a dance. She looked to Bull for his approval. "No problem, go for it."

Soon after Heather and Jason were on the dance floor, someone came over and asked Jimmy to take a few more pictures of Paul with his friends. Jimmy said to Bull and Kelly, "Why don't you guys dance . . . I'll only be a few minutes."

Bull did not hesitate to take Kelly's hand and lead her to the dance floor. The band was playing an up tempo number, giving everyone a fun workout. Then, without missing a beat, they segued into a slow romantic ballad. Bull pulled his dancing partner close, but she was careful to keep a respectable distance between them, all the while scanning the crowd for her husband. There he was, far across the room, still taking pictures, so Kelly allowed herself to be pulled into Bull's arms.

Gradually, their bodies pressed closer together. Seeing the same adoring look in his eyes as when she first arrived at the gala, Kelly could not deny the warm and tingling sensation he provoked deep within her. It was gratifying to know she had made such an impression on him. For a fleeting moment, she was Bull's date . . . a pretty girl at a dance with a handsome young man. She wished this feeling would last all night.

"You are, without a doubt, the prettiest captain at the party," he whispered.

She looked around at several 'old salts' and responded with a soft laugh, "Ha, that's not much of a compliment."

A third voice abruptly entered their conversation, "If I didn't know better, I'd say you two had something going on," teased Heather. She and Jason had made their way across the floor and were dancing next to them. Her friend's innocent remark had broken the spell. Kelly felt a sudden flush and knew her face was turning red.

Ever so subtly, she recreated a respectable space between them, after all, she was a happily married woman dancing with an eligible bachelor. Attacked by her conscience, she remembered how Bull was all she had thought about when trying on new dresses for the dance. Each time she stood in front of the mirror, she had secretly wondered if Bull would like the way she looked in it.

With Heather and Jason disappearing into the crowded dance floor, Bull wanted desperately to recapture the moment they had shared. "In case you haven't noticed, I can't keep my eyes off of you," he said.

"Bull, please don't say things like that. You know I'm a happily married woman."

"Do I? All I can say is Jimmy had better be glad he found you first, because I would surely try to sweep you off your feet."

The song was ending. She glanced across the room and saw Jimmy returning to their table. "Don't you think it's hot in here, Bull? I need to sit down for a while."

No other form of recreation compares to off-shore fishing, in terms of its potential for sudden attacks of blood rushing excitement . . . except, maybe baseball. Both can be painfully slow, but one solid hit brings everyone to their feet. It may be the spectacular leap of a mako shark or the heavy splash of a giant tuna . . . you never know what may be lurking beneath your baits.

Like most mates, Bull looked forward to every trip with anticipation, and he would not be disappointed today. Captains Paul Edwards and Stormy Pruitt had discovered a school of giant bluefin tuna about fifty miles northeast of the inlet and had put out a call to other charter boats within range. What an unforgettable sight it was! The ocean boiled with several large schools of tuna in a feeding frenzy. Each giant fish appeared to weigh three hundred pounds or more.

Captain Sid and Bull had been fishing with very little action about twelve miles to the south when they got the word. No time was wasted picking up the lines and steaming northward. When they spotted the fish from a distance jumping high out of the water, Sid thought they must be frolicking porpoises. As the 'Grand Slam' moved in closer, captain, mate and anglers alike could hardly believe their eyes. A couple of fishermen grabbed their cameras and began snapping pictures. A camcorder was filming the action. These hungry giants launched themselves out of the water as if they were tomahawk missiles being fired from a nuclear sub. Not just a few fish, there were hundreds . . . maybe thousands.

Within minutes an angler on almost every one of the twenty-five boats working the school was testing his strength against one of those powerful brutes. On this day, one charter boat out of Pirate's Cove set a new North Carolina state record for bluefin tuna, 744 pounds! As a conservation measure, federal regulations limited each charter boat to possessing only one giant bluefin tuna per day during this time of year.

Bull's most exciting moment came just as he took a wrap on the leader line and prepared to bring a giant bluefin within reach of the gaff man. David Pittman, an experienced offshore angler fishing with the party aboard the 'Grand Slam' had volunteered for gaff duty. The rope on the flying gaff was secured to a cleat, and David stood ready to set the deadly hook.

Just as Bull pulled hard on the leader, Captain Sid shouted, "There's something else back there! Another big bluish fish! Something really big is after your tuna!" Sid screamed, "Holy shit! It's a big shark! A big mako!"

Bull toiled to bring the tuna closer, "Now! David! Gaff it. Hurry up!" Bull shouted.

David deftly set the large hook just below the tuna's pectoral fin. Although their catch was secured to the boat by a half-inch rope, the real battle was about to begin.

From the flying bridge, Sid had a better view of what was about to happen and gave a play-by-play description, "Here it comes! Can you believe this? That big shark wants your tuna . . . you'd better get him in the boat fast."

Bull quickly opened the transom door and grabbed the rope to haul in the big tuna. David manned the rope with him.

Sid shouted, "He's got it! That mako's got your tuna by the tail . . . you better be careful down there! That's a terrible big shark!"

There was another member of the fishing party on the bridge with Captain Sid. He had a camcorder pointed toward the action.

Sid said, "I hope you're getting this on film."

"Yes, this is incredible!" the man answered.

The next few seconds turned into a tug of war between two determined men and one very powerful shark. The ten-foot long tuna's head was in the transom door, but Bull and David could not gain another inch from the much larger shark. The great shark's nose came out of the water thrashing from side to side; its steely cold eyes rolled up into its head as he gnawed and jerked at the tuna's body.

Finally, a third angler clutched onto the rope seeing more manpower was required. The battle ended with the three men falling backwards onto the deck as what was left of their tuna slipped through the transom door and into the boat. The lower portion of the tuna's body had been ripped away.

Buckets of fresh blood poured from the scuppers into the ocean as the giant bluefin bled to death. The thirteen-foot mako shark lingered off their stern circling the pool of blood. Bull quickly tore a chunk of meat for bait off the tuna's ravaged body, attached it to a large hook, and tossed it over. David got into the fighting chair, strapped on the harness, and prepared for the battle he hoped would follow. Not only are mako sharks excellent table fare, they are known for their spectacular leaps when hooked.

For a second, everyone got excited when the shark began to nose the bait, but he refused to take it. Apparently, the seventy or eighty pounds of tuna meat he had just eaten was enough to satisfy him.

Their mutilated fish and the story of the shark created quite a bit of interest with the tourists gathered at Pirates Cove that afternoon to see the day's catch. Even after losing the lower portion of its body and buckets of blood, the bluefin tuna still weighed 357 pounds.

As for the potentially award-winning video that would have surely made the evening news . . . Nothing! No picture, only the audio had been recorded! The crew did get a kick out of having it replayed several times, but the tape could not be played in mixed company because of all the expletive descriptions. The cameraman explained ----- it was his wife's camcorder, and today was the first time he had tried to use it. Maybe, next time, he would know to remove the lens cover.

It was the peak of summer vacation season on the Outer Banks; practically every hotel room was occupied. Beach cottages were booked solid, and the campgrounds overflowed with vacationers. The 'Grand Slam' had fishing trips scheduled every day. It got to the point where both Sid and Bull hoped for a 'blow day' so they could catch up on their rest.

Captain Sid counseled Bull, "I hope you're saving some money. You know, your paycheck will take a nose dive when these tourists are gone."

Bull was working so hard lately he did not have much time for a social life. His last date with Heather was several weeks ago. Bull had not yet met a girl with whom he wanted to develop a relationship. It seemed the only girl Bull had enjoyed spending time with was Kelly, and she was married to his best friend. When the three of them did things together, he tried not to allow himself to think of her as anything other than a friend. Just yesterday, after most of the boats came in early loaded with dolphin, Bull gave Kelly and Jimmy a windsurfing lesson in the sound. Jimmy might never get the hang of it, but Kelly caught on very quickly. While he struggled to keep his board righted, she and Bull windsurfed all the way to Whale-bone Junction and back.

There were several college girls working at the Yacht Club for the summer as lifeguards and waitresses who were actively pursuing the handsome and eligible bachelor. Bull had shown some interest in Terri, a cute waitress who worked at the restaurant and raw bar. While there that night, he invited her to go to a movie on her next night off.

At the end of the day, the raw bar was a popular place for mates to get together and enjoy a few beers as well as swap fishing stories. The topic of conversation this evening was the unbelievable girly show they had seen on the high seas today. It had taken place aboard a 60-foot private yacht called the 'Bay Lady', which had been docked at Pirate's Cove for the last several days. The ocean was very calm today; so, the owner had decided to run out to the Gulf Stream where the fleet was fishing. As the pleasure craft approached the fishing grounds, loud music could be heard blaring from large speakers on her deck. It soon became apparent the 'Bay Lady' was out for more than a joy ride. Amid the hoots and howls of several rowdy men on board, a buxom woman was dancing topless on the bow. Two other women were also performing a tantalizing dance on the aft deck.

The scofflaws aboard the 'Bay Lady' were catcalling to fishermen on other boats. One man yelled, "Hey, look at what I caught!" as he fondled the breasts of one of the strippers.

The boat cruised among the fishing fleet for more than two hours, making sure every party of anglers caught a glimpse of their voyeuristic activity. Needless to say, the mates spent much of the day untangling crossed fishing lines.

Although the display was the highlight of the day for many fishermen, not everyone was amused by the disruptive activity. Two captains called the Coast Guard and registered a complaint about the offensive behavior. Three petty officers waited on the dock in the afternoon for the 'Bay Lady' to return, but she had apparently continued her voyage down the intracoastal waterway to another port farther south.

It was Tuesday afternoon, August 13. On what had otherwise been a beautiful summer day, the blue sky began disappearing behind mountainous thunderheads. Although the sky grew dark, the ominous clouds had not deterred anyone. All along the dock, people were preparing for the Big Game Fishing Tournament which would begin the next morning. Pirate's Cove Yacht Club had been buzzing with activity all day. Last minute maintenance and repairs kept some crews busy. Others were milling about, socializing. Bull was putting new outrigger lines on the 'Grand Slam'. The engine hatch was open on the 'Carolina Pirate', where Captain Dan's fourteen year old son, Justin, and his mate, Carey, were replacing an exhaust elbow on the starboard engine to remedy an overheating problem.

Every available boat slip at the marina was occupied. High dollar prize money had attracted many of the world's top sport fishing teams who traveled the tournament circuit. There were boats from Hatteras, Myrtle Beach, and Virginia . . . some from far away as New Jersey, Delaware, and even Florida.

The threatening clouds came closer and flashed with light as if there was fire within them. When they were directly over the marina, there was a deafening thunderclap followed by a downpour that sent people scurrying for shelter into boats and under the circus-like tent which had been erected to accommodate festive activities, including the captain's meeting, the captain's ball and awards ceremony.

As rain pounded the canvas roof above them, several anglers gathered around the hospitality bar, enjoying drinks and exchanging information. Word circulated about several blue marlin recently caught. The 'Sea Dragon' had released a 600-pounder yesterday. Several days ago, a private boat reported seeing 'Bubba', the nickname given the elusive "grander" marlin. Every captain and mate who had seen the great fish agreed it weighed well over a thousand pounds. Those sightings heightened enthusiasm for the Top Mate Grander Prize of fifty-thousand dollars. It was still a mystery who was sponsoring the special prize for mates only . . . a mystery to everyone except Cap'n Willie. But, as Jason so aptly put it, "I don't give a shit who he is, I'll gladly take his money." Several mates had been speculating how they would use the money if they won. Carey wanted a new pickup truck. Kelly and Jimmy said they would pay off their house, and Jason said he would make a down payment on Paul Edwards' charter boat, the 'Ranger'. Paul was still looking for someone to buy his rig when he retired in the fall.

As quickly as it came, the storm passed, lending credence to the saying, 'If you don't like the weather on the Outer Banks, just wait a few minutes.' Once dockside activity resumed, someone noticed smoke coming from a tall piling at the end of a pier. A bolt of lighting had splintered the 12-inch diameter pole, and it was smoldering all the way down to the waterline. Luckily, the boat nearest it was not damaged.

As the skies cleared, Dan wanted to take the boat for a quick sea trial to make sure there were no exhaust leaks. As Carey released the dock lines, Jimmy and Kelly walked by. "Where are you guys going?" asked Jimmy.

"Just a quick run down the waterway to make sure I tightened all the bolts. Come on, go with us."

"Yeah, hop on," invited Dan, "help yourself to something to drink." So, they went along for the ride, helping themselves to refreshments from the 'Carolina Pirate's' always well-stocked bar. After about fifteen minutes of riding and socializing, Dan said, "The temperature is holding steady at 175 degrees, looks good to me, let's head back."

"I'll check for any exhaust leaks," said Carey, entering the engine room. Emerging a few moments later, he dropped the hatch closed and reported, "Everything's fine down there."

When Dan slowed down to turn around, Justin pointed toward a peculiar looking object in the distance and said, "Look out there, Dad! Is that a boat?"

"What *is* that?" queried Kelly.

Jimmy replied, "I noticed it a few minutes ago, but at first glance, I thought it may be a collapsed duck blind. Dan, maybe we better take a closer look." The Pamlico Sound was still unsettled from the strong thunderstorm which had passed through earlier. Jimmy and Kelly walked around to the bow for a better look, and almost immediately, together they exclaimed, "They're waving! Someone's waving for help!"

The object turned out to be a tiny paddle boat, the kind two people sit on and pedal with their feet. Instead of two people, though, there were four; a young couple in their early twenties, another female who appeared to be about 13 years old, and an *infant* of all things, not more than six months old! The small boat was swamped and barely afloat. The young mother was sitting on the water-logged craft cradling the baby in her arms. The girl and man were in the water clinging to the boat. None of them were wearing a life jacket. It was a frantic sight.

Dan carefully moved the 'Carolina Pirate' into position to help. The younger girl panicked and started swimming for the boat. Carey tossed her a life ring on a rope and pulled her to safety, Dan dared not engage the propellers until after the girl was safely on board. Kelly shouted to the others, "Stay with your boat, until we get closer!"

The tiny boat was very unstable. The mother holding the baby shifted her weight slightly and her movement caused the craft to upend and capsize. Mother and baby disappeared beneath the over-turned boat. Justin threw several life jackets toward them and Jimmy dived in to help. As Captain Dan anxiously watched, the young mother surfaced without the infant. "Save my baby! I lost my baby!" she screamed as she struggled to keep herself afloat. Jimmy swam to her rescue.

The young man, who was the baby's father, dove under the tiny vessel and resurfaced without the baby. He dove again. Kelly tossed Jimmy the life ring and he helped the struggling mother hold on to it, as Justin pulled them in. Carey was on the verge of jumping over to help look for the lost infant when, miraculously, the baby appeared! It was being pushed to the surface by the heroic young father. Carey reached down as far as his arm could extend, grabbed the baby by the collar of its shirt, and lifted it into Kelly's arms. The baby was silent, which frightened the young parents, who were being helped into the boat through the open transom door. The panicked couple feared the worst when they did not hear any sounds from their child, but when Kelly placed the baby in its mother's arms, it became obvious all had survived the ordeal unharmed. While its mother cried tears of joy, the bright-eyed baby boy was smiling and kicking as if to say . . . "Let's do that again, it was fun!"

On the way to the dock, Dan and his friends learned the Tennessee family had been camping with relatives, enjoying their first trip to the beach. The young father said they were riding on the paddle-boat in a protected cove at the campground. The water was so calm; he decided to venture out into the sound. He did not risk going very far, but when he tried to go back, he realized his mistake. They had been pedaling with the current . . . and returning, could make no headway against the tide. Together, he and his wife had pedaled as hard as they could, but their efforts were useless against the strong current. Then, the thunderstorm came through and swept them even farther out.

The mother said they had been clinging to the swamped boat for more than an hour praying someone would come and save them. She said to Dan, "Mister, God answered my prayer when he sent your boat."

The family was checked out by the Dare County volunteer rescue squad and given transportation to their campground. After the excitement was over, Bull showed up, curious to hear about the incident. Jimmy and Kelly were still aboard the boat and Bull joined everyone in the salon as the story was retold. Bull appeared to be attentive, but he barely heard a word Kelly was saying. In his imagination, he was a thousand miles away on a remote Caribbean beach . . . just him and her. If only she knew how much he longed to have her for his own. Then, Jimmy made some comment about the rescue. His voice brought Bull back from the islands at the speed of light. Glancing toward Jimmy, he thought, "I must stop thinking about her."

Kelly continued, "That helpless baby must have had a guardian angel."

"Guardian angel?" Bull expressed doubt, "you don't really believe in guardian angels, do you?"

"Of course, I do. Maybe not so much in the literal sense, but I do believe sometimes God sends a guiding spirit to protect his children. Call it divine intervention, if you will, but you must admit, something sent Captain Dan out there today."

"Oh, thanks Kelly, no one has ever referred to me in the same sentence with an angel before," laughed Dan.

To tease Kelly, Carey said, "Hey, Captain, don't you think Kelly looked natural holding that baby a while ago?"

The guys found humor in that comment, but she retorted, "I can't imagine me ever doing that for real."

"Well, I hate to interrupt all this talk of angels and babies," said Jimmy, "but we better get going, Kel. Gotta be back for the Captain's meeting by eight o'clock, you know."

A little after seven o'clock, fishing teams started gathering for the captains meeting to review the tournament committee's rules. Bull glanced at his wrist to check the time. He could see only the tan line where his watch was usually worn. Out of habit, he still looked at his wrist for the Zodiac diver's watch he had received as a gift from his mother. It had been missing for several days. Bull decided to walk around to the other side of the harbor where the 'Grand Slam' was docked and look for the watch on the boat. He hoped to find it before his parents arrived for the Captain's Ball Friday night. Their visit was supposed to be a surprise, but Cap'n Willie accidentally let it slip this morning. With everyone at the captain's meeting, the dock seemed deserted. He noticed Kelly on the 'Lucky Duck'. She was lifting the engine hatch. He jumped on the boat to give her a hand asking, "Is there a problem, Kelly?"

"No, Jimmy just asked me to make sure the battery charger is turned on. It is. Everything looked fine down there." As they closed the hatch, Kelly asked, "Shouldn't you be at the meeting, Bull?"

"Yeah, I'm going back around there in a few minutes. I came down to look for my watch on the boat."

"You still haven't found it?"

"No, and my mom tells everybody how she bought it for me at a duty free shop in the Bahamas. I know she'll be pretty upset that I've lost it. I've searched my pickup and the apartment. It has to be on the boat somewhere," Bull said, nodding his head in the direction of the 'Grand Slam'.

"I'll help you look," she volunteered, as the two of them stepped aboard. It had been quite a while since Kelly had actually been inside the salon of the 'Grand Slam'. She had forgotten how beautifully it was decorated. There was no clutter. Fishing tackle was neatly stowed away. You would never know it was a charter fishing boat if not for the dozen fishing rods hanging from the ceiling. Even the rods, black with a gold wrap, were decorative and coordinated with the gold finished reels attached to them. Most charter boats had very basic interiors with no frills, but Captain Sid's wife's background in interior design showed in their boat's tasteful decor.

18

A green runner protected the plush beige carpet along the high traffic area. The windows were covered with mauve mini blinds and accented by nautical motif curtains tied back with decorative rope. A mahogany hi-lo table, with a marlin inlaid into its surface, was centered in front of a L-shaped corner sofa adorned with colorful throw pillows. A pair of cozy club chairs were across the cabin from the sofa.

As Kelly began searching under each seat cushion for the missing watch, Bull said, "I'll check the engine room. I suppose it could have fallen off my arm into the bilge."

"Yuk! Let's hope not." After searching the salon, Kelly moved down into the galley area for a look around and as she closed a cabinet door, she glanced up to find Bull staring at her. She asked, "Did you find it?"

"Oh, no I didn't"

"Just as well, I doubt even *your* watch could survive being in a boat bilge."

"I'll check the crew quarters," he said stepping down into the narrow companion way knowing he would have to squeeze past Kelly. When their bodies brushed together, he stopped and stared at her again, wishing wildly Kelly knew what he was really feeling. His words were strained, Kelly, I . . . there's something. . ." but, his heart racing, Bull was unable to put his feelings into words.

"An air of tension fell over the cabin. Kelly asked cautiously, What, Bull?" His actions made her feel uneasy.

But her qualms subsided when the young man yielded to his conscience uttering, I . . . really do appreciate you helping me look for the watch." As he turned to enter the crew quarters, he added, "My mother would never let me hear the end of it if I've lost it."

Completing her search of the galley and moving into the master suite, she commented, "Well, for your sake, I hope it turns up."

A few moments later, just as she was about to exit the suite, Bull entered and accidently bumped into her causing her to fall backward. He reached to catch her, but they tumbled together onto the bed. At first they laughed about it, but as they gazed into each other's eyes, the two of them became quiet and for an instant, time seemed to stand still. This was more than Bull could resist. With the woman he idolized in his arms, he forgot she was the wife of his best friend.

For the moment, Kelly, too, could only think of the handsome young man whose arms were around her. They both became flooded with feeling of desire. As Bull gently caressed her cheek, Kelly knew she must control their fervor before things got out of hand. Trying to regain her composure, she urged, "Bull, don't."

"Kelly, don't you feel what I feel?"

She felt paralyzed, helpless to resist his longing blue eyes. "Bull, we really . . . shouldn't," she said ineffectually.

"It would be so easy for me to fall in love with you," he said.

"Please," she spoke softly, all the while, her lips longing to meet his. As their tender kiss became passionate, she was overwhelmed by a sea of emotions. Ever since that night at Uncle Paul's party, Kelly had tried her best not to think of Bull in a romantic way; yet, sometimes, just couldn't help herself. Now, alone together, the opportunity was there for their shared desire to be satisfied, but how far would she allow it to go? Although the kiss was wonderful . . . everything she had anticipated . . . her head filled with thoughts of how she was forsaking her husband's trust. Realizing her conscience would not allow her to continue this tryst, she pushed herself away, "I can't do this, I just can't." She quickly crawled off the bed and said, "I really don't know what I was thinking," as she ran her fingers through her tousled hair.

Feeling guilty for putting his friendship with Kelly and Jimmy in jeopardy, he said, "Kelly, it's my fault. I got carried away and I'm sorry."

"No, it wasn't *all* your fault. Maybe I've been sending you the wrong signals lately, but now, I realize. . . I just can't . . . this is wrong," she sobbed and rushed up into the salon. Bull caught her right before she left the cabin. He placed his hands on her shoulders and turned her so they stood face to face. Neither of them noticed the figure of a man walking up the dock in the twilight, watching them but unable to hear their conversation.

Bull was apologetic, "Kelly, you know I'd be lying if I said I wasn't attracted to you, but I promise I'll never put you in a position like this again. Can we try to forget it happened and still be friends?"

Confused by the myriad of emotions within her, she said tearfully, "I don't know, can we?"

"Yes, I promise," he said.

They both felt relieved the episode had stopped before it went further and Kelly found some consolation in thinking the encounter had somehow served to strengthen her character. She could now put her fascination with Bull behind her and work to strengthen her relationship with Jimmy.

She turned to walk out the door, tucking in her shirt which had become disheveled. "Don't you two look like cozy love birds?" They were startled by the vaguely familiar voice. Tommy Wilson stood on the dock. It was the first time they'd encountered Tommy since Sid had fired him and had hired Bull to take his place several months ago.

Bull asked with surprise, "Tommy! What are you doing here? I heard you were working in Morehead City."

"I came to win the big tournament, college boy."

"Oh, yeah? Whose boat are you fishing on?"

Tommy pointed down the dock about six slips over, "The 'Shady Lady', belongs to Captain Carl Lamb. We came up from Morehead this afternoon."

"Nice looking rig."

"She's a real fish raiser, too," Tommy boasted.

"We'll see about that tomorrow, won't we," countered Bull.

"Reckon we will." In his usual smart aleck manner, Tommy added, "I was walking to the boat to get my smokes; didn't mean to interrupt anything. But, let me give you some free advice, college boy. Don't let Captain Sid catch you bringing your girlfriends to the boat. I can tell you from experience; he don't like that."

Kelly spoke up, "I'm *not* his girlfriend! It's not what you think, you creep! I was just helping Bull look for something."

"Could you find it, darling?" Tommy laughed sarcastically.

Kelly responded, "You're disgusting!" She stepped up onto the dock and turned to Bull, "I'm going up to the meeting." Glaring toward Tommy she added, "My husband is waiting for me there."

Tommy ogled Kelly's behind as she walked away and teased Bull, "Whew, those legs reach all the way up to her ass . . . I can't blame you for tapping that. Tell me, college boy, how does it feel to have those long legs wrapped around you?"

Bull jumped to the dock, grabbed Tommy by the shoulder, spun him around, and said, "You son-of-a-bitch! You have no reason to talk about Kelly that way!"

Tommy threw down his cigarette and shoved Bull back a couple of steps as if challenging him to a fight. "You think you're man enough to stop me?" he dared.

"Damn right!"

"I'm gonna whip your ass right now, college boy." Tommy surprised Bull with a swift kick to the groin area. Bull fell and rolled to one side in pain. In street fighter fashion, Tommy took further advantage of Bull by kicking him a couple of times in the ribs while he was down. It appeared the fight might be over before Bull could land a single punch. As Tommy lifted his foot to smash Bull's face, he grabbed it, causing Tommy to lose his balance and fall. Jumping to his feet, Bull charged toward Tommy and hit him with a solid tackle. Tommy fell against the fish cleaning station and overturned two large garbage cans spilling fish guts and scraps. As Tommy got up from the slippery muck, Bull connected with a couple of good body punches followed by a solid right hook to Tommy's chin, landing him face down in the stinking fish carcasses. Bull waited to see if his adversary would get up for more. As he stood, Tommy picked up the head of a tuna and heaved it at Bull with both hands. As he ducked, the ten-pound fish-head crashed through the window of a parked car. At that point, Tommy was raging with anger. He jumped onto a boat, grabbed a gaff, and jumped back up to the dock. Slapping the handle of the gaff into his other hand, he dared Bull to come after him, "Come on, college boy, let's see how tough you are, now!"

Bull contended, "Is this how you want to win the fight . . . using a weapon? I thought you wanted to fight man to man."

Tommy threw the gaff back into the boat and said, "Well, come on smart ass, show me what you got."

Bull charged toward Tommy with such momentum they both plunged into the harbor. The skirmish continued underwater. They found themselves underneath the hull of the 'Grand Slam'. Tommy used the propeller shaft as a brace to kick Bull in the chest pushing him to the bottom of the lagoon. Tommy started swimming up for air. Just before reaching the surface, Bull grabbed his feet and held him under. Tommy kicked but could not free himself from Bull's tight grip. Panicked for oxygen, Tommy looked down at Bull who was gazing up with a calm smile on his face. Thanks to Bull's experience free-diving on the reefs in Florida, he was nowhere near the limit for holding his breath. Finally, Bull let go, allowing Tommy to reach the surface. Tommy gasped for air and yelled, "You tried to drown me, you son of a bitch!" He looked around expecting to see Bull. He should have had to come up for air by now, Tommy thought. He swam to the ladder on the dock obviously puzzled by Bull's disappearance.

"Looking for me?" Bull remarked in a cavalier manner, standing in the boat. "Don't you know smoking is bad for your health, Tommy? You're ruining your lungs."

"Kiss my ass," said the exhausted Tommy as he climbed onto the dock.

Bull asserted, "Just keep your mouth shut about Kelly."

"All right, all right!" said Tommy as he walked toward his boat. Looking back at Bull, he said, "Make sure you don't get too close to the 'Shady Lady' in the tournament, or you'll have a few lines cut off."

As far as the weather was concerned, it could not have been a more perfect day for the tournament to begin. There was not enough breeze to stir the American flag hanging loosely atop the flagpole at Pirate's Cove Yacht Club. Sailboaters may loathe a day so calm, but to a sport fisherman, with fifty miles to run, the slack flag symbolized a pleasant ride across smooth waters.

The fleet of more than two hundred entrants set a course for the Gulf Stream. Just off the inlet, a TV news helicopter hovered low, allowing the camera man to capture exciting footage of several sleek yachts slicing across the ocean at up to 35 knots, leaving trails of foam behind them. The TV reporter would later refer to it as a parade of power, describing the yachts as expensive platforms to accommodate sport fishermen, their specialized tackle, and high-tech electronic gear. It is true most boats over thirty-five feet in length were equipped with radar, loran, and sophisticated fish locating sonar. A few captains, even subscribed to services that faxed computer generated satellite images right to their boats, showing temperature gradients where fish would most likely be holding. With a few simple strokes on a keypad, the captain could enter the desired latitude and longitude into his Global Positioning Satellite receiver and activate his autopilot to guide the boat to the desired destination. An alarm would sound once they arrived. With first place prize money of three to five-hundred thousand dollars, tournament fishing was serious business to many; but, of course, fancy electronic gadgets were not requirements for catching a winning marlin. Some of the top money winners in previous years had fished aboard small boats powered by outboards equipped only with a radio and compass.

In fact, when all was said and done on this first day of fishing, one of the top three marlin weighed in was caught by a relatively inexperienced angler aboard a 23-foot Grady-White powered by twin outboards. The Grady-White team also picked up $5,000 for weighing in the first fish. They tricked a 408-pound blue marlin into biting a green machine trolled behind a bird-shaped teaser.

Three other blue marlin were brought to the weighmaster on the first day. Captain Paul Edwards' 'Ranger' weighed in a 486 pounder, which earned them one-half point per pound, for 243 points. His team also picked up an additional 70 points each for releasing two whites. That put the 'Ranger' team in first place after the first day with 383 points.

Down the dock, a rowdy fishing team was boisterously celebrating their second place position. Captain Sid recognized one voice rising sharply above the rest, boasting, "I told you we'd have a chance to win this thing; I can out fish most of these guys blindfolded." It was Tommy Wilson. This was Sid's first encounter with Tommy since the day he had fired him. The boat Tommy now worked on, the 'Shady Lady', caught a 452 pounder which was worth 226 points. They also received 70 points for a white marlin release, giving them a total of 296 points after day one.

A short while later, everyone watched as the 'Sea Dragon' backed up to the scales to weigh a blue marlin. Upon seeing the fish, Tommy scoffed, "Hey, Larry, there's no way your fish will weigh 400 pounds!"

Not to be intimidated, Larry jumped up to the dock, got right into Tommy's face and challenged, "How much you want to bet?"

Tommy's captain spoke up, "A hundred dollars, Tommy. One hundred dollars says his fish won't go 400 pounds." Larry took the bet. Then, a spontaneous flurry of wagering ensued as several well-heeled yachtsmen started throwing C-notes around like candy wrappers, betting whether the fish would make the cut.

A rope was secured around the marlin's tail and the fish lifted for weighing. After anxious moments waiting for the scales to settle, the weighmaster announced, with disappointment in his voice, " Close, but not close enough . . . 394 pounds."

A raucous round of haughty "I told you so's," and "I damn well knew it's" spewed from the mouths of the 'Shady Lady' team as they collected their wagers. Tommy caustically held out his hand to Larry awaiting payment. Larry reluctantly slapped a one hundred-dollar bill into Tommy's hand and walked away. Bull caught up with him and said, "Don't feel bad Larry, anybody would have brought that fish in . . . even that asshole."

Sid, who was standing nearby, added, "The crying shame is, your fish probably lost ten pounds on the way in. I'm sure it was more than four hundred when you landed it." Tournament rules stated any team entering a blue marlin less than 400 pounds would receive no points for the day; the 'Sea Dragon' was penalized accordingly.

They had also caught and released three whites, worth 70 points each, but they received zero points for them.

Bull's team scored 280 points. True to his boat's namesake, Captain Sid caught a grand slam, the only boat to do so . . . releasing a blue marlin, a sail, and not just one, but two whites. Bull had proudly run the flags up the outrigger pole for all to see. He looked over toward the 'Lucky Duck' to see if Kelly and Jimmy were still around and was very disappointed to see them driving away in their pickup. He wondered if Kelly was trying to avoid him after what had happened last night.

Tournament standings after the first day:

1st Place: 'Ranger'	486 pound marlin	243
	two whites	140
	Total	383 points

2nd Place: 'Shady Lady'	452 pound marlin	226
	one white	70
	Total	296 points

3rd Place: 'Grand Slam'	two whites	140
	one sail	70
	one blue	70
	Total	280 points

| 4th Place: 'Carolina Pirate' | three whites | 210 points |

| 5th Place: 'Grady-White' | 408 pound marlin | 204 points |

6th Place: 'Bushwhacker'	one white	70 points
	one sail	70
	Total	140 points

Although a total of nine blue marlin were caught on the opening day, no one mentioned sighting 'Bubba'. Day two was Thursday, and the ocean remained calm. Rules limited each boat to fish any three of the four tournament days. Since the forecast called for a low pressure front to move in that evening, most teams decided they would go today and lay at the dock tomorrow, when winds were predicted to be fifteen to twenty miles per hour.

However, a few seasoned captains strategically decided they would leave their boats tied today. Captain Paul Edwards, who was in first place, and Captain Sid Hilton, who was in third, felt the sea was too flat for good billfishing. They elected to fish on Friday and Saturday giving the front a chance to move through and stir up the water a bit.

Bull came up from 'Grand Slam's' engine room just in time to see the 'Lucky Duck' pass by . . . today's first boat to pull out. Bull thought it was a little unusual seeing Kelly on the bridge standing beside Jimmy instead of in the cockpit with the party. When she did not even look in his direction, Bull took it as a sign of friction between them. Paul waved as his nephew passed by and said to Sid, "Jimmy told me his charter is a family group with no offshore experience, and he was taking them on the calmest days."

Over on the 'Shady Lady', amid his team's bellyaching, Tommy was having difficulty deciding what to do. His unshaven captain was sitting in his chair at the helm pressuring in his gravelly voice, "What's it gonna be, Tommy? We going or not?"

Tommy replied, "Those guys are probably right. Fishing should get better after the front moves through. Maybe we ought'a lay at the dock today, too."

Captain Carl questioned, "What if the front is stronger than they expect and nobody gets out tomorrow?"

"I doubt that will happen," answered Tommy.

One of the other anglers on the 'Shady Lady' team popped open a can of beer and lifting it to his lips said, "Breakfast of champions!" The others laughed as their companion chugged it on down. With a satisfied sigh, he wiped his mouth on his sleeve and groused, "Hell, if those guys lay today, that just means better fishing for us. I say we go out there and kick ass while they sit at the dock!"

"Damn right!" Captain Carl agreed emphatically, "That's what I say, too." He started the engines and asked his mate, "You with us, Tommy?"

Still standing on the dock, Tommy watched as Sid and Bull got into their pickups and drove away. Hesitating, he cast off the lines and said, "Shit! Let's go catch that *big* son-of-a-bitch today," and off they went.

As it turned out, the experienced captains were right. Billfishing was very slow with only two blue's, six whites and four sails registered. However, there was quite a bit of activity at the weigh station in the meatfish category.

The 'Point Runner' weighed in a 46-pound bull dolphin which would be hard to beat. The 'Seahawk' entered an impressive 57-

pound wahoo. And finally, here came Tommy and a teammate dragging a bigeye tuna up the dock. Bull was there for the weigh-in and offered to help get the fish to the scales, but Tommy tersely refused saying, "We don't need your help, college boy."

Hearing the comment, Sid said "Well, Bull, I see Tommy still has the same charming personality."

The 'Shady Lady's' rowdy team members gathered around the scales. When the weighmaster announced 212-pounds, they whooped and hollered rebel yells! Tommy turned toward Bull and said in his cockiest voice, "Hey, college boy, this fish is gonna win $10,000 for us." Bull did not reply.

A significant change in the standings came when the 'Lucky Duck' returned with the only blue marlin to be weighed today. Jimmy and Kelly's fishing team consisted of a family of four vacationing at Kitty Hawk: John Langston, an executive for a national farm supply company; his wife Phyllis; their daughter Christie, a college freshman; and their high-school age son, Kevin, who caught the marlin. John's brother and his wife were also on the fishing team.

Jimmy and Kelly were worried the fish might not meet the 400-pound minimum weight, but her concerns changed when she saw Bull in the crowd of onlookers gathered to see the fish being lifted onto the scales. How could she look Bull in the eye, she thought, after what had happened between them night before last? Their friendship could never be the same. For Jimmy's sake, she would have to pretend nothing had ever happened. She questioned herself, how could I have gotten into such a mess.

Cheers erupted when the weighmaster announced 420 pounds. They received 210 points for the marlin, to add to the 70 points they had earned yesterday for a sailfish. Now, tied for third place, everyone was congratulating the 'Lucky Duck' team. Bull said to Jimmy, "Pretty work captain, did you see 'Bubba', out there today?"

"Not a trace. I think that fifty thousand dollars is gonna stay right where it is, in some rich guy's bank account," Jimmy joked in his usual friendly manner.

Kelly's eyes met Bull's, but neither said a word. It was a little uncomfortable. Jimmy, however, was so jubilant over the marlin, he did not detect their awkwardness; he was too busy congratulating Kevin. Kelly and Bull each tried to think of something to say to the other that would break the tension building between them. She noticed the watch on his wrist. Before she could stop herself from bringing up such a potentially sensitive subject, she remarked, "Bull, you found your watch!" As soon as she heard herself say the words, she felt a knot tighten in her stomach. Why did I comment about the very subject I wanted most to avoid, she wondered?

Bull replied, "Yeah, it was in the bait freezer up at the ship's store! Cap'n Willie found it this morning," he held up his arm and jested, "It took a lickin' and kept on tickin'."

Still feeling happy about his catch, Jimmy said, "Say, Bull, if you help us clean up the boat, we'll treat you to dinner at the raw bar."

"Sounds good to me."

As they walked toward the boat, Kelly was relieved Bull had not acted any differently toward either Jimmy or her. She hoped, maybe, after all, the three of them could continue their friendship.

Day three. Friday morning the wind was very brisk. The American flag at Pirates Cove stood out straight. The updated forecast called for northwest winds up to 25 miles per hour with waves up to 6 feet; the front was much stronger than predicted. The Coast Guard had issued a small craft advisory.

Wind whistling through the outriggers was of no concern to most of the fishing teams. Only about twenty-five boats were preparing to get underway, including the 'Grand Slam', 'Ranger', 'Sea Dragon', 'Carolina Pirate', and 'Bushwhacker'. Even though Tommy's team was not fishing today, he was up early, walking the dock while sipping on a cup of coffee. He passed by the 'Grand Slam' and said to Bull, "Hey, college boy, you better hang onto your ass today, it's gonna be rough as shit out there."

"Don't you worry about me . . . I've got a good feeling about today," said Bull as he turned his back on Tommy and walked into the cabin to secure loose items. He already knew they were in for a rough ride.

The boats passed though the inlet without a problem. In fact, with the wind out of the northwest, it was almost calm near the shore. However, about five miles out, the ocean started getting rough. Seas were soon five feet. By the time they were fifteen miles offshore, waves were running to eight feet. On their radios, some captains were talking about turning back if it got worse. Over the course of the next few miles, it actually seemed the waves were subsiding; so, the determined fishermen held their course for the Gulf Stream.

20

By the time the boats arrived at the fishing grounds, some anglers were already seasick, but once baits were in the water, action came quickly, which helped them forget about feeling queasy. "Fish on! Fish on!" Boat after boat hooked up with yellowfin tuna and gaffer-sized dolphin.

After a couple hours of this hot bite, Captain Stormy on the 'Bushwhacker' said over the radio, "Catching these forty-pounders is a lot of fun, but it ain't gonna win us any money." Stormy voiced what many other captains were also thinking. The category for largest tuna was likely in the bag for 'Shady Lady' with the 212 pounder

Tommy Wilson weighed-in yesterday. Besides, the meatfish prize was pennies compared to top money paid for billfish.

"That's what I dislike about tournaments," said Sid. "Here we are, having a terrific day of fishing, couldn't ask for better, and in the back of our minds we know it's not good enough. In a way, tournaments seem to diminish the sport. It's a crying shame."

"Crying shame or not," replied Stormy, "I'm going overboard and look around." In off-shore fishermen's jargon, Stormy meant he was going to work his way out beyond the edge of the continental shelf in hopes of finding a big marlin in deep water.

An excited voice was heard on the radio. "Committee boat . . . 'Sea Dragon' is hooked up with a sailfish."

"Time is 11:45am,'Sea Dragon'. Committee boat standing by. "

Captain Sid was not too far from the 'Sea Dragon' and saw the sailfish leaping. He watched Larry grab the leader and release the fish.

"Committee boat, give 'Sea Dragon' one scratch for a sailfish."

"Copy that 'Sea Dragon', 11:51am, first points today. Committee boat standing by."

Sid continued to work the area near where the sailfish was caught while several other boats moved out beyond the 100 fathom curve. There were seven people aboard the 'Grand Slam'. In addition to captain and mate, there were two anglers. One was Rick Murray, a car dealer from Virginia who often fished with Captain Sid. On several occasions, Rick had proven his endurance catching giant bluefin tuna off Hatteras in the winter months. In fact, Rick caught one last winter they felt certain weighed over one-thousand pounds. They will never know for sure, however, since bluefin were out of season at the time. The fish had to be tagged and released. This was Rick's first experience in a billfish tournament. He said he signed up because he hoped to join the Thousand Pound Club with a tournament winning marlin.

The first angler in the chair today would be Rick's friend, Cliff Ogg, who owned a small chain of furniture stores. Both men had their wives along with them to share in the excitement of the tournament, and, of course, the festivities that were scheduled each evening. Even though the seas were rough, the ladies were doing just fine on Sid's comfortable 54-footer.

The seventh member of the group was Thomas Eubank, the observer assigned by the tournament committee this morning. A native son of Jamaica, Thomas used to run fishing charters out of Port Antonio until he lost his boat in a hurricane. He then took a job working as narrator on an island tour bus. That was how he met the wealthy widow from Elizabeth City who had taken a cruise ship to Jamaica. A few months later, Thomas moved to the states and married her. They had a beach home in Corolla; so, of course, Thomas frequented the marinas on the Outer Banks. He was the first person to volunteer as an observer this year. Within a short time, the likeable Jamaican had everyone on board saying "No problem, mon, no problem."

Later, the wind shifted to the northeast causing seas to become much rougher in the stream, forcing most of the boats to return to the calmer green water where 'Sea Dragon' and 'Grand Slam' were fishing. By midday, just as boredom was setting in, Bull spotted what they had been waiting for. Jumping to his feet, he shouted, "Blue marlin! Hot on the right short rigger! " Cliff took his position, ready for action, but the fish did not strike. He put the reel in free-spool hoping to entice a bite by dropping the bait back to the marlin. Sid and Bull kept their eyes peeled; it was unusual for a marlin to lose interest without sampling a single bait. Then, to everyone's surprise, the long-rigger clip on the opposite side of the boat snapped open and line began to be stripped from the reel. Cliff scrambled for the bending rod and lifted it out of the holder. He dropped the rod tip toward the fish, jumped into the chair, braced his feet and set the hook. Assuming they had hooked the marlin, Sid maneuvered in a wide arc that swung the boat around in front of the fish. However, something didn't look quite right, he shouted down to Bull, "Did you see the strike?" The fish was not behaving the way a marlin typically does, and Sid suspected it might be a tuna instead.

"No, Sid. I'm not sure what we have back there," Bull turned Cliff's chair toward the line, "It's an able fish though; took a lot of line."

Captain Paul Edwards saw Sid's sudden maneuver and asked on his radio, "What'cha got over there, Sid?"

"Don't know for sure, Paul. We had a blue marlin look us over, but we haven't seen 'em air-out yet. I'm thinking now, it might be a big tuna."

For thirty minutes, Cliff fought the fish without much progress. He'd gain a little line, then lose it again. Sid said, "It'll be a crying shame if it turns out to be a shark."

"Don't 'tink dose negative 'touts mon," said Thomas in his unmistakable island accent. "Once, in 'da Port Antonio, Jamaica Marlin Tournament, I recall fightin' a fish like 'dis for near half a dey. Turned out to be a five 'undred pound marlin....wit' my line wrapped 'round his tail. We jus' took our time and we got 'em. No problem, mon," he smiled.

The rod was curved over the transom as the fish dug to greater depths. Cliff's wife rubbed his shoulders to relieve his cramping muscles. Then she gave him a drink of water to replenish his body with fluids as perspiration poured off him under the blistering hot sun.

Time ticked away . . . all the while, Sid heard radio reports of other boats hooking up with billfish. The 'Carolina Pirate' scored seventy points for a white. Captain Stormy on 'Bushwhacker' scored a double....two released whites. A few minutes later 'Sea Dragon' scored another sailfish.

Bull could see Sid was getting impatient and said, "Well, Sid, if it's a tuna Cliff has on, I hope it's more than 212 pounds, don't you?"

"Oh, yeah!" laughed Sid as he swiveled around in his chair at the helm. "Tommy will blow a gasket!" Sid turned up the volume on his radio as another boat reported a catch.

"Committee boat, 'Deep Pleasure'. Score one white marlin for us."

"Copy that 'Deep Pleasure', 1:51pm. Committee boat standing by." Sid knew he could and should be racking up some serious points during this hot marlin bite, but here he was . . . hooked up with something he didn't even know what the hell it was. Sid demanded, "We gotta get this fish to the boat now! Put some pressure on him, Cliff."

But Cliff responded, "I don't know, Sid. We've got a lot of time invested in this fish; I really don't think it's a shark. I don't want to lose it."

Rick added, "This might be a foul hooked blue marlin like Thomas said. Anyway, Cliff's gaining a lot of line now; it shouldn't take much longer."

The next radio transmission was more than Sid could stand, "Committee boat, 'Carolina Pirate' is hooked up with a big blue marlin." In the background the excited team of anglers could be heard whooping and hollering. They had obviously seen the big fish strike. Dan had decided to make this tournament a Parker family event and his wife, Marsha, was in the chair.

"Committee boat copies, 'Carolina Pirate', 1:59. Also, all vessels, please be advised, there is one hour of fishing time remaining. Committee boat standing by."

With time running out, Sid made the decision to aggressively attempt to raise their fish. He pivoted the 'Grand Slam' in a slow circle while Cliff applied full drag and pumped the rod. It was now or never. Within minutes, a flash was sighted deep beneath the boat, and, soon, the large silvery object began taking shape. Cliff brought the leader within Bull's grasp, who shouted, "Tuna! Bigeye tuna!"

Rick manned the flying gaff and by 2:15pm, the subdued fish was hauled through the transom door. The anxious captain did not give his team time to celebrate. He ordered, "Get that spread of marlin baits out! We gotta move fast!"

As Bull quickly worked to get his baits in position, he told Cliff and Rick, "I hope Tommy's around when we weigh your tuna this afternoon. I want to see his face when we take that $10,000 away from him." Everyone laughed.

Meanwhile, over on the 'Carolina Pirate', Marsha was pumping and winding with all her strength. Captain Dan was backing down to help his wife regain line. "This could be that grander!" shouted Carey. "Don't lose 'em! Just think of it as my new pickup truck you got on the end of your line," he chuckled.

"He's coming up! Coming up!" exclaimed Dan. The fish leapt out of the ocean in clear sight of several nearby boats. The 'Grand Slam' was closest, only 200 yards away. Bull watched the heavy marlin lift its head out of the water while trying to shake the hook free. He speculated to Rick, "I'll bet it's the same marlin that looked us over earlier."

"Do you think it's big enough to be a grander?" Rick asked.

"It's no grander, but it does look heavier than the one Captain Paul brought in. I hope they get 'em," said Bull.

While the 'Carolina Pirate' continued battling the big marlin, the radio channel became cluttered with numerous other boats reporting catches.

"Committee boat, score one white marlin release for 'Top Secret'."

"Copy that, 2:30, 'Top Secret'."

"Committee boat, score a white for 'Lucky Strike'."

"Also 2:30, 'Lucky Strike', committee boat standing by."

The 'Ranger' hooked up with their third white of the day. Meanwhile, on the 'Carolina Pirate', Marsha had eased her marlin closer; her teammates were urging her not to risk applying too much pressure, fearing the hook might pull free. "Let's just take our time and nurse this fish in nice and gentle," implored Dan.

"Committee boat, give 'Grand Slam' two scratches for double whites." Rick and Cliff's wives had the pleasure of catching the pair. Both fish had really put on a show, going airborne and flipping upside down.

"Copy that, Sid, two whites scored at 2:50 PM. Committee boat reminding all teams, ten minutes of fishing time remains."

Marsha admitted to Carey, "The muscles in my arms and legs are burning."

"No pain, no gain. Just hang on to that fish, whatever you do!" coached Carey.

Repositioning herself in the chair, the determined wife and mother, started working with renewed energy. All the while, the observer watched to make sure no one other than the angler touched the line or rod.

At three o'clock, the committee announced fishing time had expired for the day and asked, "Are there any boats hooked up now, besides the 'Carolina Pirate'?"

"Yes, committee boat, 'Point Runner' has a white on now."

"Grand Slam also has a white marlin hooked up . . . uh oh. We just jumped him off!"

"Too bad, Sid," said one of the other captains.

Tournament rules allowed any fish hooked and reported to the committee boat prior to 3:00 PM could be played until caught, except all fish must be through the bridge near Pirate's Cove Yacht Club no later than 6:00 PM.

Several boats moved in close enough to watch the 'Carolina Pirate' land the blue marlin; yet, carefully, they kept a safe distance in case the fish made another run. Following the last hour's flurry of activities, the radio fell noticeably silent. Carey was looking intently over the transom for the leader line to appear when he heard the next transmission echo from the surrounding boats, "Committee boat, 'Point Runner', give us one scratch, please."

"Copy that, 3:08, 'Point Runner'."

"I see the knot for the double line!" Carey shouted to his onlooking teammates.

Justin stood ready with flying gaff in hand waiting for the right moment. There was no doubt in anyone's mind this fish would exceed the 400-pound minimum weight requirement. "I've got the leader!" Carey took several wraps bringing it within reach of Justin's 8-foot gaff. The exhausted fish offered little resistance until it felt the sharp stainless steel point piercing its flesh. The marlin made one final effort to run, but it was too late; the big fish was secured to a cleat with a half-inch rope.

As the exhilarated fishing team labored to hoist the marlin into the boat, the observer spoke on the radio, "Committee boat, score one captured blue marlin for 'Carolina Pirate'."

"Copy that 'Carolina Pirate', 3:15. Congratulations! Now, let's go home."

"Pretty work, Dan," said Captain Paul. Then Paul said to Sid, "I reckon that'll take me down a notch, won't it, Sid."

"That fish will knock us all down a notch, Paul."

Then Paul asked, "How much you reckon it'll weigh, Captain Dan?"

"I'm quite sure she'll go more than five hundred pounds. She measures seventeen inches around the base of her tail. What do you think, Paul?"

"Well, from what I saw when you hauled her in, I expect that fish'll go six-hundred . . . easily. I'm glad you got 'em."

By the time the boats returned, there was an especially large crowd gathered around the weigh station. One of the charter captains always called in a daily fishing report to the local radio stations. He had reported a large blue marlin was on the way to Pirates Cove to be entered in the tournament. Tourists and participants were anxious to see how much it weighed. Kelly and Jimmy arrived as the trophy sized marlin was being lifted to the scales and made their way through the assembly to stand near Bull and his team.

Kelly also saw Tommy and his 'Shady Lady' team close by. They had stayed at the dock drinking beer all day, celebrating "the biggest tuna prize" which they thought was in the bag. They were anxiously waiting to see if it was true the 'Grand Slam' had caught a tuna larger than their's. Making eye contact with Bull, Tommy shook his fist in a hostile gesture.

The weighmaster announced, "Score 612 points for the 'Carolina Pirate' team." The rules stated that captured marlin weighing six-hundred pounds or more would receive one point per pound. The excited onlookers cheered and friends congratulated Dan and his team on moving into first place.

Next, for the meat fish category . . . Bull recruited Jimmy and Carey to help drag the big tuna to the scales. Upon seeing it, Tommy didn't even wait to find out how much it weighed. "I'll be damned!" Tommy exclaimed shaking his head in disgust and storming away. He bumped into Kelly and nearly knocked her down. Instead of saying excuse me, he spitefully blurted, "Your lover boy got lucky today, but it's not over yet. Tell him I'll get even. I'll bust his ass tomorrow!"

Shocked by Tommy's outburst, Kelly quickly looked around to see if anyone she knew had heard him. Luckily, she was surrounded only by tourists. Suddenly she felt very threatened, realizing Tommy could be a real one word. Kelly had an uneasy feeling as she watched the big tuna being lifted to the scales. The weighmaster announced, "We have a new leader in the meatfish category for tuna . . . 336 pounds for the 'Grand Slam' team."

A female voice shouted, "Grand Slam', isn't that my Bradley's boat? Yeah! 'Grand Slam'! Way to go Bradley!", she shouted.

Bull happily recognized the voice from the back of the crowd as his mother's. She was the only person who still called him Bradley. She had never approved of the nickname "Bull."

Bull's parents had come to attend tonight's Captain's Ball. Bull greeted them with hugs and introduced them to his friends. Sid walked over to meet them. "Mom, Dad, this is my captain, Sid Hilton. These are my parents, Diane and Brad Sullivan."

Diane said, "Hilton? Of the famous hotel chain?"

Sid joked, "No, they're the poor side of the family," he laughed.

When Sid and Brad shook hands, Brad said, "Oh sure, I remember Sid from when he was mate on Willie's boat."

"That's right! I'll tell you, Dr. Sullivan, you've got a very fine young man here," Sid patted Bull on the back, "and I'm mighty happy to have him fishing with me."

Point standings after day three:

1st Place: 'Carolina Pirate'	612 lb marlin	612	
	4 whites	<u>280</u>	
	Total	892	points
2nd Place: 'Ranger'	486 lb marlin	243	
	sail	70	
	5 whites	<u>350</u>	
	Total	663	points
3rd Place : 'Grand Slam'	4 whites	280	
	1 blue	70	
	1 sail	<u>70</u>	
	Total	420	points
4th Place: 'Shady Lady'	452 lb marlin	226	
	1 white	<u>70</u>	
	Total	296	points
5th Place: 'Lucky Duck'	420 lb blue	210	
	1 white	<u>70</u>	
	Total	280	points
6th Place: 'Bushwhacker'	3 whites	210	
	1 sail	<u>70</u>	
	Total	280	points

The Captain's Ball was preceded by a catered buffet dinner more elegant than anything you may have seen on one of the world's finest cruise ships. The banquet table stretched the full length of the huge, air-conditioned tent. There was a bounteous selection of fresh, local seafood including mahi mahi, blackened tuna, grilled wahoo, shrimp cocktail, clams casino, and crab imperial. There was also prime rib and steamship round being carved by a chef. The opulent salad and dessert bar would complete a meal fit for a king.

The centerpiece of the banquet table was a large ice sculpture replica of the grander blue marlin mounted in the fountain at Pirates Cove Yacht Club. This was a white linen affair with a candelabra on every table. Most of the men attending were sporting nautical blazers, while many of the women wore their finest gowns. There was a troop of uniformed waiters and waitresses to meet every need. One of them was Terri, the girl Bull had dated recently. He had invited her to accompany him to the gala, but she had already agreed to work. He was not really disappointed, though. He liked Terri, but in all honesty, he was only using her as a way to get his mind off the one he truly wanted to be with.

Bull was seated at a large round table with Sid, his wife, Grace, and also Jimmy and Kelly. Admittedly, it was somewhat awkward for Bull and Kelly to be sitting at the same table, after what had happened between them; but, everyone knew the three of them were such good friends, it wouldn't look right otherwise. There were also **21** two empty chairs being held for Bull's parents, who had not yet arrived. Making conversation, Jimmy said, "Bull, you never mentioned your father is a doctor."

"It's no big deal, really." Bull replied modestly.

Kelly said, "Well, you know I'm studying to be a nurse. Who knows, I could be working with him some day."

"Maybe you'd rather work with my mother. She's a doctor, too."

"You're kidding!"

Sid added, "Wasn't your grandfather also a doctor, Bull?"

"Yeah, the original Dr. Bradley Sullivan."

Jimmy remarked, "Bull, you're not going to be the black sheep in the family, are you?"

"I just may," he answered with a sigh, "my parents took it pretty hard when I dropped out of school."

"They are coming to the dinner, aren't they?" asked Sid.

"They'll be here soon, I'm sure. It's hard for them to get anywhere on time. If one isn't on call, the other is," he laughed.

Jimmy excused himself to greet his aunt and uncle who were just arriving. Jimmy was very close to Uncle Paul. Sid said to Grace, "Honey, let's go over to Willie's table and say hello to Miz Bitsy." Left alone with Bull, in the middle of the crowded room, Kelly used the opportunity to express her concerns about what Tommy had said earlier. Kelly took a drink of water and said, "I'm afraid Tommy Wilson may cause trouble."

"Why do you say that?"

"I'm afraid of what he might say . . . what might get back to Jimmy. Tommy was really upset about your tuna this afternoon. The creep nearly walked over top of me when he was leaving. He called you . . . my *lover boy*." Bull lifted his eyebrows with interest. Kelly continued, "He told me, 'Your *lover boy* got lucky today', and he said he'd get even tomorrow."

Trying to sound reassuring, Bull said confidently, "Don't worry about it Kelly, I really don't think he'll say anything. Besides, what could he have seen? If it ever comes up, you were just on the boat helping look for my watch, that's all." They quickly ended the sensitive conversation as the Sullivans approached. Standing, Bull said "Hi, Mom, Dad, you remember Kelly . . . "

Diane replied, "Yes, of course we do," greeting Kelly with a smile, then commenting, "Did you ever see so many devilish delights on a dessert table?"

"I tried not to look, I don't want to be too tempted," said Kelly.

Bull's father remarked, "I was too busy admiring that marlin ice sculpture."

Jimmy returned to the table just then and added, "Admire it now, Doctor Sullivan, it'll be melted before the night's over."

Sid and Grace also returned to the table, and they all exchanged polite remarks while the waiter took their beverage orders. "Please excuse us for being late, Bradley, dear; there must have been a dozen messages on our voice mail."

"No problem, Mom, but we were getting hungry at the sight of all this food. . . I think everyone's ready to visit the buffet table."

As they waited in line, Diane commented to Kelly, "Bull tells me you're a nursing student at ECU. Isn't that quite a long commute for you?"

"Yes ma'am, but I only do it three days a week. All my classes are scheduled for Tuesday, Wednesday and Thursday. Besides, I ride-share with another girl who lives on the island. The long drive gives us a chance to study."

During dinner, the Sullivans were charmed by Kelly's amiable personality. She told them about her historic island home. Bull's mother couldn't get over the idea of such a lovely young lady being a mate on a fishing boat. "You even bait the hooks, dear?"

Jimmy couldn't help joking, "Yes, ma'am, she gets up early and digs the worms, too."

"Jimmy!" Kelly elbowed him, "Please excuse him, Mrs. Sullivan. It must be the wine getting to him."

Brad laughed and asked, "So, how are you doing with your nursing classes, Kelly?"

"It's not easy, Dr. Sullivan, but I'm doing OK, I guess."

"She should be, she studies all the time!" said her husband.

"Not all the time, Jimmy, what about the days I help you on the boat?"

"That's true, I was just saying you're a dedicated student, Sugar."

Diane said, "I know you'll be glad to give up fishing once you get your RN degree."

"Not altogether, I really love being out on the ocean . . . away from everything. The world seems so rushed. Out there, I have the chance to watch the sun rise," she made it seem so romantic and inviting, until her practical side came through, "but, one of us needs a steady paycheck. In the charter business, you never know when you might lose a whole week's income because of bad weather."

"We've been lucky so far this year," said Sid. "I remember a few years back. We got an early hurricane, the middle of July. It seems like we had a string of hurricanes all the way through the fall. Put some fellows out of business."

"Jimmy doesn't think about things like that too much," said Kelly.

"Hey, we're doing OK!" the young husband objected.

"Yes, but remember, I have another tuition payment due soon."

No one spoke for a moment. Brad broke the silence asking, "What *are* your plans for the future, Kelly? Have you ever considered medical school?"

"Oh, sure, my lifetime dream was to be a doctor. If I were a doctor, I would practice right here in Manteo to serve the people on the Outer Banks, but . . . that's only a dream. I could never afford medical school. I'm just hoping to get a nursing job at the new clinic they are building at Kitty Hawk."

Brad turned to his son, "What about you, Son? Are you going to try getting back into school next semester?"

Bull, of course, could not give his parents the answer they wished to hear. Wanting not to disappoint them, nor get into a discussion in front of his friends, he replied lightly, "Ask me after tomorrow. If I catch old 'Bubba' and win that fifty thousand dollars, I just might buy my own charter boat," he chuckled.

"I'm sure you'd make a fine captain," said Sid, "but don't underestimate the value of a college degree."

A loud guitar and drums started playing music and everyone's attention was diverted to the bandstand. It was a popular group from Richmond, Virginia. All eyes were on the leggy vocalist strutting across the stage in a skimpy costume singing a popular song. Captain Sid did a double-take when he saw the performer. It was Suzette, his brother's stepdaughter! And, right up front was Tommy, watching every move she made.

Couples crowded onto the dance floor. Bull asked his mother to dance. After a set of energetic songs, the band slowed things down with a slow ballad bringing several of the older couples to the dance floor. Kelly and Jimmy continued dancing; however, Bull yielded to his father, who wanted to dance with Diane.

About halfway through the song, there was a commotion amid the dancers. Someone had fallen. A female cried, "Oh, my God, somebody help him!"

Another person yelled, "Call 911, Captain Paul's down!"

Both Doctors rushed quickly to the victim with Bull right behind them. They found Kelly and Jimmy kneeling over his uncle, Paul Edwards, who had collapsed and was unconscious. Kelly checked for a pulse on Paul's neck and wrist. "He has no pulse!" she said.

Brad took charge of the situation, identified himself as a doctor, and asked Paul's wife, Edna, if he was on any medication. "No, he's not," she answered, "he broke into a sweat and began having chest pains. I told him, 'let's sit down'. Then, he clutched his chest in pain and fell." As she talked, Brad checked to make sure Paul's airway was open. The old man's face had become ashen color and his lips were turning blue.

Diane told Bull, "Go, make sure an ambulance is on the way."

Jimmy was saying "Hang on, Uncle Paul." He looked up toward

the crowd of onlookers and said, "Everybody, please, move back. Give him some air."

Bull's parents began CPR. Diane was breathing into Paul's airway while Brad did the compressions. Brad asked Kelly to keep checking for a pulse.

"Come on, Uncle Paul, don't give up," Jimmy pleaded.

The room grew silent as the Sullivans continued CPR. Paul was not responding and many of the bystanders were giving up hope; but, the determined doctors tirelessly continued treatment. You could hear a pin drop when Kelly spoke, "I feel a pulse! Yes, he has a pulse!"

"We're getting him back!" Brad said optimistically. Moments later, Captain Paul started regaining consciousness and became combative. "Easy, Paul, I'm a doctor. Please, be still. We're trying to help you," said Brad.

As color returned to his face, Paul looked at Jimmy, who said, "You gave us quite a scare, Uncle Paul, but you're gonna be all right now. We have a couple of good doctors here helping you."

"Thank you, Jesus!" cried Aunt Edna.

Within minutes, the EMT unit arrived and after Captain Paul was stabilized, they transported him to the hospital. He was later admitted to the Coronary Care Unit at Pitt General in Greenville.

Stories would be told about what happened on the final day of this tournament for years to come. It happened on Bull's 22nd birthday. At five o'clock Saturday morning, some boats were preparing to depart. Their strategy was to get to the fishing grounds early and scout around for a color change or eddy that might hold billfish. Of course, each boat had again been assigned an observer to make sure no lines were in the water before nine o'clock and that all rules would be followed. No boat had the same observer more than one day. To keep everyone honest, they were randomly assigned each morning by the committee.

Sid and Bull saw Jimmy and Kelly arriving, and walked over to the 'Lucky Duck' for a report on Captain Paul. They had only gotten a couple of hours sleep, having returned home from the hospital late. "Uncle Paul was doing a lot better when we left him," said Jimmy.

"They're gonna keep him in intensive care a few days to run some tests. They say he'll most likely need bypass surgery," said Kelly.

Bull asked, "Who's gonna run the 'Ranger' today?"

"Nobody," Jimmy answered, "Aunt Edna told me the whole fishing team is going with her to the hospital this afternoon to visit Uncle Paul."

As they talked, several more boats pulled away. Sid said, "Looks like we're gonna be last ones out, we better get underway."

The weather was much improved over yesterday. A light southwest wind produced only a slight chop, but the boats were rocking and rolling in all the wakes. Usually, the fleet traveled in convoy fashion, one boat behind the other to eliminate wakes and make the ride smoother for everyone. Today, however, that particular rule of etiquette had been ignored by most. Right from the sea buoy, captains dispersed in all directions as it was every team for themselves.

Although the 'Carolina Pirate' team was leading with 892 points, it was still anyone's contest. A team could locate a spur of blue water loaded with marlin and completely upset the standings. There had been days when a single boat released up to twenty white marlin off the Carolina coast. Ultimately, a captured blue marlin of 600 pounds or more was every team's goal. Every mate among the charter fleet dreamed of catching 'Bubba' and winning the fifty thousand dollar Top-Mate prize. Still, the identity of the sponsor for this special category remained a mystery to everyone except Cap'n Willie. Before they got out of radio range of the ship's store, Willie put out a call on the working channel, "Well, captains, it's time for the blessing of the fleet. You know, Paul is not here this morning to lead us in prayer asking the Lord to give us a safe and successful day, so we need a volunteer."

Thanks to Captain Paul and other well-respected charter boat captains, who were also professed Christians, the daily *"blessing of the fleet"* had become a tradition for Outer Banks fishermen. Even the captains who hadn't been to church in years, cooperated by keeping the radio channel clear, so all could listen to the mariner's prayer.

Jimmy keyed his mike and volunteered, "I'll pray today, Cap'n Willie. I want to remember my Uncle Paul in our prayer. By the way fellows," he continued, "I talked to Aunt Edna, on the cellular phone a few minutes ago; she told me the doctors say Uncle Paul ought to pull through OK. I'll tell you the truth, we were lucky to have a couple of good doctors right there when he suffered his attack. Bull, if you're listening, my family is very thankful your Mom and Dad didn't give up on him. A lot of people *had* given up hope. I thought Old Paul was a goner myself, but by the grace of God, they brought him back."

After the prayer was finished, it did not take long for the marine radio to chatter with friendly conversations. This is the way many captains entertained themselves during the two-hour boat ride. Of course, they switched their radios to low power, so their trivial discussions would not be heard on shore. One captain was predicting Rusty Wallace would win the race tomorrow, another insisted it would be Earnhardt. Following a lengthy discussion on race cars, two other captains got on the subject of raising wood ducks. Then, someone else mentioned the new muzzle-load shotgun he bought at a flea market and of course a discussion on deer hunting followed. Someone finally got around to the subject of fishing. About fifteen miles from the Gulf Stream, they began speculating whether any large marlin were still in these waters.

Captain Stormy said, "Personally, I hope I don't see old 'Bubba'. If I caught 'im, first thang you know, my mate, Bryan, would take that fifty thousand dollar prize and go buy his own rig. Then, he'd be out'chere competin' with us. Sure would hate to see that happen." Sometimes it was hard to tell whether Stormy was kidding or being serious. Sid, who was just ahead of Stormy, replied, "You better *not* follow me then, Stormy, because I'm looking for 'Bubba' today." Sid noticed the boat in front of him was smoking badly, and said, "Hold on a minute fellows; looks like the boat up ahead of me may be on fire."

"What's going on up there?" asked Stormy.

"Hey, fellows . . . this is Captain Carl on the 'Shady Lady'. It's my boat smoking, but there's no fire. I've lost a turbo."

Sid and Stormy pulled back their throttles as they passed near the disabled boat so as not to throw too much wake. Sid said, "That's too bad, Captain, I hate to see anyone end a tournament like that."

"Oh, don't count us out yet. I have a diesel mechanic on our team. He's in the engine room now trying to rig up something so we can get on out there."

"Well, good luck to you, Captain," Sid waved. Tommy was standing in the cockpit watching the 'Grand Slam' pass by. When he was sure Bull was looking his way, Tommy flipped him the bird.

Rick saw the offensive gesture and said, "I thought all you mates were buddies!" "Not with that guy, he's an asshole," said Bull.

Most captains planned to fish where they were yesterday, but Sid was considering another option. He was convinced most of the larger marlin, the big females, had moved on to other feeding grounds. Lately, all the blue marlin caught had been less than 250 pounds and released, worth only 70 points in this tournament.

After completing his preparations in the cockpit, Bull climbed up to the bridge. As Sid held an easterly course, they could see blue water on the horizon. Bull was watching for any signs of fish . . . birds, bait, grass, anything floating that might attract bait. Then Bull heard Sid whisper, *Sid's Hill* and noticed his captain's eyes seemed to be looking beyond the horizon. Sid was flirting with the notion of running all the way out to where he had caught the 989-pound marlin last year. *Sid's Hill* was a distant seamount rising sharply from the ocean floor that often held large schools of bait, which attracted game fish. The weather was favorable to make the run, but Sid knew it would be a gamble. It would cost precious fishing time getting out there. The other captains had given the outlying area it's nickname because Sid Hilton was about the only man willing to run the extra thirty miles to get out there . . . across waters reaching over a mile deep. Picking up his microphone, Sid made is intentions known, and asked if anyone wanted to run with him. From the 'Lucky Duck', Jimmy quickly responded, "I'll run out there with you, Sid. Kelly can use the extra sack time. We made a deal, she's catching up on her sleep this morning, I'm gonna sleep on the way home." The 'Carolina Pirate' team also decided to go along. The three vessels continued steaming eastward, with expectations running high among the anglers. Bull felt renewed optimism he might hook up with old "Bubba" today.

Meanwhile, back on the 'Shady Lady', the crippled engine could not be repaired. It would be impossible for Captain Carl's team to reach the hundred-fathom curve, where most of the boats would be fishing. Carl was forced to remain inshore and fish the more shallow water along the thirty fathom curve. Putting out his lines, Tommy could still see the Navy's tower buoy. He was very disappointed. The best he expected here, was to catch some dolphin, maybe a wahoo, or if they were lucky, perhaps a sail. Imagine his surprise when a pair of whites came up on teasers within the first few minutes. Tommy raised hell with the unsuspecting anglers for not being ready. Captain Carl kept circling the area and said, "Don't worry boys, we'll get another shot. I see another fin cutting the water just ahead!" Carl steered toward the swirl and said cynically, "This reminds me of the old 'bad news/good news' joke. First the bad news: one of your engines blew up. Now the good news: the place it broke down was full of marlin! Ha, ha, ha," they all laughed.

"There he is! There he is! Going after the short rigger!" Tommy shouted.

As one of their anglers proceeded to hook the fish, Captain Carl's conniving mind thought, we've got to keep this honey hole a secret. He knew the observer would want to report the catch to the committee boat, which would surely cause the fleet to come racing to them. While no one was looking, Carl yanked the antenna wire from his radio. The rules stated in the event of radio failure, the observer's written report would stand; and, if an official protest was filed, he must submit to a lie detector test, if asked. Now, the other boats had no way of knowing about 'Shady Lady's' success. Tommy fished with a vengeance.

Meanwhile, the 'Grand Slam' was steaming across the vast open water with forty-five minutes to go, Bull assembled his fishing team in the cockpit to rehearse procedures. Knowing, big game fishing is not without its perils; he wanted to make sure each person knew his role in case they did hook old 'Bubba'. Since Cliff caught the big tuna yesterday, Rick had been designated today's primary angler. Bull, of course, would be wireman, and Cliff would stand ready with wire-cutters in case he got into trouble. If the time came to kill a fish, Cliff would set the flying gaff. Bull reminded them the observer would be watching closely to make sure all rules were followed. No one, except the angler, could touch the rod, reel, or line.

The observer on board the 'Grand Slam' today was Art Morgan, who owned three restaurants along the Outer Banks. Art was an avid fisherman himself, but had rather serve as an observer than enter the tournament. He said, moving to a different boat each day gave him a chance to learn from the experts.

Rick and Cliff's wives were also on board, resting in the salon. All the activities this week had worn them out, and the ladies were taking advantage of the smooth boat ride to catch up on their sleep.

About three miles before the three boats reached their desired destination, they spread out to search for signs of marlin. Suddenly, without warning, Captain Dan saw a very large sea turtle come to the surface only a few feet ahead, directly in the path of his boat. There was no time to avoid it. Everyone on board felt the dreadful thump on the hull as the boat jarred from the impact. Dan quickly brought the 'Carolina Pirate' to a stop. "Look behind us!" shouted Carey. The giant sea turtle was floundering. It's fractured shell was as wide as the hood of a car. Dan told Justin to lift the hatches and check the hull and stuffing boxes for leaks. No damage was found, but when Dan applied power, the boat shuddered with a terrible vibration. Once again, they came to a full stop. Carey opened his locker and retrieved a face mask and fins, knowing what had to be done. "Let's check this situation out," he said bravely, as he opened the transom door and slipped into mile-deep water to inspect the propellers. Captain Dan was hoping Carey would find a rope or something fouled around the shaft. But no such luck! One of the blades on the starboard prop was broken completely off. Since it was eighty miles back to the dock, the 'Carolina Pirate' immediately started trolling westward on one engine, bidding the others farewell and good luck.

Jimmy, said, "Let us know if you need anything Dan. We won't leave you stranded out here. We'll be listening for you on the side." He was referring to the sideband radio which is used for long-range communications.

Sid added, "You may as well head home, anyway, Dan. You guys probably have this thing in the bag. From what I hear on the radio, the other boats haven't seen any marlin yet, although they are catching a few tuna."

Dan replied, "I can make nine knots on one engine. I'll drag some baits just in case old "Bubba" comes along." The 'Carolina Pirate' was soon out of sight.

Within minutes of putting out his trolling spread, Bull shouted, "Gaffers!" A school of dolphin charged across the wake and crashed their baits. Three large dolphin were hooked and brought in quickly as possible. Rick and Cliff helped Bull get fresh baits over to reestablish their trolling pattern. During the next two hours, the scenario was repeated several times. Any other time, hot dolphin action like this would be welcome, but today their abundance was a hindrance. About a hundred yards to starboard, Sid spotted a piece of lumber bobbing on the surface. Not wanting to miss any opportunity, he dragged the baits past the flotsam, expecting to be covered up by dolphin again. Splash! A large wahoo went ballistic! The aggressive fish jumped in a wide arch and crashed teeth-first on a horse-ballyhoo rigged behind an orange and black plastic lure. Lucky for Rick, the big wahoo chose to hit their heaviest tackle, a 130-pound class two-speed Penn reel on a bent-butt rod. Although outclassed, the fish made a respectable run, stripping off a hundred yards of dacron line. Less than five minutes later, the trophy-sized wahoo was in the fish box. Sid remarked, "Hey fellows, that wahoo probably made it worth our trip out here . . . I'll bet it weighs sixty pounds, or better."

Rick said, "That could be another $10,000 fish! We could take first place in both tuna and wahoo categories!"

Cliff added, "Yeah man, they'll say we are meat fishermen!"

Sid had been keeping in touch with Jimmy on the 'Lucky Duck'. They too, were finding the dolphin to be a nuisance. Jimmy told Sid, "I'm thinking about taking all my baits out of the water and only pulling teasers."

"Not a bad idea, Jimmy. I'll go along with that."

Teasers are oversized lures rigged without hooks and are trolled close to the boat. The theory is large gamefish holding deep in the water column are attracted by turbulence created when a boat passes overhead. It is generally believed, pelagic fish such as marlin, perceive the propeller wash to be a school of baitfish and the teasers seem to be larger fish feeding. This is often enough to entice a marlin to rise from the depths for a chance at an easy meal. The trick is for someone to pull the teaser away at just the right moment, while an angler drops a bait back to the target.

Sixty minutes passed with no sightings. The monotonous drone of the 'Grand Slam's' twin diesel engines was interrupted by the marine radio. "Committee boat, committee boat. 'Lucky Duck' has hooked a blue marlin!" The voice was unmistakably that of Thomas Eubank, the Jamaican who was the observer on the 'Grand Slam' yesterday.

When the committee boat did not answer, Sid responded, "I don't think they can read you, Thomas, we're too far out. This is Sid on the 'Grand Slam'. How big's your marlin?"

"Looks like maybe tree hun'red pounds," replied Thomas.

"That's encouraging. Hope you get'em. We're still looking for our *first* one."

Sid continued scanning the ocean in all directions for any signs. "I see a patch of grass," he said to his team, "We'll work in that direction."

To Bull's dismay, that patch turned out to be what many mates refer to as pain-in-the-ass grass. Instead of being organized into a bed or line, the grass was scattered all around, like they were in the middle of a hayfield. Bull was kept busy, tediously shagging grass off the teasers. Sid consoled, "I know this grass is aggravating, but it may very well hold a big marlin, let's hang in here a while longer."

As was often the case when fishing was slow, a strike can catch you off guard. Bull was removing a clump of grass from the port teaser; Sid was looking across the bow, when Click! Click! Click! . . . . an rapid burst of sound came from the starboard teaser reel. Rick and Cliff were first to see a marlin attacking the daisy chain teaser. The fish let go, faded from sight, then came right back after it. As rehearsed, Sid pulled the teaser away as fast as he could while Rick dropped the bait toward the fish . . . a perfect switch! The marlin nailed the rigged mackerel. Rick knew he must allow the fish to run with the bait for several seconds before trying to set the hook. Apparently, he was a little too quick on the trigger and missed him! Angry at himself, he said, "Damn! I tried him too early!" Needless to say, everyone shared his disappointment.

That very instant, a second fish appeared, an even larger marlin, hot after a teaser! It happened so fast Bull had not yet attached another bait to his heaviest tackle. As he dashed for the bait cooler, Sid demanded from the bridge, "Hurry up down there! Looks like he's fading . . . get a bait to him FAST!" Rick grabbed the closest rod and again made a text book transfer with Sid pulling the teaser away. It was heart-stopping to see the surface of the ocean erupt with white foam as the enormous blue marlin aggressively attacked the bait. This time Rick would allow the fish to run much longer before trying to set the hook. He didn't want to miss another one.

Bull stood there awestruck, holding the now ready heavy-class fishing rod in his hands and said with disdain, "Oh shit! Rick. You've got him on a fifty!" A fifty-pound outfit would be fine for a smaller marlin, but not for a fish this large. Bull could only hope for the best. Rick was secured in the fighting chair, he braced his feet, locked the drag, lifted the rod tip and set the hook. Rick's eyes got as big as saucers when the force of the tightening line nearly lifted him out of the chair. "Whoa! Whoa!" he exclaimed. The rod bent to the verge of breaking. Bull could have sworn he heard the sound of cracking fiberglass. Instinctively, he reached for the drag setting to ease off the pressure.

"Stop! Bull, stop!" shouted Sid from the bridge. Bull froze in his tracks, realizing if anyone other than Rick touched the rod, reel, or line, the catch would be disqualified. Rick, himself, slacked off on the drag a little, and the battle was on!

Sid exclaimed, "That's him! We've hooked 'Bubba'!"

The huge marlin scorched a path across the ocean at a blistering pace, lunging into the air trying to escape the trap, shaking its head back and forth as if in slow motion. Rick exclaimed, "Jesus Christ, look at the shoulders on that fish . . . we got us a real hog here!" The fish surged out of the water again. Rick shouted, "He's smoking this reel!"

If Sid did not react quickly at the throttles, the spool of line would be stripped down to the backing in seconds. Ordinarily, Sid would have sped forward in an arc to intercept a blazing marlin on the run, but in this situation, there was not enough line left on the spool to spare. Sid threw the boat into reverse and pushed the throttles hard. White water slammed against the stern, splashing over the transom, sending spray all the way up to the flying bridge. Bull held on tightly to the arm of the fighting chair keeping Rick aligned with the fish. They were getting drenched with seawater. Cliff retreated into the cabin where the ladies were watching through the plate glass door. As the boat plowed backward, the stern dug deeper into the swells. Rick nearly became nauseous from a combination of inhaling diesel exhaust and swallowing a mouthful of seawater when a wave splashed into his face. He could hardly see through the layer of salt covering his sunglasses, but he never stopped cranking the handle. Bull coached, "Reel! Reel! Reel!" The water was standing six inches deep in the cockpit by the time Bull signaled up to Sid, "We're OK, we've gained back enough line for now, Captain!"

As Sid brought the boat to idle, the observer, Art Morgan,

picked up the mike on the marine radio, and with Sid's permission, said, "Committee boat, 'Grand Slam is hooked up with a blue marlin. A big one! This may take a while."

In scratchy radio reception, "Copy that 'Grand Slam', 12:59 PM, committee boat standing by."

From five hundred yards away, even before hearing the radio transmission, everyone on the 'Lucky Duck' had seen the great fish leaping behind 'Grand Slam'. The cloud of smoke created when Sid backed down had gotten Jimmy's attention.

"Is that what I think it is, Sid?"

"We've got big 'Bubba' hooked up, Jimmy. In all the years I've been fishing, I've never seen a fish run like this one. Damn near spooled us!"

"I hope you get 'em."

"Thanks, Jimmy."

A forty-five minute standoff followed. Putting forth a tremendous effort, Rick had regained over half the line. As his wife gave him another sip of her soda to help clear the taste of seawater from his mouth, he commented to her, "Honey, my arms feel like they are turning to jelly."

Sid told Rick, "There's no need to rush, just hold what you got. Save your strength. We have got plenty of time to tire him out." All the while, Sid was using a little known captain's trick to wear the fish out faster. He maneuveared the boat to keep the fish swimming against the current at all times.

After ninety minutes had passed since the monster was tricked into taking the bait, the team was unusually quiet. They knew what was at stake here. This fish would be worth well over $400,000 in prize money, plus an additional fifty thousand dollars to Bull for top-mate prize, but of course, only if they were lucky enough to land it.

Sid tried not to allow himself to get too optimistic. He could remember several times when a large marlin had pulled off after the mate got his hands on the leader. For an instant, he found himself wishing Tommy was in the cockpit. Tommy had done such a masterful job handling the 989-pounder last fall. Sid was sure the fish which Bull faced today was considerably larger. He was concerned Bull might be overwhelmed by the imposing sight of a *grander*. Then, trying to think positively, Sid reassured himself Bull certainly was every bit as strong as Tommy . . . and what Bull lacked in experience he made up for in determination.

In the cockpit below, Bull's mind was also racing as he impatiently stood by the fighting chair watching the rod bend to its limit.

Rick continued to pump and wind, managing to regain a few more feet of line. Then, suddenly, the rod straightened. Bull got a sickening feeling in the pit of his stomach as he saw the line go slack. Rick exclaimed, "What the hell happened? I didn't feel the line break!"

Sid immediately applied power, moving the boat forward, and shouted, "Reel! Reel! Reel! He's coming to the boat!" Rick cranked as fast as he could. Sid shouted down another instruction, "Rick, slack up on your drag!"

Seeing the spool fill with line, thinking the fish was lost, Bull fretted, "I don't think we've got him, Sid!" He waited at the transom watching the water, knowing the Bimini twist knot tied to the leader would appear any second, when suddenly, he visualized the form of the giant marlin emerging from beneath the boat. The rod arched sharply and Rick exclaimed, "Holy shit! He's still with us!"

As if the mighty fish wanted to demonstrate it had a seemingly inexhaustible supply of strength, it leaped into the air again, thrashing angrily . . . giving everyone on board the opportunity to behold it's bulk. Art was flabbergasted by the numbing sight, "He's really lit up! Look at its colors!" he said.

Cliff's wife, Kathy, had presence of mind to snap several photos of the once in a lifetime spectacle. The powerful and aggressive fighter's dorsal fin was fully extended. Its huge dark eye seemed to make contact with the camera lens. It's thick back was cobalt blue. Bright sunlight glistened on its silvery white flanks highlighting the lavender vertical stripes on the marlin's broad side. The mammoth hulk fell back into the ocean shattering the surface with a colossal splash. Rick kept a tight grip on the rocking rod as the marlin streaked off again and Bull watched helplessly, hoping the line would hold. Art removed his cap and spoke in awe, "Captain, I've never seen anything like that before. That fish is every bit of 1200 pounds . . . maybe more!"

Meanwhile, the 'Lucky Duck' had hooked a blue marlin of their own. Even though the two boats were almost 500 yards apart, Bull noticed Kelly was on the bridge running the boat. He could tell it was her by the bright lime-green cap she always wore. After a blue marlin was hooked up, it was not unusual for Kelly to run the boat and let Jimmy work the cockpit.

As Rick battled to bring his fish closer, Donna, his wife, wiped sweat from his brow. She cleaned his sunglasses and gave him cool water to drink. It was a blistering day with no breeze at all, but not relenting, Rick slowly refilled the spool inch by inch. Finally, the marlin's broad back and silvery side became visible to Sid and Art who were watching from the bridge. The fish was making lazy circles about forty feet beneath the boat. Bull became anxious, knowing the wire would soon be in his grasp; it would be up to him to control a fish as heavy as his pickup truck. With his feet planted firmly on the footrest of the fighting chair, Rick lifted the bowed rod three more feet, bringing the leader to the surface. Bull stretched out his arm . . . almost there . . . a little more . . . "Got It!" he exclaimed taking two wraps on the 20-foot length of heavy number 12 wire.

This was Bull's moment of truth . . . like a matador facing an angry brahma, the young mate must now test his true self. Would he have the courage to face this Goliath? This would be his greatest conquest, and perhaps, his riskiest. Every big-game fisherman has heard horror stories of wiremen becoming tangled in the leader and snatched overboard. Some mates have even lost their lives. It was now, when the safety procedures Bull had reviewed with his teammates this morning, came into play. Cliff stood at the ready with wire-cutters, in case Bull could not get his hands free; and Rick immediately eased off the drag pressure of his reel. If the fish made another run, they did not want the line to break; should Bull be pulled overboard, it would become his lifeline.

From Sid's vantage on the bridge, he could tell the fish was hooked solidly in the lower jaw, and coached, "Looks like a good hookup! Hold on to him, Bull."

The determined mate managed to take another wrap, and Cliff reached out with the flying gaff just to get an idea of its range. "Careful not to spook him, Cliff. Let me get him close." Bull was careful not to make any sudden moves that might dislodge the hook. He tugged gently, yet firmly, applying every ounce of strength he could muster while trying to get another wrap on the wire. The strain of each passing minute was taking its toll. Bull's fingers on his right hand grew numb from lack of circulation as the taut wire squeezed around his glove. He would soon have to let go of the line or find some way to relieve his aching hand. He managed to get the leader around the starboard cleat and free his right hand for just a second. He felt the relief as blood rushed to his fingertips. At that precise moment, the fierce fish lunged upward as if intent on attacking Bull with its spear-like bill. The terrifying sight of a thousand thundering pounds charging to within inches of his face caused Bull to jump back. When he did, the leader became fouled around the cleat.

Everyone on board felt the sudden jolt when the wire became taut . . . like a bulldog reaching the end of his chain. For a split second, the fish seemed to hang in the air close enough to almost fall into the boat. Witnessing the full length and girth of this magnificent marlin, Art, who was still on the bridge with Sid, said, "Good God! It reaches clear across the transom . . . must be fifteen feet long!"

Noticing the immense fish's thick belly hanging heavy with eggs, Sid lamented, "It's a crying shame to kill this noble creature."

The marlin crashed down into the foaming ocean with such a splash everyone in the cockpit got soaked! Frightened of what the truculent fish might do next, Kathy and Donna dashed back into the cabin and watched through the windows.

The great fish attempted to sound deep causing the wire to cut into the teak cover board. Fearing the leader would break, Bull managed to free it from the cleat and again wrapped the wire around his hands. He could sense the fish was growing tired; the last jump had taken a lot out of it. Bull became confident it would be just a matter of moments before the trophy would be within reach of Cliff's waiting gaff. Rick was still in the fighting chair, keeping a tight grip on the rod in case the fish made another run. He, too, felt sure the battle was almost won.

No one could have expected what was about to happen. Above all the commotion coming from the cockpit, Sid heard Kelly's voice screaming in the radio. "Mayday! Mayday! Oh, my God! Jimmy's fallen overboard! Help! Oh, God! ...Help!"

Looking toward the 'Lucky Duck', Sid picked up his microphone, "What's going on Kelly?" When Kelly keyed the mike again, Sid heard screams of horror from the other members of her team.

"We just got hit by a freak wave," she cried. "Jimmy fell overboard! He's tangled in the leader! Oh, God! I don't see him now! The fish pulled him under!"

Standing right over the noisy engine exhaust, Bull was oblivious to the mayhem unfolding on the radio. He was focusing all his energy on getting the big marlin a little closer to Cliff's waiting gaff. They could taste victory.

After hearing Kelly's anguished cries for help, Sid knew Jimmy was struggling to escape death. There was no other boat close enough to offer assistance. He shouted down, "Bull, cut the leader!" The three men in the cockpit could not believe their ears. They all turned and looked toward the captain, who repeated the order, "Cut the fish off, now!" Seeing the urgency and distress in Sid's face, Bull complied. The great fish was released and made a dash for freedom with their hook dangling from its jaw.

Black smoke poured from the exhaust ports as Sid applied full throttle pushing the "Grand Slam' into the direction of the emergency. The freak wave Kelly mentioned was coming toward him. It appeared to be a six to eight foot swell working its way across an otherwise calm ocean. It's probably a submarine wake, he thought. By now, Bull was climbing to the bridge, curious to learn the reason for Sid's sudden urgency. When he was on the third rung of the ladder, Sid shouted, "Hold on!" The boat rocked violently as they crossed the tall wave at high speed.

Bull pulled himself up and saw they were heading straight for Jimmy's boat. A very angry Rick came up the ladder on Bull's heels, demanding, "What the hell are you doing, Captain? Don't you know that fish was worth a fortune!"

They were shocked when Sid told them what had happened. "If we're gonna help that boy, we don't have a second to lose," he said. Kelly and Thomas were on the bridge of the 'Duck', frantically waving their arms and pointing in the direction Jimmy was last seen. But the ocean had concealed all traces of him. Bull asked on the radio, "Kelly, is the fish still on the line?"

"No! It broke as soon as Jimmy went over! Hurry, Bull. Please, hurry!"

23 It had been only a minute, or so, since Sid first heard Kelly's cry for help. As he pulled back the throttles, allowing the 'Grand Slam' to drift into position, Bull instinctively dove from the flying bridge, knowing he must try to rescue his friend. With wire-cutters in hand, he propelled himself downward into the clear blue water, straining his eyes to see. There! Something moved far below him! He could not discern whether it was man or fish. Without regard for his own safety, Bull forced himself deeper, but he could get no closer to the object below him. It continually moved away, growing smaller; then, finally, it was just a dot disappearing in the abyss.

By now, Bull's starving lungs were burning. With his eyes fixed on the hulls of the two boats floating far above him, he swam upwards, wondering if he could complete the ascension before lack of oxygen rendered him unconscious.

Art looked at his watch and said, "It has been more than two minutes since Bull went in." All eyes anxiously scanned the surface for any sign of either of the two young men. Fearing the sea may have swallowed them both, Kelly prayed for a miracle. Then, after what seemed like a breathless eternity, Bull appeared, gasping for air as if there was not enough oxygen in the world to fill his empty lungs. Sid threw him a life line. Exhausted, Bull could barely hang onto the ring. He was too weak to reply to questions being shouted to him about whether he had seen Jimmy. Looking at Kelly with an expression of defeat and disappointment on his face, Bull shook his head, no. Realizing her husband was lost, she became hysterical. Thomas Eubank tried his best to console her.

Sid maneuvered his boat alongside the 'Lucky Duck' and dutifully called the Coast Guard on his long-range radio to relay the events that had transpired. They immediately dispatched a rescue helicopter from Elizabeth City. A second helicopter was dispatched by a Navy aircraft carrier, which happened to be only thirty miles from the scene. The carrier was on its way to the Norfolk Naval base.

While they waited, Kelly pensively sat on a bench staring at the floor in the stifling hot cabin of her idled boat, not knowing how to deal with the sudden loss of her husband and lifelong friend. Sid and Bull lashed the two vessels together side-by-side and placed bumpers between them. Stepping aboard the 'Lucky Duck', Bull kneeled before the weary young woman who sat with her face in her hands. Several seconds of empty silence passed. Not knowing what to say, he spoke with despair in his voice, "I'm sorry, Kelly, I'm so sorry."

She put her arms around him, resting her head on his shoulder, and cried "Why, oh, why? Bull, please tell me this is only a bad dream, that it didn't really happen!"

Her heartbreaking moans brought tears to the eyes of all the others. No one wanted to admit it, but of course, they had all given up hope of finding Jimmy alive, although they continued watching the water for any sign of him. Kelly was becoming weak and pale. Sid feared she may be on the verge of going into shock. He convinced her to move over to the 'Grand Slam' where the cabin was more comfortable. Several of the others helped steady her as she made her way to the other boat.

A few minutes later, the pilot of the Navy helicopter called the

'Grand Slam' to confirm Sid's position. His ETA was ten minutes. The boats had been drifting with the current in the mirror calm Gulf Stream waters for half an hour. Once at the scene, the two helicopters swept the area all the way back to the coordinates where Jimmy had fallen overboard.

When four o'clock came, the Coast Guard advised Captain Sid, the two boats should return to port; the choppers would continue the aerial search until dark. Thomas Eubank took the helm on the 'Lucky Duck' and followed the 'Grand Slam' for the three and a half hour journey back to the dock. To Kelly, the events were only a blur. She lay on the sofa of Sid's boat, curled into the fetal position, and soon wept herself to sleep.

At about six o'clock, still an hour and a half from the marina, the cellular phone rang on the bridge of the 'Grand Slam'. Sid was below resting, Bull was at the helm and answered. Reception was broken. " Hel-o is this Cap----Sid -ilton?"

"Yes, this is Sid's boat, who is calling?"

"This -s Jack Edwards, Ji--my's father."

"Mr. Edwards, this is Bull. Sid is down below right now. We're still pretty far off the beach and the reception on this phone is not too good. I'll tell him to call you in a few minutes. Are you at home?"

"Yes, I am."

"I'll tell Sid to call you. Goodbye." Bull asked Rick to hold their heading while he went below to get Sid. Before returning the call to Jimmy's father, Sid contacted the Coast Guard and learned the search had turned up nothing. He made the call and gave Jack Edwards the grim details of what happened to his son. Jack was hoping to hear his son's body had been recovered. Jimmy's mother was taking it very hard, and he thought it would be very difficult for her to accept their son's death if his body was forever lost to a watery grave. Sid assured Mr. Edwards it had been an unfortunate freak accident, and they had done everything possible to try to save his son.

Before they reached the inlet, Kelly awakened and wanted to talk about the ordeal. Kathy and Donna told her about the great fish they had been fighting, and how Sid reacted quickly as possible to her distress call. "He ordered Bull to cut the fish off without even giving it a second thought," said Kathy.

"My husband was pretty upset, but after he found out what was going on, he was very understanding," said Donna. "We are all so sorry about what happened."

Kelly walked out into the cockpit where a melancholy Bull was sitting on a cooler gazing morosely into the boat wake. She sat down beside him and placed her hand on his arm. "Are you OK, Bull? You had us all worried when you stayed under for so long."

"Yeah, sure, I'm fine, how about you?"

"I still can't believe this has happened. I keep hoping I'll wake up from a bad dream."

"I wish it could be that easy."

Changing the subject, Kelly said, "They told me you had a really big marlin on----a grander for sure. I'm sorry you had to cut it free. I know it cost you the tournament." She was choking back tears as she talked.

Bull put his arm around her and said, "Don't worry about that, Kelly. We did what we had to do. Jimmy would have done the same for me."

"What am I going to tell his parents?"

"I know it's not gonna be easy for you."

As Sid made the final turn to enter the harbor, Kelly stood up and wiped the tears from her eyes, determined to be strong when she saw Jimmy's and her parents.

Word of the tragedy had spread quickly to shore. Several captains had been monitoring Sid's radio communications with the Coast Guard; by the time the two boats reached Pirates Cove, a large crowd had assembled. Many were wondering, how such an accident could have happened to a fisherman with as much experience as Jimmy Edwards?

Kelly's parents, Barbara and Charlie Fisher, met her at the dock. After the expected flood of tears, they left for Jimmy parents' home. His mother was too upset to come to the marina.

Three members of the Coast Guard were also waiting at the dock. They boarded the 'Lucky Duck', conducted a safety inspection, and interviewed the passengers about the accident. The assigned observer, Thomas Eubank, who piloted the captain-less boat back to the dock, conveyed the following account in his rich Jamaican accent, and this is the story which circulated around the community:

"Da marlin was not very large, actually . . . not even tree-hun'red pounds. Da angler was Miss Langston . . . her first marlin. We were all s'prised how quickly she brought da fish to da boat. Jimmy said da fish was probably still green, but when he took a wrap on da leader, da fish seemed to give up. It just lay there beside da boat." Thomas paused to think for a moment, "Before releasing da fish,

Jimmy asked Mrs. Langston if she wanted to get a photo. As she was focusing her camera, he said, 'Wait a second, let me lift da bill out of da water for a better picture.' Jes as Jimmy reached down, da boat was hit by an unexpected wave. Da sea was calm except for dat one surprise wave; we never saw it coming. Jimmy flipped overboard, head first; I fell down myself. Somehow, his feet became entangled in da leader coiled on da deck. We saw da fish pulling him away as he struggled to get free. He managed to surface once and got a breath, but dat's da last we saw of him before he was pulled under for good. We all wanted to jump in and help him, but neither of da two Langston gentlemen nor myself was in good enough physical shape to do it. Dere was not'ing could be done. I was amazed how quickly Captain Sid got to us. Dat mate of his is very strong. He dove under for da longest time, but . . . it was too late. Jimmy was lost." Thomas paused and looked around at those listening intently to his story and in a superstitious nature, added, "In my homeland, dere is ancient belief . . . dat when a good man dies at sea, his spirit will dere remain to watch over future generations."

A short while later, the tournament director made an announcement on the public address system. "Ladies and gentlemen, out of respect to the family of Captain Jimmy Edwards, the awards ceremony and activities scheduled for tonight are canceled. Tournament winners' names will be posted in the ship's store by noon tomorrow. The winners can pick up their checks there, between noon and six p.m.. Thank you very much for participating in this year's tournament. We hope to see you back here again next year under happier circumstances. And in closing, we ask you to please keep the family of Jimmy Edwards in your prayers."

For the next several days, Kelly was housebound by grief. On Thursday afternoon, Bull visited to see how she was doing. When he pulled into the driveway of her parent's home, where she was staying, Bull saw Kelly sitting on the front porch grooming the family dog, Backlash.

He walked over and said, "Looks like you could use some company."

"It's just me and Backlash. Daddy's on his workboat crabbing, and Mama went to the grocery store."

"How's it going, Kelly?" Bull sat on the step by her tail-wagging dog and petted it.

"These last few days have been like a nightmare."

"I'm sure it's been hard for you."

"Bull, I'm glad you came by. I've been wanting to talk to you about something."

"Sure, Kelly. What?"

"I want to thank you again for trying to save Jimmy. I know you risked your own life, and I'll never be able to repay you for that." She hesitated, not knowing how to express what she really wanted to say without hurting his feelings. "There's something else I need-ed to speak to you about, and I . . . I hope you will understand."

"What is it, Kelly?"

"Well, my parents, and Jimmy's too, are quite old fashioned, you know. They may not understand our relationship, ah, friendship."

"Come on, what are you getting at?"

"Bull, you're a very special person to me, but I feel we should try to keep our distance for a while. Being seen together could make things a little awkward, especially, if Tommy tells anyone he saw us together on Sid's boat."

"I told you before, don't worry about Tommy, besides, he's al-ready gone back to Morehead. You know, that jerk won second place in the tournament. They got into a good bite and caught eight marlin on the last day . . . claimed their radio went out and didn't report to the committee boat the way they were supposed to."

"Well, it does make me feel better knowing he's gone."

"Kelly, I don't think there is anything wrong with us being seen together. Everyone knows we're friends, and nothing really ever happened between us. You remained true to Jimmy."

"That's what you say, Bull, but I can't help feeling guilty about what almost happened on Sid's boat the other night," hesitating, she continued . . . "Oh, I'm so confused right now. Jimmy was the only man in my life before I met you." Her eyes filled with tears, and Bull placed an arm around her. "Losing Jimmy like that . . . it's more than I can deal with. Please understand, Bull. I need time to get over this."

"Sure, Kelly. Whatever you say." As Bull walked to his car, he turned and said, "Just remember, I'll be there if you need anything."

* * * * * *

The following Sunday, a memorial service was held on the grounds of the marina for family and friends to pay last respects to Jimmy. The service was set for six p.m. so charter boat captains who fished that day would be able to attend. The tournament commit-tee's podium and stage, which were never used for the awards ceremony, had been converted into an outdoor chapel adorned with flowers. There was not a dry eye in Manteo as the town mourned the untimely loss of such a well-liked young man who had grown up in their community.

The girls, who worked in the ship's store at Pirates Cove, had learned Jimmy died with no life insurance benefits. They made an arrangement with a local florist to offer a single white carnation for five dollars to each person attending the service, with proceeds benefiting the young widow.

At the conclusion, Bull was among the many mourners who set their carnation adrift in the harbor in memory of their friend who had lost his life to the ocean he loved. Few would ever forget the sight of several hundred white carnations floating around the boats at Pirates Cove Yacht Club that day.

The following Tuesday afternoon, Cap'n Willie and Miz Bitsy paid Kelly a visit. "I'm sure she'll be happy to hear what we came to tell her," said Bitsy. There was no answer when they knocked on the front door of her parent's home, but they heard a small dog barking as it came running from the back yard. Presently, Kelly appeared around the corner, chasing after it, saying, "Quiet down, Backlash." The obedient dog silenced and she picked it up as she greeted her guests. "Hello! Cap'n Willie and Miz Bitsy, how nice of you to visit. Everyone's in the back yard sitting under the shade tree."

Miz Bitsy looked upon Kelly's face with special affection. She and Cap'n Willie had often commented to each other about how much Kelly resembled their deceased son. They had always suspected Barbara may have been pregnant with his child when she left town so quickly after his death. Their suspicions became stronger when Barbara and her new husband returned a few years later with a child. The time frame matched Kelly's age, but Cap'n Willie never followed up on his hunch, because he did not want to embarrass the family.

Miz Bitsy smiled lovingly and said, "Kelly, dear, I brought you and your folks some home-made bread and a coconut cake."

"Oh, thank you so much," said Kelly, trying her best to sound cheerful. "Won't you come around back and visit for a while?"

In the back yard, they were greeted by Kelly's mother, Barbara. "It is good to see you, Miz Bitsy, thank you for coming. I saw you at the memorial service, but didn't get a chance to speak to you."

"I think the whole town was there," said Miz Bitsy as she was offered a seat. "Jimmy sure had lots of friends."

"Look, Mama, Miz Bitsy brought us some of her homemade bread and a coconut cake. I'll take it inside."

"Thank you, Dear." As Kelly entered the house, Barbara continued, "And thank you, Miz Bitsy, that was so thoughtful. I'm glad y'all came to visit."

"Have a seat, Cap'n Willie," said Kelly's father while packing his well-used pipe with tobacco.

"Don't mind if I do, Charlie . . . feels mighty nice out here under this old elm." Charlie struck a match on the arm of his weathered rocking chair and puffed the fire into his pipe to get it started. If anyone ever looked the part of a waterman, he did. Charlie's overly tanned face was mildly wrinkled from years of exposure to the sun's rays reflecting off the water. His forty-six year old body was lean and muscular from pulling up two-hundred crabpots a day. Taking the pipe from his lips, he spoke in his easygoing manner through the thin layer of rising smoke, "I'd rather sit out here in the shade than inside under that air conditioner . . . as long as the mosquitoes don't bite."

Bitsy leaned toward Barbara, placed her hand on her forearm, and asked with concern, "How is Kelly doing?"

"Today is the first day I've not seen her cry. It'll take a long time for my Kelly's heart to heal."

"Willie and I plan to visit Jimmy's parents tomorrow. I do hope Mae is doing better. You know, I understand just how heartbroken she must feel."

"I'm sure you do, Miz Bitsy," Barbara lamented, "it must be terrible losing your only son."

"They say time heals all wounds, but it never removes the scar," Miz Bitsy responded meekly. Hearing the squeaky spring as the screen door on the porch opened, she turned and saw Kelly emerge adding, "But, my Gene will never be completely gone. I feel his spirit is alive."

Kelly walked to the old-fashioned swing hanging from a bough of the tree. She remembered the last time she sat there; Jimmy was standing behind her, pushing her gently and talking about the two of them taking a long overdue vacation. He had always wanted to visit the Bahamas. She did not allow the swing to move as she sat there thinking how lonesome her life would be without him.

Willie noticed the sadness on her face and pondered how she was too young to be a widow. Then Charlie broke the silence saying, "Cap'n Willie, don't you miss running fishing parties? I'll bet you feel like a fish out of water sometimes."

"To tell the truth, Charlie, I do miss it a little . . . that's why I took my part-time job at the marina. Gives me a chance to keep up with what's going on out there." Willie took his handkerchief from his pocket and wiped a little perspiration from his brow . . . "How's crabbing these days?"

"I had a fair catch this morning. Not getting anything for 'em, though. When there's plenty of crabs, the price is low. 'Course when the price is good, we can't catch any. Seems like that's the way it always is."

"I know what you mean, you can't win for losing." Cap'n Willie turned his attention to Kelly and said, "Let me tell you what really brings us over here today, young lady."

At those words, Barbara moved to the edge of her seat full of anxiety about what Willie might say. She was apprehensive Willie may know Kelly was his own granddaughter, and perhaps, he intended to reveal her secret. Then again, she silently assured herself, even if he does know, surely he wouldn't mention it now; not so soon after the heartbreaking tragedy.

The dignified old gentleman leaned forward with an elbow on each leg, "Kelly, I'm sure you knew about the fifty-thousand dollars top mate prize."

She interrupted, "Cap'n Willie, I feel so bad about Bull not winning. He certainly deserved it. Everyone knows they had the winning fish on when . . . when," her eyes welled with tears.

"Now, don't you worry your pretty little head about that, young lady. I talked with Bull and Sid yesterday; they have no regrets about cutting the fish off. Sid says if it ever came down to it, he'd do the same thing again. Besides, who knows, that fish could have gotten away from them anyhow. I've lost many a fish right at the boat. I always said the fish has the advantage as long as it's in the water."

Charlie waved his pipe and asked, "What about that fifty-thousand dollars, Willie?"

"Well, for one thing," the old captain paused, "the prize will never be offered again. At least not by this gentleman. He's afraid it may cause mates to take unnecessary risks. He feels terrible about what happened to Jimmy, and wants to put the prize money he offered to good use. He sent me here to make your daughter an offer."

"What kind of offer?" asked Barbara.

"If she will accept it, he is offering to provide a scholarship to Kelly to attend med-school." Kelly looked astonished as he continued, "If she agrees to become a full-time student at the East Carolina University School of Medicine, her tuition will be paid."

"Is this for real?" Kelly was bewildered. "Who is this person?"

"Well, that is one thing I still can't tell you. He insists on remaining anonymous."

"Must have plenty of money," remarked Charlie.

"Well, let's just say he's been fortunate."

"I don't know what to think!" said Kelly, overwhelmed. "It's always been my dream to go to medical school, but I don't know if I could get in."

"That's already been looked into," Willie replied. "You are near the top of your nursing class. The university has already said they will accept you in the program, if you only apply. . . and you'll receive full credit for the classes you've already taken."

Kelly said, "But, the fall semester is already starting."

"You could begin classes next week, if you choose to," said Willie. "The university said there would be no problem changing your curriculum."

Kelly thought aloud, "This is so sudden. I don't know what to say. There is so much to think about."

Her mother said, "Kel, don't worry about the details, they can be worked out. This is a wonderful opportunity for you."

Charlie asked skeptically, "Is this for real, Willie? This sounds too good to be true. A complete stranger footing the bill for my daughter?"

Willie looked at Charlie and pulled an envelope out of his pocket, then turned to Kelly in an almost grandfatherly way, and said, "Honey, I have a certified check right here. If your answer is yes, when I leave here I'm going straight to Citizens Bank and establish the account. You can trust me. So, what do you say?"

"What can I say? Oh, yes! Thank you, Cap'n Willie!" For an instant, Kelly beamed with happiness, until her bliss was dimmed when it occurred to her the opportunity was only made possible because of what had happened to Jimmy. Her eyes filled with tears. She suddenly felt all alone in the world without a husband to share her joy.

Wondering what had dampened her enthusiasm, Willie said, "I thought you'd be happy!"

With a strained smile, she replied, "Oh, I am happy, Cap'n Willie. It's just that . . . well, Jimmy knew it was my dream to attend medical school, but it was financially out of the quest . . . "

Barbara interrupted, "I'm sure he would be happy for you, dear. We all are."

Willie smiled at everyone, slapped his hands on his knees and said, "Now, that settled, what'ya say we cut into Bitsy's coconut cake?"

For the next few days, Kelly hurriedly went about getting her affairs in order so she could become a full-time student. After learning all the dorms on campus were full, she checked the bulletin board in the student cafeteria for possible apartments to rent. By Friday afternoon, she had found an apartment to share with a third-year accounting student from Fayetteville.

Kelly had been thinking about what she would do with the 'Lucky Duck', knowing she could not afford to keep it. The way she felt now, she never wanted to see the boat again. She couldn't bring herself to even go near the marina . . . the memories were too painful. She decided to ask Cap'n Willie if he would help her sell the boat; after all, she needed to pay the mortgage on her house in Wanchese.

It had been ten days since Kelly had last spoken to Bull. She had seen him at the memorial service, but he had kept his distance, as she had requested. Now, she regretted not saying anything to him . . . after all, he had tried so desperately to save Jimmy's life. That evening, she dialed Bull's phone number.

"Hello," he answered.

"Bull, this is Kelly."

Of course, he recognized her voice, "Kelly! How are you doing?"

"Actually, these last few days have been like a whirlwind."

"Yeah, I heard you're going off to school. I'm gonna miss you."

"You know, I'd be foolish to pass up an opportunity like this."

"I'm really happy for you."

"How 'bout you, Bull, are you going back to school?"

"No, I'm going to stick with fishing for a while. Sid's talking about us going to Mexico this winter."

"How did your parents react when you told them?"

"Surprisingly, very well. They did cut off my allowance though, but that's OK, I'm making good money working with Sid." Then, Bull changed his tone a little. He sounded like a bashful teenager, saying, "Say, ah, Kelly, I really would like to see you before you go. How about having dinner with me tomorrow night?"

His tone was so sweet, Kelly didn't want to say no, but felt she must. Quickly thinking of an excuse, she replied, "I'm sorry, Bull . . .I'd really like to, but I haven't finished packing. I'll be moving to an apartment in Greenville."

"When are you leaving?" he asked.

"Sunday afternoon, my first class is eight o'clock Tuesday morning."

"I'd be glad to help you move, if you need a volunteer. We don't have a charter this Sunday . . . Sid's going to a wedding. Besides, it'll give me an excuse to visit Mom and Dad."

"That's very sweet of you. Sure, I could use another truck," Kelly agreed. "I'm going to church with my parents. Why don't you come over around one o'clock; we'll load everything and be on our way."

"I'll be there, goodbye." Not hanging up the phone, Bull pushed the button to get a dial tone and called his mother. "Hi, Mom, I'll be home Sunday night."

"Wonderful, Bradley, your father and I will be happy to see you. Can you stay for a few days?"

"No, I've got to come back Monday afternoon. We have a charter to run Tuesday."

"Bradley, dear, I hope you're being careful out there on the ocean. I worry about you so much . . . especially since that terrible accident happened."

"Oh, don't worry about me, Mom. I'm always careful." He continued, "I'm helping Kelly move to Greenville on Sunday afternoon."

"Kelly is moving here?"

"Yeah, remember the fifty thousand dollar top mate prize nobody won? Well, they're using the money to set up a scholarship for her to go to medical school."

"That's wonderful, dear, and how nice of you to help her move."

"Yeah, she's a great girl. This is a lucky break for her."

Around five o'clock Sunday afternoon three compact pickup trucks stopped in front of the apartments at Tar River Estates. Bull's truck was loaded with Kelly's bedroom furniture; the Fisher's had a sofa, desk, and TV; and Kelly carried her stereo, clothes and personal belongings. Her new roommate, Dana Hinson, was there and helped them unload.

After everything had been carried inside, Bull felt like he was in the way. Approaching the door to leave, he said, "Unless you need me for anything else, I'm gonna head over to my folks' house now."

"Thanks Bull, Mom and Dad are going to help me get things arranged," Kelly said as she walked with him out onto the porch.

"Good luck in med school, Kelly, I'll be seeing you."

She touched his hand saying, "Thanks Bull . . . thanks for everything."

Bull called through the open door, "Goodbye, Mr. and Mrs. Fisher, and nice meeting you, Dana." Quieting his voice, almost to a whisper, he said, "Kelly, call me if you need anything."

After he left, Dana remarked, "Kelly, don't tell me that hunk lives here in Greenville."

"Well, actually, he's living down at the beach, but he is from here. His parents live over on, ah, Edgewater Lane."

"Edgewater Lane? Have you ever been to his house?"

"No, why?"

"Because every house on Edgewater is a mansion with either a Lexus or Mercedes parked out front, that's all," Dana explained. Kelly found herself feeling slightly jealous her new roommate was showing such interest in Bull.

Kelly's father interrupted her thought, asking, "Kel, honey, where do you want me to put the TV?"

A month later, Kelly was driving along route 64 on her way to Pirate's Cove Yacht Club. Cap'n Willie had found a buyer for the 'Lucky Duck', and she was going to transfer ownership today. There is a saying, the two happiest days in a boater's life are the day he buys, and the day he sells. To the contrary, this was not a very happy occasion for Kelly. She dreaded going aboard the boat, but she needed to get the documentation papers and also collect some personal belongings. She had promised to give Jimmy's photo album to his mother.

To make matters worse, the last few weeks, Kelly had been enduring a private struggle . . . with feelings of guilt. She had not mentioned it to anyone, but Kelly blamed herself for the accident that took her husband's life. She had suffered many sleepless nights unable to get the nightmarish picture out of her mind, of him struggling, then disappearing beneath the ocean's surface. 'I was at the helm,' she reasoned, 'I should have seen the rogue wave coming and warned him. Why wasn't I paying closer attention to what was going on around us, instead of looking back at them taking pictures of a stupid fish? It's all my fault,' she thought.

Trying to clear her mind, she turned up her car radio, thinking perhaps, music would help. But what she heard was the familiar voice of one of the girls who worked in the ship's store at Pirate's Cove. Judy was giving the daily fishing report. A grander had been brought in. Kelly missed the part mentioning which boat caught it. She hoped it might have been Sid's.

Entering the yacht club grounds, she saw a crowd of tourists gathered around the weigh station admiring the large fish hanging there. From where she parked, she could read the numbers 1031 written in white paint on its side. The 'Grand Slam' was moored in its slip, but then, so were most of the other boats. She walked over to find out who had made the lucky catch and was delighted to see Bull, Sid, and their anglers Rick and Cliff posing for pictures with the trophy fish. Rick had finally become a member of the Thousand Pound Club.

Bull happily greeted her, "Hi, Kelly, good to see you. You look great!"

"Hi, Bull, you too!" Kelly acknowledged Sid, Rick, and Cliff, "Looks like you guys had a good day," she laughed.

"They kept us busy," said Rick, pointing to the six marlin flags displayed on their outrigger pole.

Cliff added proudly, "We had four whites and another blue besides this one!"

"Wow, that's terrific!" she said.

"Yeah, it was some day!" exclaimed Bull. "So, what brings you to Nags Head?" he asked, although he already knew. Cap'n Willie had mentioned she would be coming.

"I'm selling the 'Lucky Duck'. I came to sign the papers."

"Oh, yeah, Cap'n Willie told us . . . to a really nice couple from Williamsburg."

Sid said, "I hear they're gonna move it up to the Chesapeake Bay."

"Sounds like a good place for her to retire," said Kelly. Turning to Bull, she said, "I need to get some things off the boat, and I'm . . . a little nervous about going aboard. Would you come with me? I may need a little moral support."

"Sure," he said with empathy.

Walking down the dock, Kelly and Bull approached Captain Dan's boat slip. As usual on Friday afternoons, several of the mates were gathered around having a few beers and shootin' the breeze. Dan greeted Kelly with a friendly hug saying, "Kelly, it's so good to see you. Everything going OK in college?"

"I have to do a lot of studying, but yes, Dan, everything's fine, thank you."

"I'm glad to hear it, you know I'm an ECU alumnus myself; some of my fondest memories are from there. You keep up the hard work, and I know you'll be fine."

"This isn't your boat, is it Dan?"

"Oh, yes it is!" laughed Bull.

"How do you like my new toy?", Dan asked showing pride.

His wife, Marsha, who had been inside reading a mystery novel, heard them talking and stepped out to say hello. "Hi, Kelly. Come aboard, let me show you around our new boat."

"Oh! Hi, Mrs. Parker, this is beautiful," said Kelly, entering the spacious salon.

As it turned out, their 612-pounder had held on to win first place in the tournament. It was a narrow victory over the 'Shady Lady' team, who had an excellent catch of marlin on the last day to come in second. Dan used his prize money to upgrade to a 54-foot custom built boat, the 'Carolina Pirate II'.

Once she was on the dock surrounded by friends, Kelly soon lost her anxiety about going aboard the 'Lucky Duck'. On the boat, she recalled many fond memories of happy times she and Jimmy had shared on the water. She found the documentation papers needed to transfer ownership and picked up her belongings, including the photo album Jimmy was so proud of. As Bull walked with her to the office where she was to meet the boat's new owners, he asked, "Could you have dinner with me tonight, Kelly?"

She stopped walking, turned to him and explained, "Bull, it's not that I wouldn't like too, but I don't think I should. It's been less than three months since the accident. You may think I'm old fashioned, but . . . it's just too soon. Besides, I already have dinner plans." Bull was obviously disappointed, but tried to look understanding. Kelly continued, "I'm meeting Heather for dinner at the Blue Pelican. I don't see any reason why you can't join us."

"Great! I'll see you there." Bull returned to his duties as Kelly entered the office.

After spending time with her at dinner, Bull found it hard to suppress his desire to see Kelly again. He thought about her almost all the time and wondered if she knew he was in love with her. He dared not call, knowing she needed time to get over Jimmy . . . if ever. Bull understood, but several times, he had picked up the phone to call her, dialing most of the numbers before changing his mind and hanging up. A few days later, he gathered enough courage to call. There's no harm in asking how she was doing, he thought.

"Hello," answered Dana.

Bull was surprised when Kelly's roommate answered, "Uh, hello, this is Bull Sullivan. Uh, hi, Dana, may I speak with Kelly?"

"Sure, handsome, hold on."

Dana handed the phone to Kelly, whispering she was leaving to pick up their dinner at the nearby Chinese carry-out. As she left the apartment, Kelly was happily talking to Bull, but when Dana returned a short time later, Kelly was obviously discouraging him, saying. "Bull, I still need more time. My life is hectic right now, I have to maintain a 3.0 average to keep the scholarship, and I'm finding medical school to be much more demanding than nursing classes."

"I can appreciate what you are saying, I hope you don't mind my calling, though, I care about you."

"Thanks Bull, you're a good friend."

When Kelly hung up Dana teased, "I know it's none of my business, but if I were you, I wouldn't let a good thing like him slip through my fingers." Handing Kelly her dinner, she added, "It seems to me you're more to him than just a friend."

Over time, the scars began healing, and Kelly came to realize she need not take responsibility for what had happened. It was not her fault. It was only an accident.

Lately, she found herself often thinking of Bull, and wondered if he still thought about her. She had not heard from him in a while and was afraid he may have given up on her. Then, on her birthday, November 29th, she received a lovely floral arrangement of twenty-two roses. The card attached read, "Has enough time passed for an old-fashioned girl to accept a dinner invitation from a guy who cannot stop thinking about her?" signed, "Love, Bull." Nothing could have made her happier. That night she telephoned him . . . and they talked for hours.

* * * * * * *

With the holidays so near, bookings for fishing charters dropped off sharply. Some of the captains and mates were making use of their commercial fishing permits and had been doing very well, but when tuna prices fell, Sid decided to take his boat out of service until the giant tuna showed up off Hatteras in mid-January. He told Bull to go home for the holidays, and call him after New Year's. He also reminded Bull of their plans to depart for Cancun, Mexico the first of March.

Driving home to Greenville on the second day of December, Bull was in an especially good mood because he and Kelly had planned their first date for that evening. "Hello! Mom, I'm home," he called out entering the familiar surroundings of his family's kitchen. "Bradley, this is a surprise!" Although Diane kept a busy schedule with her own practice as a pediatrician, this was her day off. She was making a floral arrangement. Gardening was her favorite hobby. "It's so good to see you. I hope you are home for the holidays."

"Yes, Mom, I'll be here through New Year's!"

"That's wonderful, Dear. It'll be so nice having you home."

"So, what's up?" he asked.

"I'm hosting the garden club meeting this afternoon. My guests should be arriving any minute."

He gave his mother a kiss on the cheek, grabbed an apple from the fruit basket on the table and started walking toward the foyer. "I need to get cleaned up," he said as he trotted up the circular staircase to his room. "I'll visit with you after your meeting, Mom." His mother followed him to the bottom of the stairs and said, "I know your father will be glad to see you. Maybe the three of us can go out for dinner tonight."

"Afraid not tonight, Mom. I have a date."

"A date? On your first night home? With whom, may I ask?"

"Kelly Edwards." Stopping at the top of the stairs, he said with a boyish smile, "Oh, by the way, Mom, don't wait up."

Bull arrived at Kelly's apartment looking more handsome than ever in a sport coat that really brought out his ice blue eyes. When she answered the door, Kelly looked striking with her hair pulled up in a French twist. She was wearing a pearl necklace and dangling earrings to match, and her black satin dress clung to her shapely figure. Bull walked in and surprised her by lifting her and swinging her around while saying, "I told you if I ever got the chance, I would sweep you off your feet."

"Oh Bull!" She laughed in delight as he eased her down, giving her an unexpected kiss. For the first time, she felt completely relaxed in his presence. Kelly was ready to move on with her life. She returned his kiss without any inhibition.

"I love your dress, Kelly, you look terrific."

"Thanks, it belongs to Dana; she insisted I wear it." Her roommate had gone home for the weekend. Kelly had the apartment to herself.

"You do things for this dress Dana never could," said Bull. He drew her to him and they kissed again . . . only this time more passionately. Kelly pulled away breathlessly and said, "I think we should go to dinner now."

"I have a special treat in store for you," holding her coat, "we have reservations for a candlelight dinner at DeFazio's."

At four-thirty the next morning, Bull opened his eyes. It was the usual time his body was accustomed to awakening during fishing season. Kelly's head rested on his shoulder, and her arm lay across his bare chest. He thought how sweet she smelled . . . how beautiful she was . . . and how wonderful their night together had been. Her hair was silken; her skin was soft. Kelly was even more sensuous than he had ever hoped. Bull knew he was in love. He wished he could lie there forever, but felt he really should get home. He didn't want his parents to know he had been out all night on their first date. Bull whispered, "Kelly . . . Kelly."

"Hmm," she responded sleepily.

"I think I'd better be going now."

"I'm never gonna let you go." She rubbed Bull's chest and slid across his body. As she pulled herself on top of him, and their lips almost touched, she whispered, "Can't you stay a little longer?"

An hour later, Bull found himself rushing home. At eight o'clock, he got up and went downstairs to the kitchen. His parents were having coffee by the bay window, enjoying the last of the scenic autumn colors in their back yard along the river bank.

"Good morning, Mom. Hi, Dad," Bull said as he entered the room and opened the refrigerator, taking out a bottle of orange juice.

"Hello, Son, it's good to have you home. I didn't hear you come in last night, you must have been very quiet," said his father.

Bull's mother poured Brad a fresh cup of coffee, and said, "I was just about to make breakfast; your father is having French toast. What would you like, Dear?"

"That'll be fine Mom. I'm starved."

"Your mother tells me you're home for a while."

"Yeah, Dad, probably till early January. We have to get the boat ready to go down to Hatteras the latter part of January, and Sid says we're going to Mexico the first of March."

"Sounds like that will be an adventure."

"Yeah, I'm really looking forward to it."

Diane asked, "How is Kelly doing, dear?"

"Great, Mom. Kelly's great."

"She's such a delightful girl."

"I'm supposed to pick her up around noon to go shopping. She wants to get her mother a Christmas gift."

"Why not bring her back here for lunch?" Diane said. "You'll be around, won't you, Brad?"

"Yes, but please make it an early lunch, Dear. I'd like to get in a round of golf this afternoon, even if it's only nine holes. There won't be many more nice days like this."

When Bull returned with Kelly about eleven-thirty, Diane showered her with attention and gave her a tour of the house. When they came to the kitchen, Kelly offered, "Can I help you with anything, Mrs. Sullivan?"

"Oh, please call me Diane. *Mrs. Sullivan* sounds so old," she laughed. "And no, thank you, Dear, I have everything under control." Diane turned to her son and said, "It's such a lovely day, Bradley, why don't you show Kelly around outside while I get lunch on the table."

"Sure, Mom." He took Kelly's hand and led her out onto the patio. They strolled past the large swimming pool which was covered for the winter. They walked hand in hand across the yard to the riverbank---where they stopped to talk. When she leaned against a large tree, Bull took advantage of the opportunity to trap her with his arms and steal a kiss, saying, "I think I'm falling for you."

His romantic gaze was interrupted by a loud bell. Diane was ringing the dinner bell hanging by the back door, just like she did when Bull was a youngster. He laughed as they walked toward the house, "Mom hasn't rung the bell since I was in boy scouts."

During lunch, their plans changed slightly. Kelly and Diane went shopping while Bull played golf with his father.

Over the next few weeks, Kelly was all but adopted by Diane. Bull's mother still had the spark of youth and enjoyed Kelly's company very much. On one occasion, while they were preparing a dinner salad together, Diane confided to Kelly, she regretted never having a daughter. She had become pregnant after Bull was born, but she miscarried. It was a girl. There were complications, and she was never able to conceive again.

Since their first date, Bull and Kelly had been almost inseparable. Not a day had gone by without them seeing each other. As Christmas week approached, his parents were preparing to go down to their condo at Fort Lauderdale. They had hoped he would join them; instead, he wanted to stay with Kelly. She planned to stay with her parents in Manteo for the holidays. She had not seen them since Thanksgiving. When she called to say she was bringing a friend with her, her mother was surprised to hear it was Bull. "Why would Bull want to spend Christmas with us, Kel?"

"Not *us*, Mom. Me!" Kelly confided to her mother she had been seeing a lot of Bull recently and they wanted to be together for Christmas.

"Oh my goodness!" Barbara responded, "What will the Edwards' think? They live right next door, you know."

Kelly understood her mother's reaction. She, too, felt it would be awkward so soon after Jimmy's death. "Mom, he won't be staying here, he'll be at his apartment. I just want to invite him to spend Christmas Eve with us, then come back for Christmas dinner."

In the end, Barbara and Charlie welcomed the young man into their home knowing it was what their daughter wanted.

28

Late Christmas eve night after her parents had retired, Kelly and Bull cuddled by the fireplace talking in whispers while Christmas music played softly on the radio. As they gazed at the lights twinkling on the tree, he took her hand and tenderly said, "Kelly, I have loved you since the day I first saw you. I never dreamed I'd be able to say those words to you, but it seems destiny has brought us together. I know you'll say it's too soon, but that doesn't stop the way I feel. I love you . . . and want to marry you."

"Oh, Bull, you know I've fallen in love with you too, but . . . but don't you think we're rushing things enough as it is? I want to finish college, and my parents; oh, God, my mom would freak if I told her I was already thinking about getting remarried!" trying to keep her voice down.

Still holding her hand, Bull opened a small box containing a sparkling engagement ring. "I will wait for as long as it takes. You can even keep it a secret, for now, from your mother if you want to. But, I know in *my* heart you're the only one for me. Kelly, will you, someday, be my wife?"

She did not hesitate to answer, "Yes . . . yes, Bull, I will." Taking the ring, she slid it onto her finger . . . and they sealed the engagement with a kiss.

* * * * * * *

On Christmas morning, as they worked side by side in the kitchen, Barbara noticed the engagement ring on her daughter's finger. "What did Santa Claus bring *you*, young lady?" Her mother's reaction was a mixture of surprise, bewilderment, and Kelly knew she would worry 'what will the neighbors think.'

Kelly put away the dish she was drying and turned to her mother, speaking in a respectful yet determined tone, "Mama, I thought my world ended when I lost Jimmy. He was a wonderful husband, and I will never forget him. But, now, I need to move on with my life. I love Bull and I know he loves me. I was hoping you might share in our happiness."

"You know I want you to be happy, dear, it's just that....." The dog started barking, signaling Bull's arrival.

"Please don't let this spoil your Christmas, Mama. If it's any consolation, we plan a very long engagement." Kelly opened the door and when Bull walked in, Barbara could see the love in his eyes, and the way her daughter beamed when they hugged.

A smile spread across Barbara's face, too. Wiping her hands on her apron, she walked toward them with outstretched arms saying, "Congratulations, I *am* happy for you. It's been so long since I've seen you this happy, Kel."

Bull later telephoned his parents in Florida and told them of their engagement.

"You work pretty fast, don't you, Son," Brad teased.

"I know a good thing when I see it, Dad."

"She is a very lovely girl, and I'm sure your mother will be very happy for you, too. Have you set a date?"

"Oh no, Dad, we plan on a very long engagement. Kelly wants to finish school first."

"That's smart, Son. Tell Kelly that we look forward to having her in the family . . . oh, hold on a minute, Son, your mother wants to talk to you."

"Bradley, I am so happy for you. You know how much we love Kelly. Why don't the two of you come down to Florida and join us for New Year's, to celebrate your engagement?"

"Mom that would be wonderful, but I don't think I can afford it after buying the ring."

"It'll be our treat, Dear."

"Hold on, let me ask Kelly about it." It did not take long for them to decide. "Thanks Mom. We'd love to come down. I'll call you in a couple of days, OK?"

"Wonderful! Goodbye, Dear, I love you, and Merry Christmas!"

"Merry Christmas, Mom. Love you too. Goodbye."

Following their whirlwind trip to Florida, it was time for Kelly's classes to resume. She found it difficult to get back into the college routine. She thought about Bull and their future constantly. Kelly confided to her roommate, Dana, that she had never been more in love. "The first time Bull made love to me, it felt like the earth moved!" she said.

Dana replied, "Yeah? Well, if you ever decide to ditch him, let me know, OK? I could go for an earth-shaking romance," she laughed.

"Don't hold your breath," Kelly replied, "but to tell you the truth, I'm almost relieved Bull's gone back to work in Nags Head. At least now, I can spend more time on my studies." As she opened one of her books, she pondered who the mysterious benefactor of her scholarship might be. Who would want to pay for my college education? But then, Kelly mused, what difference does it really make. I promised to do my best, and that's just what I intend to do. As she turned the page, trying to concentrate, her thoughts involuntarily turned to Bull and how much she already missed him. They would not see each other again until she returned home to Manteo the following weekend.

Bull drove through the open gate of the Wanchese boatyard and, for the first time, saw the 'Grand Slam' up on dry dock. Her proud bow loomed high above him. The boat appeared larger than he expected. Sid and one of the yard hands were working underneath the boat, scraping barnacles off her shafts and rudders. Taking advantage of the unusually mild winter day, they had just hauled her out that morning.

During the next couple of weeks, Bull and Sid would work fervently to get her shipshape for another season. They had thirty charters booked to run out of Hatteras before their planned departure for Mexico on March 2nd. The report they had awaited came on January 20th . . . two charter captains, scouting the offshore wrecks, reported the giant bluefin tuna had returned. A large school was feeding around the *British Splendour,* one of the shipwrecks about twenty-five miles south of Hatteras Inlet in an area known as the Graveyard of the Atlantic.

With a quick phone call, Sid was able to arrange a fishing trip for the very next day. So he and Bull ran the boat sixty miles down the Pamlico Sound to Hatteras Village and docked at Teach's Lair. The marina was named for Edward Teach, better known as the legendary pirate, *Blackbeard,* and is advertised as North Carolina's closest marina to the Gulf Stream.

Until recent years, this remote fishing village at the end of a tiny spit of sand jutting out into the Atlantic would be practically deserted during the dead of winter. Not much ever happened until the Spring run of red drum and bluefish in the surf, which brings droves of fishermen to its wide sandy beaches. Since it was discovered in recent years that schools of giant tuna winter only a few miles off the Carolina coast, the village's motels, restaurants, stores, and marinas enjoy a flourishing commerce from mid-January through March. Even though it is mostly catch and release, big game anglers come from around the world to test their endurance against these giants of the sea. The Coast Guard closely monitors the daily catch and requires each boat to have a special permit. Only fish under 73-inches in length can be kept . . . and only one per boat, per day. Sid said it would be easier to smuggle drugs than to try to bring an illegal tuna to the dock.

His booking calendar was filled for the next thirty-five days. But, it would be the weatherman who had the final say on how many days they would actually get to fish. Winters are generally mild on the Outer Banks, except for an occasional cold front passing though, which can cause strong winds to blow for days at a time . . . . shutting down fishing altogether. That was just what happened near the end of January. The Coast Guard closed the inlet due to gale force winds. While Sid telephoned his affected parties, Bull eagerly got on the road to Greenville; he could hardly wait to be with Kelly.

Three days later, the ocean righted itself and the 'Grand Slam' enjoyed twelve consecutive days of fishing before the weather flared up again. Their next trip was on Tuesday, February 14th. As much as Kelly and Bull would have liked to spend Valentine's Day together, it was not possible. They were separated by a three and a half hour drive aside from other obstacles . . . she had classes, he was fishing, and the roads were covered with snow. A major winter storm had dumped up to 24 inches on the interior of the mid-Atlantic states. And, for the first time in six years, Hatteras Island was dusted with a blanket of snow. However, the morning sky was clear and the forecast called for temperatures to rise steadily. It promised to be a good day for fishing.

The 'Grand Slam's' party arrived looking more like duck hunters than fishermen. Three men and a boy, all dressed in heavy camouflage coveralls, left their footprints in the snow as they walked to the boat. The boy was thirteen and obviously thrilled about going fishing in the ocean for the first time. Until now, his fishing experience had been limited to farm ponds. They were a family of dairymen from Charlottesville, Virginia. Luckily, they had driven to Hatteras the day before the snowfall.

Bull joked with the boy, "They let you out of school to go fishing today?"

"I'm not missing school," the boy replied with a grin on his face, "school's closed anyway because of the snow. Charlottesville has eighteen inches!"

"Well, aren't you lucky." Bull said, extending a hand to help him aboard, "Hi, my name is Bull, I'm the mate."

"*Bull?*" the lad smiled, "My name is Jay. At home we have a cow, ah, I mean a bull, named *Bull*. He's mean as they come. He chased me across the pasture the other day!"

"Well, Jay, I promise I won't chase you. But, when you get one of those giant tuna on you line, you're gonna think he's *strong* as your bull."

"Strong as *Bull*? No way!" he laughed.

"You should have seen the one we caught yesterday . . . a thousand pounds easy."

The excited boy's eyes and mouth opened wide as he looked at his father and uncles in disbelief, "I don't think I could bring in anything *that* big."

"Sure you could; it's all in having the right equipment . . .uh oh," Bull jumped to the dock, seeing a troop of hungry pelicans coming toward his bait. "We've got company," he said. It was apparent the pelicans made themselves right at home around the marina. Bull took a step toward them and yelled, "Get away from here!" They moved back a few yards, but watched with vigilance, as Bull loaded three forty-pound flats of baitfish onto the boat.

"What are *they*?" asked the inquisitive teenager.

"You've never seen pelicans before?" Bull kidded.

"Of course I know what pelicans are! I mean the fish!" he said, picking one up, "these are about the size of the perch I catch in the pond on the farm. They're real good fried up for breakfast.."

"I don't think you'd want to eat one of these. I'm surprised the pelicans will eat 'em, they're so bony and oily. Folks around here call 'em fat-backs; they're menhaden fish. Crabbers use 'em to bait their traps, and we use them for chunking."

"Chunking?"

Bull tossed one amid the eager passel of pelicans, and as they scrambled for the prize, said, "I hope those tuna will be hungry as these guys." Jay was still holding one of the fish. He waved it at arm's length, teasing the big birds by moving it side to side. It was comical the way their heads moved in unison following the movement of the tempting morsel. He tossed it into the water watching the clumsy birds go after it, "Looks like Pete got it again," said Bull.

"How do you know which one's Pete?" asked Jay.

"They're all named Pete!" laughed Sid. "Let's go fishing!" The lines were cast off, and they got underway. It took only an hour to reach the sunken tanker where the tuna were holding. Three other charter boats were already there, and each was hooked up with a fish.

"Who's our first victim today?" Bull asked as he came out of the cabin with a very large rod and reel. Jay's father and his uncles agreed the boy should have first crack. The eager lad jumped into the fighting chair.

Sid shouted from the bridge, "We're right over the wreck and fish are here! Heavy marks on the fishfinder, down deep. Chunk 'em, Bull. Bring 'em up!" On the way out, Bull had filled a five-gallon bucket with baitfish cut in half. He scattered a double handful of chunks over the stern. Within seconds, they saw a quick splash and a glimpse of one of the aggressive tuna hitting a chunk of bait. From the size of the boil on the surface, they could tell the fish was very large. Then, another darted by. The teenager got a good look, "Wow! Did you see that?"

"What did I tell you?" Bull said as he placed the heavy rod in the gimbal of the chair between Jay's knees. He connected the wide reel to a harness, which had been fastened around Jay's waist.

"But, what is *he* hooked to?" asked Jay's father, somewhat concerned after seeing the size of these giants.

"Good question! We don't want to lose your son *or* this rod 'n reel. It cost over fifteen hundred bucks; I don't know how much you have invested in Jay," teased Bull as he secured a safety rope to the boy. Bull baited Jay's hook, tossed it over saying, "Are you ready to rumble?" The boy tightened his grip and braced his feet anticipating the strike. His father peered through the lens of his video camera at the bait gently floating about thirty feet behind the boat. Bull started counting aloud. "One, two, three, four, five, six, seven, eight, nine."

Wham! Splash! The torpedo sized fish crashing the bait was captured on film, and so was the teenager's scream of excitement, "Holy cow!" cried Jay as the powerful tuna streaked away with his line in tow. The rod, which had seemed to be stiff as a broom handle before, now arched into a semi-circle lifting the young angler several inches above his seat. His anxious father, not trusting the safety line, grabbed his son's harness and held on to him for dear life. The one hundred-foot section of monofilament leader quickly disappeared. It was secured with a strong knot to a spool of bright, neon-green dacron line which zipped up through the guides and over the rod tip, penetrating the clear blue water like a laser beam. The high-visibility line was used so other captains could avoid it, since the boats worked in such close proximity.

"Less than ten seconds to get hooked up today, Captain," boasted Bull.

"The snow must have made 'em hungry," replied Sid as he gunned the 'Grand Slam' into reverse, backing down on the fish, and getting away from the crowd of boats.

"Crank that handle, Jay!" coaxed Bull. "Use the muscles in your legs and back to bring that monster up as fast as you can. I want to get him tagged and released before he gets too stressed."

As the boy labored with the fish and his father fumbled with a video camera, Sid called down, "Bring your camera up here. You'll get a nice view from the bridge."

Climbing the ladder, he asked, "Captain, you say we're over a shipwreck?"

"Yes!" Sid replied, "the *British Splendour,* a big tanker that fell prey to an undersea raider during World War II."

"You mean a submarine?"

"That's right! A German U-boat."

"I never knew the Nazi's came this close to our shores."

Sid explained, "Oh sure, especially in the first part of 1942. My father was in the Navy during the war and told me all about it. Back then, the military classified such attacks as top secret. Maybe they didn't want the American public to know Germans were so near. To this day, many Carolinians don't realize how close they were to front line action. Dozens of freighters and tankers were torpedoed off Diamond Shoals, and hundreds of men lost their lives, before the U.S. Navy finally sank a few of them and chased the rest out of here."

In the chair, the lad grunted, "ugh," as his stand-off with the big tuna continued.

"Can you handle him, Jay?" asked one of the boy's uncles.

"Ugh, yeah. I'll get him . . . sooner or later," he strained to reply.

Jay's father couldn't help teasing, "Are you sure it's a fish? Could be a dead body you snagged from the shipwreck under us, Jay."

"If it is," replied Bull, "he has a lot of life left in him."

The strong farm boy soon won the battle, and Bull grabbed onto the leader. A moment later, he tossed aside the tagging stick and shouted up to Sid, "I need the measuring line. This fish may be under 73-inches!"

No other boats were near, so Sid came down from the bridge long enough to assist. Bull was right, the tuna measured 71-inches and was hauled aboard. The captain congratulated the young angler, "Pretty work, son, you've got meat to take home."

"How much you think it weighs?" one of the men asked Sid.

"Close to two hundred pounds," Sid replied, ascending to the bridge. Then, looking back he added, "I hear the Japanese will pay as much as fifty dollars a pound for a fish like that!" He could tell the farmer's eyes were calculating, no doubt trying to estimate the value of their fish.

"Holy cow, that's ten thousand dollars!"

But his hopes were dashed when Sid said, "Don't get any ideas; you need a special commercial permit to sell it, and we don't have one."

Before their day was over, the group had caught and released seven more fish. The largest was estimated by Captain Sid to weigh over eight-hundred pounds. In each case Bull carefully removed the hook from the tuna's jaw. It was rewarding to see these magnificent giants swim away still strong. Perhaps they would be caught another day off New England, in the Mediterranean, or right back here at Hatteras.

That night, when Bull and Kelly talked on the telephone, the young lovers promised nothing would keep them apart next Valentine's Day. Kelly mentioned she visited Diane that afternoon, "Your mother said tell you hello, and she loves you."

"Mom really thinks a lot of you, Kelly. She told me you were like the daughter she never had."

"I love her too. She always knows just what to say to cheer me up."

Kelly also mentioned her upcoming spring break. She and Dana, along with a few other college girlfriends, were planning to drive down to Fort Lauderdale and stay in the Sullivan's condo. An idea occurred to Bull. Since the boat was departing for Mexico about the same time, he suggested Kelly and Dana cruise down the coast with them and meet up with their friends in Florida. Sid's wife had already made plans to cruise with them as far as Florida and then visit her aunt in Winter Haven.

Bull's plan came together nicely. On the evening of March 1st, Bull and Sid were loading provisions on the boat when Diane's Mercedes pulled into the parking lot at Teach's Lair Marina. Bull's mother had given Kelly and Dana a ride to Hatteras Village. The 'Grand Slam' would embark on its journey to Cancun at daybreak.

Kelly had been somewhat uneasy about going. This would be the first time she had ridden on a boat since that horrible day Jimmy was lost at sea. But, knowing she and Bull would be separated for two months while he fished in Mexico, her strong desire to spend time with him overshadowed her apprehension.

As it turned out, Kelly could not have asked for a more enjoyable spring break and found it difficult to leave Bull, knowing she wouldn't see him for many weeks. When she returned home, she was glad her new semester started the following day. It would help keep her from missing Bull. Sometimes she caught herself worrying about him. In light of what she had been through seven months earlier, this was only natural.

On the following Friday, Kelly awoke feeling nauseous. She stayed home from school and canceled plans to attend a weekend garden show with Diane. Playing down her illness to her future mother-in-law, Kelly assured her, "It's nothing serious, I'm sure I'll be fine in a couple of days." But, in reality, she was scared. This was the second time she had missed her period. The first time went almost unnoticed, as she was so preoccupied by her whirlwind romance and heavy college load. Realizing this queasiness could be morning sickness, she anxiously took an at-home pregnancy test and confirmed her worst fear.

Kelly was devastated. Her troubled mind filled with questions. Why wasn't I more careful? What will Bull think? What about medical school and my scholarship? She felt as though her life was ruined. Never thinking she would consider it, going to an abortion clinic seemed to be her only practical option. Kelly reasoned, "After all, Bull is in Mexico. He'll never know anything about it. No one will have to know."

Having made her decision, Kelly went to bed, but sleep did not come easily. When she finally did drift off, she awoke wrestling with her conscience . . . this is Bull's child, too, conceived by two people in love. I don't have the right to terminate this baby without even telling him. How could I live with myself?

The stress brought on by Kelly's predicament took its toll. She came down with a terrible cold and missed several more days of school. Concerned after having not heard from her for days, Diane stopped by the apartment. She was surprised by Kelly's appearance, "Dear, you look terrible. Are you no better?"

"It's just a cold, Diane. I'll be fine," said Kelly while trying to suppress a cough.

"I'm the doctor; you're the student; let me decide." Placing her hand on Kelly's forehead, she said, "Oh, honey, you have a fever! You may need antibiotics."

"No, really, Diane. I feel much better today. I'll probably be back in school tomorrow."

Seeing Kelly on the edge of tears, Diane sensed she was holding something back. As she sat down beside her on the sofa, Diane spoke in a caring and gentle tone, "Dear, I care about you as a doctor and friend. Please tell me what's upsetting you."

Choking back tears, the distressed young woman began to reveal her burden, "Oh, Diane, I didn't want to tell anybody."

Diane hugged her, "Oh, honey. It'll be all right. What's the matter?"

"I'm pregnant."

Wide eyed with surprise, Diane asked, "Are you sure?"

"They claim those tests are 99% reliable. Yes, I'm sure."

Diane reached over and hugged Kelly gently, "Please don't be upset, Kelly. This is wonderful news! My Bradley's going to be a father!?"

"Yes, I'm afraid so," she replied wiping her tears. Seeing how happy Diane was at the prospect of being a grandmother, a smile slowly emerged on the troubled girl's face. "Yes, I'm going to be a mother." For the first time Kelly considered the possibility of motherhood.

"Does Bull know yet?" asked Diane.

"No one knows. I wasn't sure what to do. I was so confused, I even thought about having it aborted."

"Oh heavens, no! Kelly!"

"But what will I do? How can I go to college and care for a baby? I don't want to give up my scholarship."

Diane took a bottle of Tylenol out of her purse. Giving Kelly two tablets with a glass of water, she said, "The first thing we have to do is treat your cold." Taking Kelly's hand, Diane reassured her, "Dear, don't you worry about a thing. We'll work this out. I wish you had told me sooner. You just don't know how pleased I am. Let's make an appointment for you to see an obstetrician right away."

The next day, Kelly's fever had broken and she was feeling much better. She accepted Diane's invitation to come to her house for dinner.

Over dessert Brad said, "Of course, Diane told me the news, Kelly."

She blushed and responded, "I'm really sorry it happened, Dr. Sullivan. I should have been more careful."

"Don't try to accept all the responsibility yourself," he said.

"That's right dear. It takes two to tango," added Diane.

"But I am concerned how I will continue my studies and take care of a baby at the same time."

"Diane and I have discussed that," Brad responded.

"Where there's a will, there's a way," said Diane.

Brad placed his dessert dish on the table and said, "The first thing we need to do is figure out a way to get you down to Mexico so you can tell Bull in person." He poured himself another cup of coffee and continued, "Don't you worry, Kelly. Diane and I have come to love you almost as much as Bull does . . . and besides, you may be carrying my namesake, Bradley Sullivan, IV."

Diane quipped, "Oh, Brad! Don't say that, I'm counting on a granddaughter to spoil."

Kelly's emotions were welling up inside her. "You are the kindest people I have ever known, and I love you both." She felt as though a great burden had been lifted from her shoulders.

The telephone rang, and Brad answered. It was Bull calling from Cancun.

"Tell me about your trip across the Gulf, Son."

"It was great, Dad, didn't have any problems. We made the crossing with a couple of other boats. It's a 335-mile run from Key West to Cancun----took us about eighteen hours."

"How close to Cuba did you get?"

"Very close, actually. We had to watch the loran to make sure we stayed clear of their waters . . . and you can bet we kept our left eye peeled for Cuban patrol boats."

"Sounds like a real adventure, Son."

"It was Dad. It was great! I wish you could come down here and go fishing with us one day. You won't believe this, but we start trolling as soon as the boat leaves the marina. We're catching as many as fifteen sailfish a day and never leave sight of land. It's incredible. You really should come on down!"

"Well, if I did come, would it be all right if I brought a couple of ladies with me?"

Bull was taken by surprise, "Sure Dad! Is Kelly there now? I didn't get an answer at her apartment."

"Yes, she's here, Son. She's really not feeling too well, though. She's just getting over a cold. I'll put her on in a minute, but let's get back to this fishing trip. You check with Sid and see if Saturday week is available. If it is, we'll fly down on Friday before."

"Great, Dad! I'll call you back and let you know."

"You do that Son, now, here's Kelly."

"Tell Mom I said hello."

"All right, Son, and she sends her love."

Before Kelly took the phone, Diane whispered to her, "Dear, I don't think you should mention anything about 'you know what'. Wait till we get there."

Kelly nodded in agreement.

While Kelly talked with Bull, Brad said to Diane, "That worked out well. I was afraid we would have to come up with some kind of lame excuse for sending Kelly down there. This is perfect."

"And if I know our son, he'll be happy when he hears the news. Don't you think, Dear?" commented Diane.

"Well, it's hard to predict what young people think nowadays. We'll know soon enough."

Kelly hoped Bull would be as supportive as his parents had been. She had returned to her studies with renewed enthusiasm. Being a top student, she experienced little difficulty catching up on her work.

Their flight arrived in Cancun the following Friday at about three o'clock in the afternoon. It was only the second time Kelly had flown; the first was when she and Bull had visited Florida for New Year's. The Sullivans and Kelly took a cab to the Marina Hacienda del Mar and were standing on the dock to meet the 'Grand Slam' when it returned from fishing. Seeing the boat enter the harbor, Kelly trembled with anxiety.

When Sid spun the boat around to back into the slip, Bull happily waved and shouted hello to them and threw a kiss to Kelly. She managed a smile and returned the gesture. Brad commented about both outrigger poles being lined with billfish flags. As the boat's engines were silenced, Brad called to Sid, "It looks like you had a good day, Captain."

"Yes, we did. They really turned on this afternoon. We raised twenty billfish today! Caught thirteen: ten sails and three whites."

As soon as the dock lines were cleated, Bull jumped up onto the dock and gave Kelly a hug and kiss. The first thing he said to her was, "Baby, you're a sight for sore eyes!". He greeted his parents, then gave Kelly another hug as he lifted her off her feet.

31

Kelly thought, that's strange, he's never called me *baby*, then said, "I have really missed you too. You better enjoy being down here now, because after we're married, I don't think I could stand being apart from you for so long."

"Baby, I feel the same way. I'm going nuts down here without you."

As he kissed Kelly again, she thought, how odd, he called me *baby*, again.

Turning to Sid, who was still on the boat with the fishing party, Bull commented, "Cap'n, if it's all right with you, I'll be back to clean up the boat after I get them settled in the villa."

"Don't you worry about the boat, Bull. It doesn't need too much attention today. I'll give it a quick rinse. You go spend some time with your family."

After everyone had a chance to freshen up, they went to the Hacienda Restaurant for dinner. Given a choice, they decided to dine on the screened-in patio overlooking the harbor. Most of the other patrons were dining inside where it was air conditioned, but Diane said it was so cold when they left North Carolina this morning, she wanted to enjoy the warm air. After they were seated, Bull complimented Kelly, "I can't get over how great you look. I've never seen you look better."

Kelly said modestly, "Bull, I think you've just been in the sun too long."

"No, It's something about you. I don't know . . . your lips seem fuller."

"Buulll," Kelly demurred, thinking his compliments were a bit too persistent.

"I'm serious, you're radiant. Your face is aglow," he taunted.

Diane lifted an eyebrow as she gave Brad a suspicious look, thinking it was a little out of character for her son to be so verbose. She detected a slight smirk on Brad's face.

Kelly laughed, "Maybe it's the Mexican air, but it's nice to be appreciated by the man I love."

The waiter appeared at the table to take drink orders. Looking first at Diane, he inquired, "Would you like something from the bar?"

"A margarita, please, no salt."

He then turned to Kelly, "And you, Señorita?"

Kelly considered aloud, "Let's see, what would I like . . . hmm"

"May I suggest our house drink, the Matador?" said the waiter.

"That sounds interesting, what's in it?"

"Pineapple juice, lime juice, and Tequila."

Bull interrupted, "Hold the Tequila, please, she's not allowed to have any alcohol." Looking at Kelly, he said, "She's going to be the mother of my child."

Diane's mouth fell open as she looked at Brad with reproach. "I knew it!" she exclaimed.

"So, I've got a big mouth," he confessed.

Feeling both surprised and relieved, Kelly smiled happily and said, "How long have you known? I should have known something was up when you kept calling me *baby*. You've never called me *baby* before."

Bull leaned toward Kelly and put his arms around her. She

beamed with joy when he said, "We're going to make terrific parents. You know how much I love you."

Kelly was elated; tears of happiness filled her eyes. "I was so worried about how you might react."

"I only found out last night, really."

"I confess," said Brad. "I knew how apprehensive you were about telling Bull the news. So, I thought it might make things easier if I just gave him a call. Kelly, I hope you'll forgive me if I spoiled your surprise. I promise never to meddle again."

Diane quipped, "Kelly may forgive you, but I'm not going to let you off so easily. Why didn't you tell me you had called Bull." Then she laughed, and said joyfully, "This calls for a celebration, after dinner let's go to Pedro's, across the street, where the loud music was coming from. I feel like dancing."

During their short weekend in Mexico, they set the wedding date for Saturday, May 12, in the Sullivan's back yard at Greenville. Bull did not mention it would take place one year to the day since he spotted Kelly leaving Pirate's Cove on the 'Lucky Duck'.

The following Monday, Bull accompanied his parents and fiancé to the airport for their midmorning departure. He was also supposed to pick up a party of three anglers who were arriving on the same plane, including: Jerry Mitchell, who owned a thirty-eight-foot Bertram which he kept at Pirate's Cove; his friend, John Carver; and John's son, Mike, who worked as a dock boy at the marina a couple of summer's ago. They were scheduled to fish that afternoon and the next two days.

Of course, saying goodbye was difficult for the newly engaged couple . . . there were hugs, kisses and tears; but for Kelly, her tears were tears of joy, for her heart was so much lighter than when she arrived a few days ago. She was filled with optimism about their future together. Bull stayed with her until she had to go through customs, then he went around to meet the arriving fishermen.

The second he entered the baggage claim area a voice called out, "Hey, college boy, where the hell have you been? We've been waiting for fifteen minutes."

Needless to say, Bull was utterly shocked to see Tommy Wilson standing there with Mike, John, and Jerry. After welcoming them, Bull said, "Tommy, I didn't know you were coming along, too!"

"I wanted to surprise you," that familiar devious laugh followed his smart-aleck remark.

Jerry spoke up, "Bull, you don't think Sid will mind we brought

Tommy along, do you? Mike's working for a boat broker now. He ran into Tommy a couple of weeks ago in Morehead City and invited him to come along with us."

Bull knew the three men had no inkling of the rift between them. Wondering how Sid would react but knowing there was nothing he could do, Bull hesitantly replied, "No problem. Let me help with your bags."

"Carry this one," said Tommy handing him a canvas tote. "You'll be needing what's in there. I brought my personal rigs, including some secrets Sid doesn't even know about."

Bull dropped them off at the nearby motel and returned to the boat. Walking down the dock carrying Tommy's bag of gear, he thought, "This is just great; now I've got to put up with this jerk showing me how to fish for the next three days."

Sid saw him coming and asked, "What's the matter with you? You look like you're mad at the world."

"Guess who's coming to dinner," said Bull.

"What are you talking about?"

Bull looked toward the motel and saw the group walking their way and said, "Your friends brought a guest."

"So, what's the problem?"

"It's Tommy Wilson."

"You're kidding, right?"

"No I'm not. Apparently Tommy ran into Mike and got himself invited."

When the group arrived at the boat, Sid did a good job concealing his dismay at learning Tommy was among the party of anglers. "Well, this will be a change for you, Tommy. You'll have the opportunity to catch a few fish without having to do all the work."

"I'm gonna watch the way Bull does things this afternoon, but he's already agreed to let me do my own thing tomorrow . . . if that's all right with you, of course."

"That'll be fine,' said the captain, "as long as everyone has fun and catches fish."

A short while later, they were underway. It seemed almost nothing went right for Bull that afternoon. Maybe it was because he was aware of Tommy watching everything he did. Several marlin came into the spread but appeared skittish. The same rigs he had been so successful with lately, were not working today. They finally managed to hook one sailfish, and Mike caught it. Returning to the marina, Jerry said optimistically, "That's OK guys, we'll get 'em tomorrow."

"Yeah, tomorrow I'll pull a few tricks out of my bag," Tommy chided.

Terrific, Bull thought in silent contempt. That night, he telephoned his fiancé to make sure she had arrived home safely. Kelly was so obviously happy with the way things had turned out, "I want to go back down there where it's nice and warm, it is freezing here! They're calling for snow tonight." When he told her about his encounter with their mutual nemesis, she said, "Don't even think about him, honey, keep your mind on me."

"I do! I think of you all the time," he replied.

She laughed teasingly, "Yeah, me and those billfish." She went on to tell Bull how his mother wanted to make their wedding a big to-do. "I was hoping to keep it simple," she said, "but, really I'm happy to have her help. Biology is giving me a fit this semester."

For a while longer, Kelly and Bull talked of life and love. At times, their conversation lulled to silence, but they were content . . . just hearing the sound of each other breathing bridged the distance between them.

Sure enough, the next morning Tommy was on the boat an hour before anyone else, rigging baits. Bull arrived, sipping from his mug of hot coffee, trying to be friendly, greeted, "Morning, looks like it'll be a nice day."

"Morning," was Tommy's one word reply. Bull couldn't help but watch with interest as Tommy prepared his rigs. Everything needed to be ready when they left the dock, because in Cancun, the outriggers are dropped and lines in the water almost as soon as you clear the jetties. Bull paid particular attention to the teasers Tommy rigged . . . a daisy chain of a half dozen Hawaiian Eye lures with blue 'n white skirts. They hung from the chain like the limbs of a Christmas tree and each lure was rigged with a ballyhoo. Bull couldn't help but say, "For a man who loves to fish naked, you sure are rigging a lot of skirts."

"Two reasons for that, college boy. It's because of all the flying fish I saw out there yesterday. I always pull plenty of blue 'n white skirts when flying fish are around."

"What's the other reason?"

"I saw how skittish those fish were acting. We're gonna pull four teasers like this and drive those marlin wild; you watch. You and me both are gonna have to be on our toes. I don't want to lose these teasers."

About that time, Sid and the others arrived and they were soon underway. Within a short time, Bull felt humbled watching Tommy work the cockpit. No matter what else Tommy had said or done, he quickly gained Bull's respect for what he did best, raising marlin. They scored early and often. Within the first hour, two whites and two sails had been caught and released. Bull wanted to convince himself the hot action was only because the fish were cooperating today, but Sid told him from what he heard on the radio, the other boats were not having as much success. Then they saw two marlin come up at the same time after one of Tommy's teaser chains. Bull was convinced . . . the man knew his stuff. They missed both fish. One of them was quite large . . . Tommy estimated more than six hundred pounds. "I'll get your ass," Tommy called out to the fish, reaching for his bag of tricks. He produced a short piece of stout wire to which was attached a small, but very strong treble hook, with three razor sharp points.

When Bull saw it, he said, "Sid's not gonna like it. He doesn't approve of stingers."

"How's he gonna find out, college boy? You gonna tell on me?" Bull turned away and Tommy discreetly attached the stinger hook to the mackerel, which he had rigged earlier. He placed the deadly rig in a bucket of water near his work station, at the ready.

The party landed several more marlin and soon other captains were calling Sid on the radio asking what his secret was. Sid answered, "Nothing particular, it must be the boat. You hang in there, though, you'll get 'em."

The generally peaceful mood aboard the boat was suddenly interrupted by Tommy bellowing, "He's mine! He's mine!" Grabbing his specially rigged bait, he scrambled to the stern, nearly running over Jerry, and started feeding back line. Everyone saw a huge marlin chasing one of the teasers. It looked to be at least twice as large as any other fish they had seen today. As Tommy dropped his deadly rig back to his target, Bull quickly pulled in the teaser. The fish turned its attention to Tommy's bait. The water splashed with commotion! "He's picked it up!" said Tommy, putting the reel into free-spool. "Who wants him?"

Jerry said, "It's John's turn!"

"No Jerry, let Tommy get 'em!" said John.

The others agreed. Bull was caught up in the excitement too, "Try him, Tommy!" he urged. Tommy pushed the lever on the reel up to strike position. The line tightened and a great fish leaped into the air far behind the boat. "You got him!" shouted Bull.

When the marlin leaped a second time, it became obvious the hook was deep. Blood flew from its gills as the fish shook its head back and forth. It was a sickening sight to which Sid commented, "Damn, that's a crying shame."

At the same time, Tommy was in the cockpit laughing with joy, knowing the fish was hooked well. Bracing his knees against the transom, Tommy skillfully pumped the arching rod, as if trying to break the fish's will to survive. He yelled, "I've got the *big Kohuna* today, boys!" Again it jumped and danced atop the water with blood streaming down its sides. "Look at him, I'd say he's having a *bad* day!"

Hearing Tommy's wicked laugh, Bull lost his enthusiasm. "No need to release that one," he lamented to Sid.

Life drained quickly from the grand fish and by the time Tommy got it to the boat, he was pulling dead weight. There was no fight left in her. As Bull and Tommy drug the heavy fish through the transom door, onto the deck, it showed one final spark of life. As if making a desperate effort to save her species, she spewed out millions of tiny eggs. The mass spilled across the deck, enough to overflow a five-gallon bucket.

Witnessing this sight, Sid recanted his trademark phrase, which he used to describe any manner of catastrophe, no matter how major or minor, "It's a crying shame."

Regardless of how the captain and mate felt, the others were excited to have landed such a fish. Although Sid would have preferred tagging and releasing the fish and perhaps getting a few pictures on video, he did not want to dampen their enthusiasm. He pointed the bow toward the inlet, and said, "That's a good way to finish the day fellows. We'll go see how much this one weighs." He knew it was good for business to bring one in now and then; it creates excitement around the dock. And besides, the meat would feed a lot of hungry Mexican kids.

Bull scooped up double handfuls of her eggs and returned them to the sea in hopes a few of them might somehow survive. Tommy lifted the fish's bill and opened its mouth appearing to retrieve his hook. In reality, he was cutting the wire leader close to the stinger hook which was lodged deep within the fish's throat. When he was satisfied it would not be visible, he looked at Bull and said, "Our secret?" With some hesitation, Bull nodded, giving his promise not to say anything to Sid, but vowing he would never let Tommy get away with it again.

After the six-hundred pound fish was weighed, pictures were taken, and arrangements made for the meat to be used by some local families in need. Tommy and Bull returned to clean up the boat. The cockpit was still splattered with blood and fish eggs. As they walked down the dock, a new boat was arriving at the marina. It was a sleek 65-footer with European lines. Tommy said, "Hey, that's one of those new Donnie Wood Yachts." The boat's name and hailing port were 'Naughty Gal', Boca Raton, Florida.

Bull said, "Hey, I saw that boat advertised in a magazine. It's a new hull design, supposed to cruise at 40-knots."

"Now there's a boat with an attitude! Let's go check that baby out!"

As much as Bull would like to get a closer look, he saw this as an opportunity to get rid of Tommy for a while, "You go ahead, I'll start cleaning up the boat."

About an hour later, Bull was finishing his cleaning chore and saw the new yacht docking in a vacant slip nearby. He couldn't help but feel envious when he saw Tommy on the bow of the awesome boat, tying dock lines. Bull walked over to be friendly and to lend a hand. A heavyset middle-aged man standing at the stern threw him a line and Bull cleated it to the dock. A moment later, Tommy walked around the cabin, hopped down on the deck and secured the other stern line. "Nice rig, huh?" he commented to Bull.

The captain, a slightly younger and thinner man than the other, shut off the engines and spoke in a thick Long Island accent, "Get the spring lines, Hector."

Tommy looked up at him and said, "I've already tied the spring lines, Mr. Reno. You're all set."

The captain looked at the lines with surprise, "I'll be damned, Tommy, you're fast. It usually takes Hector and me a half-hour to get her tied."

Bull was amazed at how quickly Tommy had gotten to know the strangers . . . already on a first name basis. But then, Tommy has always been a fast operator, he thought. The salon door slid open, and two gorgeous women emerged. The dark haired beauties were much younger than the two men . . . closer to Tommy's age. Mr. Reno came down from the bridge and gave his new friend a pat on the back, "Thanks for your help, Tommy, and I want to take you up on your offer to go fishing with us tomorrow. Right now, though, we need to get these ladies over to the motel. I know they're ready to get off this boat for a few days."

Bull remarked as he and Tommy left the marina, "So, it looks like you got yourself a new ride for tomorrow."

"Yeah, man! That boat is bad to the bone; never been fished! Tomorrow's the trial. If we raise several marlin, the builder is sending a film crew down here to document how well she fishes."

"Sounds like Sid and I are gonna have some stiff competition out there tomorrow."

"You bet your ass. This is my big chance. I'm gonna try to talk these guys into hiring me on full-time. They don't know shit about catching marlin. The only place they've fished is Montauk Point, mostly for tuna."

The following day, fishing was much better. Ocean currents had brought in cooler water which made the billfish more eager to take the bait. The top boat was flying fifteen flags. The new boat was flying eleven. The 'Grand Slam' had nine. Tommy had adequately proven his worth to the newcomers, and they offered him a job.

Sid had taken his party to the airport to catch their evening flight home, and Bull was invited aboard the "Naughty Gal" to celebrate their good catch. Over cocktails, he learned quite a bit about Mr. Reno and his friends. He had just taken delivery of the boat a few days ago. He planned to move it up the coast to Long Island in a couple of months. That is where he lived and owned a box factory.

"A box factory?" Tommy had asked thinking his new employer surely must be in some more glamorous profession.

"Think about it, young man," his convincing executive nature came through as Mr. Reno pointed his index finger at Tommy and said, "Almost everything you buy comes in a box. Your shoes come in a box. Hats come in a box. Even when you die, they put you in a box! Everybody uses boxes. Hey, I know boxes; you know fishing; Hector, there, he knows engines." The surly Hector sat uninterested, drinking straight bourbon over ice. He was Mr. Reno's chief mechanic in charge of the box company's fleet of trucks. Because of his knowledge of diesel engines, he had accompanied his employer on the trip across the Gulf.

Tommy said, "Speaking of fishing, Boss, we need to get this boat into the tournaments. You could win some big money with this fast rig and I know every inlet up and down the east coast."

With a quick glance toward Hector, Mr. Reno answered, "So you know all the inlets, huh?"

"Yes, sir! I can take this baby anywhere you want." At this remark, the stone-faced Hector seemed to come alive as a faint smile took shape. He returned Mr. Reno's look, as if they were thinking the same thing. . . as if they were in cahoots.

"We'll, I'm glad to hear that," Mr. Reno remarked. Tommy had no reason to believe these guys had any other interest in him other than fishing. Bull, though, was somewhat suspicious of them. He felt an undercurrent of dishonesty.

Over the next few weeks, to Bull's chagrin, he found himself competing with Tommy in the fishing grounds. Mr. Reno had long since returned to Long Island, but he often sent customers down for Tommy to take fishing aboard the 'Naughty Gal'. Bull could not help feeling jealous of his rival, who had made an overnight transition from mate to captain. The new status had gone to Tommy's head. He hired a teenage Mexican boy named Carlos to work as mate. He ordered Carlos around all day, and did very little work himself. The poor boy was overwhelmed with long hours of cleaning and polishing, but he did not complain.

Tommy lived aboard the boat, so Bull could not avoid seeing him every day. It was not unusual to see a young Mexican girl leaving his cabin early in the morning. Hardly ever the same girl twice. Tommy had bragged about how cheap it was to get 'laid' in Mexico.

By the first of May, Bull was ready for their departure on the following Thursday. He was yearning to be home and in the arms of his waiting future bride. Romance during their time apart had been limited to telephone conversations and the love notes they exchanged. On several occasions, Bull had sent a trinket of jewelry made by one of the local artisans. Recently, he had sent the loveliest gift of all. It came from the Mexican silver mines, a braided necklace with a heart-shaped locket inscribed, *without you, days seem like weeks.*

With their wedding date fast approaching, the bride-to-be was growing understandably anxious, worrying something might happen to delay his return. Kelly knew from experience boats can be unpredictable, and break-downs never occur at a convenient time.

Three-thirty Thursday morning, the 'Grand Slam' was preparing to depart for the return trip home. Sid fired up the engines and Bull jumped onto the dock to release their lines. He thought he heard someone call his name; or maybe he didn't. It was such a muffled and distant sound. There it was again, accompanied by pounding and knocking. Walking toward the commotion, he soon discovered its source . . . the 'Naughty Gal'. He found Tommy in the engine room where he had been trapped all night. By accident Tommy had discovered a flaw in the boat's design. Before turning in, he had gone below to check the engine oil levels, since he had a fishing trip the next morning. Apparently, the engine hatch did not lock open properly and fell shut. This allowed the cabin door to swing open preventing Tommy from lifting the hatch. There was no way out until someone closed the door. As Bull lifted the hatch, Tommy emerged mad as a hornet, "I'm gonna call that damn Donnie Wood and tell that son-of-a-bitch he caused me to spend the whole friggin' night in the goddamn engine room!" Picking up a pack of cigarettes and lighting one up, he continued raging, "Trapped in there with no goddamn cigarettes!"

In the days that followed, Bull and Sid laughed about the predicament many times, recalling the sight of a humiliated Tommy standing on the dock in his underwear, smoking cigarettes like there would be no tomorrow. As the 'Grand Slam' left the dock, Bull had shouted, "You just missed the perfect chance to kick the habit."

"Kiss my ass!" came Tommy's simple reply, his standard response to any comments he found annoying.

Back at home on the Outer Banks, Bull, like most young grooms, grew nervous as the wedding day neared. But standing at the alter, his jitters turned to joy as he watched his beautiful bride approach. The happy couple stood before the minister, as the organist faded the traditional march to a close. Kelly was somewhat disappointed because rain had ruined their plans for a beautiful garden ceremony by the Sullivan's pool. The wedding was taking place down the street in the church where Bull had been christened as a child. The chapel was filled with the Sullivan's guests, although there was good attendance by Kelly's friends and family from Roanoke Island. Captain Sid had cleared his fishing calendar so he and Mrs. Hilton could attend. Cap'n Willie and Miz Bitsy rode with them. And, as it turned out, the storm responsible for bringing the rain enabled many of Bull's fellow mates to attend the ceremony as well.

After honeymooning in Florida, the newlyweds moved into the house Kelly owned at Wanchese. The young couple seemed to have everything going for them. Bull loved his work, and Kelly enjoyed her free summer days. Several weeks passed. Being a wife and preparing for the birth of their child kept her contentedly busy.

32

Kelly's pregnancy had been trouble free until she became concerned when her ankles were continually swollen. At her next checkup, lab tests revealed blood in her urine and there was an increase in blood pressure. The doctor said these were symptoms of pre-eclampsia, a disorder of pregnancy in which the mother's blood pressure rises and there is excess fluid in her body. The doctor asked if she had experienced headaches, blurred vision, or nausea, to which she answered, no. He also asked if she had any kidney problems; again, she replied, no. She had never been treated for any illnesses except childhood measles. The doctor decided, since her case was mild and she felt perfectly well, she could go about her normal activities. He reminded her not to miss any prenatal checkups, so they could detect any change in her condition early.

It was that night, after the visit to the doctor, she first felt the baby move. Bull was already asleep. She woke him up so he could feel it too, but the baby did not move again. Bull said, "He's gone back to sleep . . . exactly what I'm about to do."

"What makes you so sure it's a boy?" she teased.

It was also that night she first had a dreadful dream, a recurring nightmare that would disturb her repeatedly. She interpreted it as an unwelcome prophecy of something so unthinkable she dared not mention it to anyone, for fear it might come true. Over the next few weeks, the same nightmare returned with such regularity Kelly would not allow herself to sleep at night. Bull became concerned about his wife's restlessness, but she convinced him it was a normal part of being pregnant. When she woke up a few nights later, screaming and nearly scaring him to death, he insisted on knowing what was wrong with her. Placing Bull's hand on her stomach so he could feel their baby kicking, she assured him it was nothing; she had only experienced a bad dream, which was not uncommon during this stage of pregnancy. Bull believed her, and before long he drifted back to sleep, unaware she lay there still agonizing over the vivid scenes from her dream.

She had just relived the dreadful memory of Jimmy's death. Once again, she saw her entangled husband pulled overboard and dragged away by the marlin. The scene in her mind was so realistic she could feel the sun on her face and taste the salt on her lips. She had watched once more in horror as Jimmy struggled to the surface to grab a breath of air. Only the face that surfaced was not Jimmy's . . . it was the face of a child. A young boy she did not recognize . . . . looking straight at her and pleading, 'Mommy, Mommy, please help me!' The unnerving experience left her with a premonition of a terrible fate awaiting her unborn child.

In the days that follwed Bull noticed how Kelly had become aloof and at times seemed a million miles away, deep in thought. Trying to think of a way to cheer her up, he suggested they have a 4th of July cook-out at their house. "It'll be no problem for you at all, Honey. I'll do most of the work," he said, and she agreed half-heartedly.

Down in Cancun, Tommy was docking the 'Naughty Gal' after a disappointing day of fishing with Mr. Reno and a couple of his associates. After apologizing for the slow action, Tommy said, "Boss, this time of year, the boat needs to be in Carolina. We should be fishing the tournaments."

"I have plans to take some very important customers fishing over fourth of July weekend. Can you have the boat up there by then?"

Tommy thought for a minute, "That'll be cutting it close, but this baby can make it." Sounding convinced, Mr. Reno told Tommy and his mate Carlos they it would be possible for them to leave right away, as soon as Hector serviced the engines. Tommy and Carlos went out immediately to pick up provisions for their journey. When they returned, Hector said, "Everything will be ready as soon as we pour fresh oil into the engines. Except, I found a problem with the auxiliary generator; you cannot use it."

"The primary gen set is OK, isn't it?" asked Tommy.

"Yeah, that one is fine, but you cannot use the auxiliary until I get parts to fix it. The battery cable has been disconnected. Don't screw around with it, you understand?"

"No problem, Hector," said Tommy, "you can fix it when I get to Pirate's Cove." Tommy and Carlos soon departed.

A few days later, their journey nearly completed, the 'Naughty Gal' approached Nags Head. Tommy spotted another boat in the distance, returning from the fishing grounds. At the angle they were running, he knew their paths would intersect just south of the inlet. Tommy was hoping it would be the 'Grand Slam', but it turned out to be 'Bushwhacker'. Knowing Stormy would not recognize his boat, Tommy decided to have a little fun with him. He pushed up his throttle just enough to assure the 'Naughty Gal' would get there first.

Stormy, of course, saw the flashy boat and thought it was just another transient heading up the waterway. However, when the 'Naughty Gal' took a short cut to the inlet, unmarked by buoys, about which only local captains knew, Stormy keyed his two-way radio microphone, "Are you on here, 'Naughty Gal'?"

"Hey, Stormy! What do you think of my new ride?" came a cocky reply.

"Who've I got up ahead there?"

"Tommy, Tommy Wilson."

"Tommy? Well I'll be a monkey's uncle. Got yourself a fancy ride there . . . you working for an oil sheik or something?"

"Naw, I'm running her for a fella up in New York. He owns a big box factory. We're gonna hit the tournament circuit."

"What's she got in her?"

"A pair of 12-cylinder diesels. I'm making thirty-two knots right now, but she'll do forty-five top end." Tommy couldn't resist a demonstration. He unleashed all her power and quickly put distance between him and Stormy.

His young Mexican companion, Carlos was caught up in the excitement and yelled, "Let her eat, let her eat!" He was beginning to pick up some of his captain's slang expressions.

Blasting under the bridge Tommy saw a boat up ahead. It looked like an outboard puttering along on the edge of the channel. No problem, he thought, I'll just blow by him. He did not realize, until it was too late, it was actually a 24-foot Coast Guard vessel with a disabled boat in tow. "Holy shit!" Tommy exclaimed, realizing his mistake, but it was too late to slow down now. As he zoomed past, one of the 'coasties' gave him an angry glare but did not signal for him to stop. Tommy could only hope nothing would ever come of it.

Once he and Carlos got the boat settled into the slip at Pirate's Cove, Larry came by to say hello and get a better look at the glitzy yacht. Tommy gave him a tour and just as the two of them were coming out of the engine room, Mr. Reno showed up. He bellowed, "What the hell is this, an open house?!"

"No problem, Mr. Reno," said Tommy, shocked by the owner's reaction, "just showing the boat to one of my old buddies, that's all."

"Yes sir, this is one bad boat!" said Larry, trying to be nice, yet confounded by the owner's unfriendliness. Feeling embarrassed, Larry said, "Tommy, I'll talk to you later on tonight," and quickly left.

"Just remember, I like my privacy, Tommy," said Mr Reno as he and Hector marched into the salon. "Don't turn this into a damn showboat." Then, very businesslike, he handed envelopes to Tommy and Carlos containing their month's pay and said in a gentler tone, "Nice job getting the 'Naughty Gal' here on time. There's a little bonus in there for each of you."

"Thank you sir, I'm sorry about Larry," said Tommy, "I promise you it won't happen again."

"Fine, Tommy, just so we understand each other," said Mr. Reno, reaching into his pocket, withdrawing a fat roll of folded money. "I want you and Carlos to have dinner on me," handing Tommy a couple hundred dollar bills, "and get a room someplace. Hector and I are staying on board with our guests tonight. We'll probably be up late, so don't bother waking us till we reach the fishing grounds. Is that understood?"

"Sure, boss, whatever you say."

Tommy and Carlos packed their overnight bags and quickly left. Mr Reno closed the cabin door behind them and breathed a sigh of relief. Hector went into the engine room and returned a moment later, saying, "It's all here; hasn't been touched! That idiot captain you hired never suspected a thing."

Mr. Reno smiled with satisfaction saying, "That's why I hired him. He don't give a shit about anything but fishing and fucking."

Hector sneered, "And by the time those two get back tomorrow morning, we'll be long gone with the candy," he laughed deviously.

The next morning, following his instructions, Tommy and Carlos cast off the lines and departed with the fleet. Tommy was proud to show off his new status to the other captains and mates, especially those who had ridiculed him in the past. His only regret was the 'Grand Slam' remained at the dock today. Sid made it a practice to always take the 4th of July off to be with his family. That is why Bull had planned a picnic on that day.

With his boat's swift speed, Tommy easily outdistanced the others and would be first to reach blue water. After making the forty-mile run to the Gulf Stream, Tommy slowed down to trolling speed and started dropping the outriggers into position. He thought it was peculiar not to have seen any sign of Mr. Reno or his guests, but he reasoned, "They must have partied all night long." Tommy was unaware Carlos had found a message which had fallen from the salon door earlier. The young Mexican mate had unlocked the cabin to retrieve the rods and reels. He noticed a piece of paper on the floor in the doorway, but since he could not read English, he thought nothing of it, and placed it on the table.

Tommy shouted down to the mate, "Let the boss know we're here!"

Carlos went inside and knocked on the stateroom door. He heard no reply. He knocked on the two guest salon doors. Likewise, no response. He opened all three doors and discovered the beds had not been slept in. Realizing the paper he had found on the floor must have been a message, the dumbfounded boy came yelling from the cabin, in his native tongue, "Aqui no hay nadie! . . . there's no body here!" He promptly handed the note to Tommy:

> *Sorry Tommy, urgent business came up.*
> *Had to leave for New York. Will call you in couple of days.*
>
> *Signed, Mr. Reno.*

"Son of a bitch!" the irritated Tommy exploded into a tantrum hitting his fist on the chair, and yanking the outriggers back into the upright position.

Carlos asked sheepishly, "Does 'dis mean no fish today, boss?"

"Hell no! No fish today!" he mocked, "get those damn lines in!"

For their 4th of July picnic, Bull and Kelly had invited their parents as well as Larry, Heather and a few other friends. The Sullivans were first to arrive, and immediately Kelly's spirits lifted. She had not seen Diane and Brad since the wedding. When her own parents, the Fishers, showed up with a bushel of just steamed crabs, she started acting more like her old self again. Bull took charge of grilling fresh tuna steaks, and Kelly joked to Heather, "I can't get Bull to make toast in the kitchen, but when it comes to cooking fish on the grill, he's a master chef."

"Ouch!" shrieked Bull as he jumped back from the flames.

Larry cautioned, "Careful Bull, you'll singe your eyebrows!"

Heather joked, "He only likes cooking when there's danger involved."

They were really having a good time until Larry said to Bull, as he handed him a beer, "Guess who I saw on the dock late yesterday."

"Give me a hint."

"Well, his initials are . . . Tommy . . . Wilson."

"What's that asshole doing back here?" asked Bull, obviously not thrilled.

"He's running a private boat, a 65-foot Donnie Woods. It is something else!"

"Yeah, Yeah. I've seen it, 'Naughty Gal'. He got hooked up with it down in Mexico."

"I'm surprised you didn't notice it at the marina yesterday."

"I must have left before he got there . . . to tell you the truth, Larry, I've not been hanging around the marina much lately after I finish work. Kelly's not been feeling well, so I've been coming straight home."

Through the sliding glass doors, Larry and Bull could see Kelly standing next to her mother at the kitchen counter helping prepare a potato salad. They were chatting with Diane, who was at the table tossing the garden salad. Seeing the women laugh, Bull assumed his mother had made one of her amusing wisecracks. It was obvious where Kelly got her good looks; mother and daughter shared the same unforgettable smile. Larry commented, "You could have fooled me, Kelly appears to be doing fine now."

"Yeah, she looks great doesn't she?" Bull smiled.

"Yeah, well anyway," Larry continued, "Tommy gave me a tour of the boat . . . that is one sweet machine. When we were coming out of the engine room, his boss showed up and gave him holy hell for showing me around. The guy was a real jerk."

Bull sighed, "Well, he and Tommy ought to make a good team. Sounds like they deserve each other!"

Kelly came out onto the deck, asking, "Honey, is the tuna ready? Everything else is."

"Yes, dear, dinner is served."

At the end of the day, as the sun sank behind the trees, Brad and Diane helped clean up and said their goodbye's. Bull invited them to go see the fireworks at Kitty Hawk, but his mother said she was looking forward to a quiet evening in their recently purchased condo at Pirate's Cove. This would be their first night there. "We'll be able to comfortably watch the fireworks from a distance, on our balcony," she said, "but thank you for inviting us."

Barbara went inside to help with the final clean up. Bull and the others were still out on the deck. As the mother and daughter stood together in front of the kitchen sink, washing and drying the serving bowls, Kelly asked, "Mama, are you and Daddy going with us to see the fireworks?"

"No, I don't think so Kel, your daddy wants to get home soon. He has to be up at three AM, you know." Handing a dish to Kelly for her to dry, she commented, "Kel, it's obvious Bull's parents think the world of you."

"Yes, Mama, the Sullivans have been so kind to me. I thought they would be very upset by us having a baby coming so soon, but his parents say they want to help us. After the baby comes, they want me to live with them so I can finish medical school." Kelly placed the dried dish in the cabinet and then added, "Diane even says she'll hire a nanny, can you believe that?"

"Well, I suppose they're determined to have another doctor in the family, and it looks to me like you're their only chance, unless Bull goes back to school."

"They might as well forget about Bull ever returning to medical school. He says he can't stand being around sick people," Kelly laughed. "He may return to college someday, but he'll never become a doctor of medicine. Right now, his goal in life is to run his own charter boat."

"Dear, have you ever wondered if the Sullivans may be the ones paying your way to college?" asked her mother.

"Sure, the thought has crossed my mind. But don't you think they would have told me by now? They're not the type to keep secrets from a family member."

That comment about keeping secrets from a family member pierced Barbara's conscience like a knife. She felt compelled to confess who her daughter's real father was. She walked across the kitchen, closed the door, and turned to Kelly, "Kel, I've had something on my mind lately I've wanted to discuss with you."

"Discuss what, Mama?"

"Well, I'm not sure just how to begin."

Having no idea what her mother could be referring to, Kelly immediately assumed the worst . . . one of her parents must be sick. "Are you OK, Mama?" Kelly asked with concern.

"Oh, yes, Kel, I'm fine."

"What about Daddy?"

"He's fine too, really." Her mother's words of assurance did not concur with the look of uncertainty on her face, and Kelly was puzzled. Then, remembering her promise to Charlie, Barbara hesitated, not knowing what to say to her daughter.

Their conversation was interrupted when Bull opened the kitchen door and said, "Honey, the others are leaving to see the fireworks over on Jockey's Ridge. Are you about ready to go?"

Kelly looked at her mother, who said, "Don't let me keep you, Dear. We can talk later. It's really nothing important anyway. Run along now and go with your friends. I'll lock the house for you," she smiled.

When they drove past Pirate's Cove on the way to Jockey's Ridge, Bull looked across the harbor and saw the 'Naughty Gal'. "Larry's right, that boat is something else," he commented to his wife.

Meanwhile, Tommy was sitting up at the raw bar getting reacquainted with his old friends, and bragging about how he had made the trip from Cancun to Nags Head in record time. Then, leaning toward the bartender said, "Dave, you won't believe what happened to me today . . . "

Tommy left the bar around ten-thirty with an old girlfriend on the pretense of showing her the luxurious yacht he was now running. They both knew what he really had in mind. But what Tommy did not know was, the Coast Guard wanted him for questioning. The guardsmen who were rocked by his wake yesterday had reported the incident and a trace was run on the boat's documentation. The 'Naughty Gal' had been found to belong to Anthony Reno, who had been suspected of dealing in illegal narcotics in New York. The D.E.A. had not been able to produce enough evidence to charge him. This could be the break the authorities were waiting for.

A van carrying three officers and a drug sniffing dog named Spray arrived in the parking lot. Before they got out, the driver saw Tommy and the woman coming down the dock. "Hold everything. That looks like the guy who was running the boat yesterday."

When Tommy stepped onto the boat, the guardsmen moved in. The officer in charge shouted, "Freeze! United States Coast Guard. Are you the captain of this vessel?"

Seeing three officers and a dog, Tommy sneered, "Wow, aren't you guys overreacting a little. All I did was throw a little wake."

"Sir, we are going to board this vessel and conduct a safety inspection and issue you a citation for reckless boat handling and failing to yield to a vessel-in-tow."

Aghast, the girlfriend he had picked up said, "I didn't do anything, I'll see you later, Tommy." They allowed her to leave.

Two officers went aboard, the other officer and the dog stood on the dock. As soon as they stepped into the cabin, they smelled the sweet aroma of marijuana and one officer said, "Somebody's been smoking grass, how much you got on board?"

"It's that stupid Mexican mate of mine. Just his own personal stash. I caught him smoking one earlier and kicked him off the boat."

"Then, you won't object to us looking around."

"Go ahead, but I tell you there's nothing here except," he opened a drawer and produced a couple of joints, "this is all that's left. You guys are not gonna charge me with this are you?"

"Spray!" When the guardsman called his name, the dog snapped into action and started working the cabin. Spray had been trained to scent cocaine. He was not locking in on anything, although he was showing much interest. One of the officers lifted the engine room hatch and Spray eagerly jumped in. Tommy didn't know what to think when the officer who followed the dog in said, "We may have something here, Joe . . . Damn! We're too late!" At that, the second officer went into the engine room, leaving the third in the cockpit to keep an eye on Tommy. The usually self-confident Tommy was getting very nervous. He strained to hear what the officers were saying.

The first officer said, "Spray is going nuts all around this generator. Problem is, someone just installed a new muffler; and look, the dog keeps coming back to it."

The second officer said, "Judging from the size of it, they could have easily stashed two or three million dollars worth of uncut Colombian in the old one. Do you want to take the captain in for questioning?"

The whole ugly picture came to Tommy's mind in an instant. He'd been had! Unwittingly, he had become a drug runner for Mr. Reno. Panicked, and only thinking of how he could escape, Tommy slammed the engine room hatch closed and threw open the cabin door, trapping the officers and dog inside, just the way he, himself, had been trapped before. Then, he struggled with the third officer and managed to push him overboard . . . making his getaway.

The fireworks celebration at Jockey's Ridge in Kitty Hawk was spectacular. Aerial bombs exploded in sync with patriotic music blasting through large speakers. Dazzling pinwheels and fountains of fire rocketed high above the Wright Brothers Monument, splashing the evening sky with brilliant colors. Bull was happy to see Kelly in high spirits. The picnic and fireworks display seemed to have done the trick; she was acting more like her old self again. They said goodnights to their friends and walked arm in arm to their car.

On the drive home, they talked about how much fun it would be to bring their children to see fireworks in the years to come. As they crossed the high-rise bridge to Roanoke Island, out of habit Bull looked over to the harbor where the charter fleet was docked. At a glance, he could tell Sid's boat looked fine. Approaching the intersection, he noticed the stoplight ahead change to green. Then suddenly, from the corner of his eye, he saw a blur of red. It was a pickup truck; the driver had failed to stop and darted into their path. The collision was unavoidable. Kelly screamed when she saw headlights coming straight toward her side of the car. Instinctively, she tried to shield her baby by turning her back to the oncoming headlights a split second before impact. The crash made horrendous sounds as metal twisted, glass shattered and tires skidded across the pavement. Finally, their crumpled car came to a stop. The smashed pickup sat only a few feet away, with steam billowing from around its engine. Bull was dazed and bleeding badly from a deep cut over his eye. Kelly applied pressure to his forehead and shouted, "Bull, are you OK?"

Although groggy, he quickly became aware of the situation. "Don't worry about me, what about you?"

Before Kelly could finish saying, "I think I'm OK," she felt a piercing pain, starting in her lower back and running up through her abdomen. She winced and held her stomach. "Oh, no, something's wrong, Bull, the baby!" He tried to release her seat belt, but there was too much pressure on it; it was in a bind. He ended up cutting it with his pocket knife. All the while Kelly repeated, "Get help, Bull! Oh, God, please don't let me lose the baby!" she prayed.

At that particular moment, there were no other cars on the road. Bull looked toward the mangled pickup that had caused the accident and saw a cellular antenna mounted on its roof. He ran to the truck. The windshield was shattered where the driver's head had hit it. The door was jammed. He ran around to the other side; it was jammed shut, too. He jumped onto the hood and kicked in the broken windshield. It was then he saw and recognized the driver, Tommy Wilson! His apparently lifeless body was slumped against the steering wheel. The floor of the pickup was littered with beer cans. Bull yelled, "You son of a bitch!" as he quickly reached for the phone and called 911. Then, remembering his parents were close by, he fumbled in his pocket for the number at their condo. His father answered. "Dad!" said his frantic son, "We've been in an accident, right here at the entrance to Pirate's Cove. Kelly's hurt! Please hurry!" Bull ran back to check on her.

She said, "Bull, it hurts, it hurts. You've got to help me get out of this car."

"I'm afraid to move you, baby. Help is on the way. I just called 911 on Tommy's phone."

"Tommy's here?"

"Yeah, he's the one who hit us. I don't think he made it."

Then they heard a dreadful thud . . . like the combustion sound a gas grill makes when you light it, only louder. Bull saw flames jumping from beneath the hood of Tommy's truck. He ran toward it to try and pull Tommy clear, but before he got there, an explosion engulfed the truck in fire. Afraid spilled gasoline might also ignite their car, Bull promptly carried his wife to safety.

By now, other cars had stopped at the scene. One of them was a Coast Guard vehicle and a couple of guardsmen were trying to extinguish the blaze. When the Sullivans arrived, Kelly was obviously in a great deal of pain. Diane placed a blanket under her head and held her hand while taking a pulse. "Where's the pain, dear?" she asked.

"In my back and stomach. I feel like I'm going to throw up, and I'm getting dizzy." The scared young woman grabbed her mother-in-law's arm and pleaded, "Please, save my baby!"

Moments later, medics arrived and immediately called for the medivac helicopter. They were suspicious Kelly may be bleeding internally which could jeopardize the life of her and the baby. Bull wanted to ride in the chopper with his wife, but the crew told him there was only enough room for the patient. Within a few minutes, he and his parents were on their way to the hospital in the Sullivan's car. Bull called the Fishers and told them what had happened. He also called Sid and informed him of the accident, "Kelly is in a helicopter on the way to the hospital and I'm with my parents on the way there now."

"What about you, Bull? Are you OK?"

"I only got a cut on the head and need a couple of stitches. They wanted to take me to the local clinic, but I insisted on going to be with Kelly."

"Take as much time off as you need, Bull. I'll find someone to fill in till you're back."

"It was Tommy Wilson who ran into us. He didn't make it."

As Bull put the cell phone down, Diane applied a clean bandage to her son's forehead and said, "Looks like you'll need quite a few stitches, Dear, that's a nasty cut."

It seemed like the ride to the hospital took forever.

The scene in the emergency room was organized panic as the gurney carrying the young woman was rushed into pre-op and the medical personnel assembled to evaluate her condition. Kelly looked critical; pale and unconscious, a tube in her nose, and an IV in each arm. A phone could be heard ringing in the background as the trauma team began assessing her injuries. The flight nurse told the doctor in charge, "She's twenty-five weeks into her pregnancy; the baby's heartbeat is sounding more distant and the mother's blood pressure is down to 80 over 40, doctor."

"We may have to take the baby to save the mother," the doctor thought out loud. "Get an OB-GYN on standby and a pediatrician here, stat!" he ordered.

A nurse behind the counter spoke up to get the doctors attention, "Dr. McCloskey, excuse me . . . Dr. Sullivan's on the phone. Your patient is his daughter-in-law."

Dr. McCloskey knew the Sullivans well. He often played golf with Brad. He hurried over and took the phone, "What the hell happened down there, Brad?"

"Looks like a drunk pulled out in front of my son and daughter-in-law, Mack. I've got you on the speaker phone. Diane and Bull are in the car with me, what's her situation?"

"We're getting her stabilized now, but she is a very sick young lady. Looks like she took quite a blow to her lower back. Abdominal girth increased significantly during the flight which, of course, indicates internal bleeding. I think she may have a ruptured aorta. We won't know for sure till we perform the exploratory Lap."

"Doctor, what about the baby?" asked Bull.

"We're hoping we won't have to deliver it, but we're calling in her OB-GYN just in case."

"Take care of our girl, Mack, we're counting on you," said Brad. "We're on our way."

The patient was prepared for surgery. The medical team worked with determined precision. Within minutes, vital monitors were connected to Kelly and her baby and the surgeon proceeded with the Laparotomy. He located the source of internal bleeding. As he suspected, it was a ruptured aorta near one of her kidneys. Once the surgeon repaired the rupture, Kelly's vital signs improved quickly. They found the patient's right kidney had suffered a severe contusion as a result of the impact. The surgeon remarked the damage looked irreparable, but he would leave the kidney intact in hopes it would heal itself. He also mentioned it should not be a real problem for her since one kidney can do the work of two.

At this point, they had not yet made the decision whether to take the baby, whose vital signs appeared normal. The real question, however, was, 'Can Kelly safely continue the pregnancy with her injuries?' The lab technician came in with the results of her blood tests. Unusually high amounts of toxins were in her system . . . as if neither kidney were functioning. Then, the OB-GYN noticed her ankles had swollen even more, which suggested a problem with renal function. Since the young woman had suffered such a severe contusion to her lower back, it was decided they should take a closer look at her other kidney; could it be both organs were injured? This is when an unexpected discovery was made . . . Kelly had only one. Her left kidney was a mere fraction of the size it should have been and apparently had never functioned since birth. Her obstetrician mentioned this might have been the reason for an early, though mild, case of pre-eclampsia. Dr. Mack said, "I believe our young lady will be in the market for a new kidney soon." The doctors all agreed the baby should be delivered now, so the OB-GYN team went into action.

Several hours later, Bull was quietly sitting in a chair by his wife's bed in ICU. Unable to sleep, he had been awake all night, listening to the monotonous pump on the artificial kidney machine and watching the steady rhythm of her heart monitor, wondering what he would say to her when she awakened. He had plenty of time to think about how they had been robbed of the opportunity to experience the natural birth of their son. Kelly had already arranged for them to take Lamaze classes. Looking on the bright side, though, at least both his wife and son survived the horrible accident. "That damned Tommy," he thought.

Several hours ago, after receiving the good news their premature grandson appeared healthy, both sets of grandparents left for the Sullivan's home to rest. They tried to convince Bull to go with them, but he would not leave his wife's bedside. A while later, he noticed a slight movement in Kelly's hand which he was holding. Slowly lifting her hand to her stomach, she realized she was no longer carrying the baby. As her eyes opened and saw Bull, she asked in a weak and anxious voice, "My baby, what happened to my baby?"

He was quick to assure her, "Our baby's fine. Don't worry, everything's going to be OK. I just saw him a little while ago."

"We have a son?"

"He's tiny, but he's perfect. Wait till you see him; he's the cutest little thing. He's in an incubator, but they say he has a strong heart. I've got a new fishing buddy," Bull said with pride as he kissed his wife.

"I want to see him," she said as she tried to get up, but she was weak and still groggy from the surgery. Kelly looked at the tubes in her arms and the machine beside her bed. As a nursing student, she knew what a dialysis machine looked like. "What's wrong with me?" she asked.

Not really wanting to tell her, Bull replied, "You're gonna be fine. The doctor will be coming around in a little while. He'll explain everything."

"No, Bull, you tell me," she demanded weakly.

Holding her hands in his, he sighed and said, "The doctors said if you hadn't turned your body to shield the baby from the crash the way you did, he would have surely died. You saved our son's life. But, in doing so, the blow to your back destroyed one of your kidneys."

"Well, that's not the end of the world, is it? Lots of people do fine with only one kidney," she said.

"That's very true, but honey, the problem is, you only had the one kidney to start with."

"What do you mean, only one kidney?"

"The doctors were just as surprised as you. Apparently, your other kidney never developed."

Sounding frightened and desperate, Kelly said, "So, what does this mean?"

"The doctor is coming by later today, and he's bringing a transplant specialist with him."

"Transplant?" she seemed shocked . . . "I want to see my baby!"

"You can't right now."

Louder, Kelly demanded, "I want to see my baby!"

A nurse came over and said, "Please calm down, Mrs. Sullivan. We'll take you to see your baby very soon, very soon. Don't worry. The doctors want you to bond with your baby as soon as possible."

The next day, Kelly was transferred to the renal unit for recovery and treatment. She had come to terms with her situation and was trying to be optimistic that a suitable donor could be found soon. She had been allowed to visit the maternity ward to see her son. Though her arms ached to hold him, she knew it was impossible until the baby was removed from the incubator. "Perhaps tomorrow," they said.

The baby was named Bradley Sullivan, IV. Kelly nicknamed him "Buddy" because it was the first thing Bull called his son, "My new fishing 'buddy'."

Bull and his mother-in-law, Barbara, happened to be in the room with her when Dr. McCloskey came by to introduce the kidney transplant specialist, who assured them Kelly was an excellent candidate for the operation. She was young, strong, and healthy. He expected she would resume a completely normal life once she received a healthy donated kidney.

At that point, Bull eagerly volunteered; however, the doctor explained, "The main problems in a kidney transplant are rejection and infection. Although immuno-suppressive drugs reduce the chance of rejection, we still like to use a donated organ matched as closely as possible to the patient by tissue and blood type."

"I understand," said Barbara.

"Are there any siblings?" asked the doctor.

"No, I only had one child, Kelly."

"Mrs. Fisher. What is your blood type?"

"I...I honestly don't know," she answered.

"Don't feel bad, lots of people don't know their blood type. I feel sure either you or her father could be a suitable donor. Perhaps, both of you are. So, of course, we would like to test both of you for compatibility before we look for other possible donors."

Eager to be approved for the procedure, Barbara said, "Doctor, can you please arrange to test me now?" She desperately hoped she would be compatible, knowing full well Charlie would not be. The doctor reached Barbara later in the afternoon while she was still at the Sullivan's home and gave her the disappointing news . . . she would not be a suitable donor. He asked her to please send Mr. Fisher in for a test the next morning.

The following afternoon, when Barbara visited her daughter in the hospital, Bull was there, too. Kelly seemed to be in much better spirits. "Hi, Mama, we just went to see little Buddy. They let me hold him. I was a little nervous at first, with those tiny IV's in his arms. I think he's grown some. I can't wait to see him again this afternoon."

"Yes, Kel, I'm sure the little fellow will be just fine. Bull's parents have already started setting up a nursery. They seem to be counting on you and the baby living there while you go to school."

"Honey, I'm afraid our son is going to be spoiled," said Bull.

Kelly smiled, "After what he's going through, he'll deserve a little special treatment. Mama, who do you think the baby looks like?"

There was a long pause before Barbara answered, "Kel, I think he looks exactly like your father."

"Daddy?" she asked in a puzzled tone. She did not see any resemblance there.

"The child has your father's eyes, and so do you."

Smiling, but not taking her seriously, Kelly asked, "Where is Daddy? Wasn't he being tested for the transplant today?"

"No . . . dear, no, he wasn't."

Bull immediately seemed a little upset, "Why not?"

Barbara was obviously getting uncomfortable and said to Bull, "Could you please let me talk to Kelly, privately, for a few minutes?"

The young couple looked at each other somewhat perplexed. "Mama, I don't think you could possibly have anything to say to me Bull couldn't hear."

"Very well, of course, you are right." She paused, then started speaking in a slow and steady tone, "My dear, you have Gene Davis' eyes, Gene *Kelly* Davis."

Those words dazed her daughter. Kelly's arms fell to her side as she asked, "What are you saying, Mama?"

Barbara sat down in the chair near the bed and confessed the long held secret identity of Kelly's true father, who never lived to see his only child. She explained how, in those days, their small close-knit town was less understanding to unwed mothers. She had run away to conceal her pregnancy and that is when she met Charlie, who was a wonderful and caring husband. She told Kelly of the promise she had made to him years ago. Even though she had wanted to tell Kelly the truth many times, she had never been able to bring herself to do it.

"This is what you were trying to tell me the other night, isn't it, Mama?"

"Yes, Dear."

To say the least, the shocking revelation left Kelly with mixed emotions: angry her mother had not told her sooner, yet glad to know the truth. She also felt compassion for Charlie, her daddy. "Where is Daddy, Mama?"

"Just outside the door, dear."

"Ask him in," Kelly nodded to Bull. Bull opened the door, and Charlie entered. There were a few emotional moments as they shared their true feelings. Charlie said he wished she had learned the truth sooner. He had not expected Barbara to keep the promise beyond Kelly's eighteenth birthday, but he hadn't brought it up himself because of his love for Barbara and his desire not to drag up any painful memories for her. Kelly hugged him and said, "You may not be my biological father, but Charlie Fisher is the only daddy I've ever had. I love you, Daddy." They hugged.

Bull spoke up with an idea, "Cap'n Willie!" The young husband looked at his wife with a glimmer of hope in his eyes and said, "Don't you see, Cap'n Willie is your biological grandfather. He may be a suitable donor."

Charlie said, "We've already thought of that. We talked with Willie last night, and he knows everything. In fact, he came in for the test this morning in my place."

Just then, the door opened and in walked the doctor with Cap'n Willie and Miz Bitsy. The doctor said, "We have very good news, young lady. Your grandfather is the perfect match, and he has agreed to be your donor."

The proud grandfather went to Kelly and gave her a big hug saying, "We're gonna have you home changing diapers in no time, my dear granddaughter."

Kelly sat in stunned silence for a few moments and then said, "Cap'n Willie, you have always been a special person in my life. I've always admired you, and now I learn we are so closely related . . . it's such a shock. And to know you are willing to be a donor and restore my health. I can't say 'thank you' enough. I love you."

Six weeks later, Bull took a few days off from work to bring Kelly and their son home from the hospital. Her body had accepted the new kidney without rejection problems, and little Buddy now exceeded five pounds.

Fortunately for the young family, the insurance company that covered Tommy's truck paid all their medical expenses. Incidentally, Mr. Reno was never charged. His lawyer claimed his client had no knowledge of his boat ever being used to smuggle contraband. If it were, it was entirely the actions of the deceased captain. Tommy was, after all, running from the Coast Guard when he crashed into Bull and Kelly.

The young family moved in with the Sullivans, just in time for Kelly to start the fall semester. As first-time grandparents, Brad and Diane were almost as excited about the baby as Kelly and Bull. Diane beamed, "This is just what this big old house needs, the pitter-patter of little feet!" They spared no expense in setting up a nursery for their new grandchild in the room across the hall from Kelly's.

During that first week home, Bull stayed with Kelly to help care for Buddy. He was a proud father and seemed to always be holding his son. Kelly lightheartedly complained, "The only chance I get to hold the baby is either when it's time to feed him, or he needs changing."

Barbara and Charlie returned to see the baby and brought with them Kelly's newly discovered grandparents, Willie and Miz Bitsy. "How's our great-grandson doing?" Willie asked.

"He's just fine, Grandad," answered Kelly.

"How's that kidney you borrowed doing?" he asked with a little laughter mixed in his voice.

"Its just fine, too," she gleamed, "I hope you haven't missed it."

"To tell you the truth, I can't even tell it's gone."

Grandma Bitsy was more truthful, "He was quite sore there for a while, but he's fine now."

At the end of the week, Bull reluctantly went back to work, leaving his wife and son in the capable care of his parents.

In the weeks that followed, Bull drove to Greenville to be with his family every chance he got. He telephoned every night and in one conversation shared something with Kelly that made her very happy. Captain Sid had decided not to return to Mexico next spring, saying by the time he paid expenses, he'd be better off staying on the Outer Banks and fishing for bluefin tuna.

Bull then said, "Someday, when I have my own boat, the three of us . . . you, me and Buddy will spend our winters chasing the sun. We'll go down to the islands. It'll be like a never ending summer for us."

Kelly replied jestfully, "Well, maybe you and Buddy can, while I stay home and work. One of us needs to bring in a paycheck," she laughed. "I must agree, though, it's nice to dream about doing that."

There was a long pause in their conversation. Kelly finally asked, "What's the matter, darling?"

"Oh, I guess I'm just feeling lonely. I wish I were there with you and Buddy right now. I've been thinking . . . maybe, I should give up fishing. When Buddy gets a little older, I won't even be able to play ball with him if I'm out fishing every day."

"Nonsense, Bull, you know you wouldn't be happy doing anything else. Besides, the holidays are almost here. You'll have almost two months off. You can play with Buddy then."

To that, Bull jokingly replied, "I think I'd rather play with Buddy's mother, now that I think about it . . . a game called chase mommy around the bedroom."

Kelly laughed, "Bull, you're terrible, but I love you anyway. Good night."

Their first few years together were truly happy. Although there had been no recurrence of Kelly's dreadful dream, she never completely erased it from her memory. Perhaps that was the reason she sometimes seemed overly protective of her son.

The Sullivans hired a nanny to care for Buddy while his mother attended classes. Kelly arranged her schedule to have Mondays free. On weekends, she and Buddy drove to Roanoke Island to be with Bull. They also stayed on the island during semester breaks and summer vacations.

When Buddy was about three years old, he discovered the beach. He loved to watch the waves roll in and frequently asked his mother to take him there. Their favorite place was the public beach access next to the beautiful Ocean Side Hotel. Bull joined them whenever he could, and together they would build sand castles, swim, and comb the beach for shells to add to Buddy's collection. It was on one of these beach outings Kelly and Bull talked about having another child. They were lying on a blanket watching Buddy play in the surf with another little boy and girl. Bull mentioned it first, saying he did not want Buddy to grow up an only child . . . the way he did.

Kelly agreed, saying, "I was an only child too, you know. Although . . . ," she couldn't help but think about Jimmy, her childhood playmate, turned husband.

"Although what?" Bull asked. Kelly seemed a million miles away as she gazed across the ocean, dotted with whitecaps, and hearing only the constant roar of the rolling surf. Bull wondered what his wife could be thinking, "Although what?" he repeated.

In that brief moment, the horrible dream flashed into her mind. The dreadful vision of a drowning child struggling for a breath of air and the haunting cry, 'Mommy, Mommy, please help me.' Kelly snapped back into reality and quickly scanned the beach to locate Buddy, making sure her son was safe.

Finally, she answered her husband, "I . . . I'm sorry, I was just thinking about Jimmy. You know, it's funny. I remember him more like a brother than a hus . . . ," she stopped short, not wanting to say or think any more about the terrible vision that had just popped into her mind. She smiled at Bull and said, "Honey, I agree. I think it's time Buddy had a little sister . . . or brother." Their conversation was interrupted by their son running up to them, yelling, "Fish on, Daddy! Fish on!" The youngster pointed to the bouncing fishing rod Bull had set up on the beach in front of them. Little Buddy reeled in the fish all by himself.

"You caught a flounder!" said his mother.

"Nice catch, son!" praised Bull.

Buddy squealed with delight. It was a small flounder which they carefully released. As Buddy watched it swim away, he said, "Bye bye, fish."

Although Buddy, whom everyone loved dearly, came as a surprise in more ways than one, next time Bull and Kelly set the perfect example for planned parenthood. They even discussed the matter with the Sullivans. Diane was thrilled with the possibility of having a granddaughter to spoil. They were all very happy when Kelly became pregnant in September . . . perfect timing; the baby was born during Kelly's summer break and named Kelly Diane Sullivan. Diane finally had her granddaughter. Bull called his daughter, "Di, my little princess".

The next few years seemed to pass quickly. Under Sid's tutorage, Bull had successfully passed the Coast Guard exam and held a USCG captain's license, although he continued to serve as mate aboard the 'Grand Slam'. Dr. Sullivan had been talking about investing in a charter boat for Bull to run. His accountant was checking to see if there would be any tax advantage for him. Bull was excited about the prospect but tried not to allow himself to get his hopes up too high. He knew his father was a shrewd investor who preferred real estate deals.

Kelly continued to be a top student in medical school. For a while, she became obsessed with trying to learn the identity of the generous benefactor who provided the funding for her education. Her grandfather, Cap'n Willie remained loyal to his promise saying, "Someday soon, my dear Kelly, I will tell you. But for now, just concentrate on getting your degree."

37

Having almost completed her residency, Kelly learned from her mother that their family practitioner, Dr. Lewis in Manteo, was looking for an associate who would eventually take over his medical practice. It had always been Kelly's dream to serve her hometown community, so she immediately scheduled an interview with him. Three days later, he called and invited her to come work with him after she completed her residency and received her doctorate from the university.

Her many years of hard work and dedication to studies were finally paying off. Kelly's dream of becoming a doctor in her hometown would soon become a reality. With medical school almost completed, Kelly looked forward to living on her beloved Roanoke Island and being with her husband every night.

Bull's dream of becoming captain of his own charter boat was also materializing. His father decided to have a new 54-foot Carolina sport fishing charter boat built. Bull would operate it for his father the first few years; then, eventually, he would buy it for himself. The boat would be constructed at Mann's Harbor in a small, but highly renowned boat yard.

One year later, the gleaming new boat, with its hull painted a distinctive rich kelly green, was christened 'Dr. Hook'. On the occasion of the boat's maiden voyage, the Sullivans drove down from Greenville to join Bull, Kelly and their children, eight-year-old Buddy and four-year-old Di, for the leisurely cruise around Roanoke Island to 'Dr. Hook's' new home at Pirate's Cove.

Like any good mother, Kelly kept a close watch on her children during the short trip. At one point, the entire group was up on the flying bridge. Brad was steering while his granddaughter sat in his lap. Bull kept a close eye on the narrow channel to make sure they did not run aground. Inquisitive young Buddy was opening every locker and investigating behind every door. Diane and Kelly were chatting, when suddenly the young mother started screaming, "Buddy! Oh, my God! Buddy get down from there!" The child could not hear her shouting over the loud roar of the engine exhausts. Unnoticed, little Buddy had climbed down from the bridge and was in the cockpit alone. He was leaning over the stern with his feet dangling above the deck, watching the water race from beneath the boat. The boy had an unusual fascination with boat wakes. He loved to watch the turbulent water rush swiftly from beneath the hull, curling up into a frothy white v-formation that seemed to chase the boat. It was such a sharp contrast from the color of the ocean, the boy had once asked his father why the boat made the water turn white, like milk.

Kelly scurried down the ladder screaming, "Buddy! Get down right now!"

She rescued her son and scolded him, "Buddy, that was very dangerous! Don't you ever hang over the boat like that again!"

"I wasn't going to fall over, Mom. I was holding on," Buddy protested.

"The boat could have hit a wake! You could have easily fallen overboard!" Kelly continued her lecture, "We have a new rule now, Buddy. When you're in this cockpit, you keep your feet flat on the deck; that goes for everyone. No more hanging over the side! Is that understood?"

"Yes, ma'am," Buddy pouted as he went stomping into the cabin.

Then, Kelly looked up at Bull and said, "We should make the kids wear life jackets when they're on the boat." Even though Bull thought Kelly was slightly over reacting, he replied, "Sure, honey, whatever you say."

Not much was said for the next few minutes. The Sullivans were a little surprised by Kelly's maternal outburst; yet, at the same time, Diane was proud of Kelly's ability to assert her authority when it came to keeping her children safe.

A few minutes later, Bull adeptly maneuvered his new boat into the slip without touching a single piling. Captain Sid and several other friends were on the dock to welcome the newest boat in the charter fleet. Among the well wishers eager to see their new boat, was Kelly's grandfather, Cap'n Willie. The open house on the boat lasted for the rest of the afternoon.

Midway through the celebration, Cap'n Willie said his goodbyes; saying he must get home to Bitsy. Before Willie left, Bull invited him to go along on the fishing trip the next day, and he had accepted. Kelly got off the boat and walked with Willie down the dock toward his old truck. "How is Grandma Bitsy doing?" she asked.

"You know, she's recovering from knee surgery and I don't like to leave her too long. I'm gonna get her sister to stay with her tomorrow while I go on your fishing trip." He smiled at Kelly and added, "Could be my last chance to see the Gulf Stream, I'm not getting any younger, you know."

"Oh, Grandpa Willie, don't talk like that. Tell Grandma Bitsy I'll visit her again real soon. I want to thank her again for the pictures of my father."

"You bear a remarkable resemblance to him, I guess that's why your mother named you Kelly when you were born. Bitsy and I had always thought of you as our granddaughter, even before we found out for sure."

Halfway down the long dock, they stopped for Willie to rest on a bench. He said, "Kelly, your grandmother and I are so proud of what you have accomplished. I know you've seen your share of whitecaps . . . losing a father and a husband to the sea; and that close call you had when little Buddy was born; but, look at you now with a fine family and promising career." With a chuckle, he added, "And, I know for a fact you've got a good kidney; I never had a minute's trouble with it."

"Grandpa Willie, you're right. I do have a lot to be thankful for.

And I owe a special thanks to my benefactor who made it possible for me to attend medical school, if you ever decide to tell me who it is."

"Captain Dan."

"What about Captain Dan?" asked Kelly, wondering why he would change the subject.

"I think it's time you knew. Dan Parker, he's the one you can thank."

Kelly was astonished by this revelation. For years she had thought Bull's parents were somehow responsible. "I don't understand why. Why would Captain Dan do something like that for me?"

"Y'see, granddaughter, it was Dan's idea to spice up the tournament for the mates by offering the fifty-thousand dollar Top Mate Grander Prize. You know how well he has always gotten along with most of the mates; he just wanted to do something special for them."

"I didn't know Dan had that kind of money to throw around."

"He didn't," answered Willie. "He got together with an insurance agent up in Virginia and took out a special policy. Insurance would have paid the fifty-thousand dollar prize if a grander *were* caught."

"You mean you can buy an insurance policy to cover a prize like that?"

"Sure. It's done all the time in fishing tournaments for anyone who sets a new state record. They do the same thing in golf tournaments, to cover a special hole-in-one prize," Willie took off his glasses and started cleaning them, continuing his explanation. "Dan told me the premium cost him around a thousand dollars, and the insurance agency bartered it out for advertising on his radio station. So, y'see, it really didn't cost him any cash to offer the prize . . . just some radio time. Good arrangement, don't you think?"

"Yeah, but what about the college tuition money? Where did it come from?"

"From the money he won, taking first place in the tournament. Between that and the calcutta prizes, Dan ended up with over $450,000! But, under the circumstances, it was a bitter-sweet victory for him. With Dan being the generous person he is, he decided to set aside $50,000 of the winnings to memorialize Jimmy in some way. He told Sid and me about it, but he wanted to remain anonymous and asked if we had any ideas. Sid mentioned he had heard you say your dream was to become a doctor. It was Sid who suggested setting up the scholarship fund. Dan couldn't think of a better way to use the money. He was happy when you accepted, since he's a big ECU Pirate's booster . . . that's why he named his boat 'Carolina Pirate'."

Kelly said, "Dan's son is a student there now, I've seen him on campus."

"As I recall, with the prize money, Dan funded your scholarship, opened an annuity for his son's college tuition, gave his mate a new pickup plus a cash bonus, and with the balance he and his wife traded up to a new boat." Willie slapped his hands on his knees and concluded, "So, my dear, like the man on the radio says . . .*and now, you know the rest of the story.*"

She hugged the kindly old gentleman and said, "I love you, Grandpa Willie, and thank you for being such an important part of our lives. And I owe a debt of gratitude to Sid and Dan."

Meanwhile, back on the boat, Bull and his father were talking about where they would try fishing tomorrow. Bull's first official charter was scheduled for two days later, but he was anxious to see if the new boat would raise fish as well as the 'Grand Slam'. As a shake down trip, the Sullivan family planned to go fun fishing. Brad and Diane had invited a couple of their hospital associates to join them. Kelly and little Buddy would be going too, on the eight year old's first trip to the Gulf Stream. Little sis, Di, would spend tonight and all day tomorrow with Kelly's mother, Barbara. Bull was thrilled Cap'n Willie was also going along for the ride. After all, he felt he owed it all to Willie. Bull often commented, "If it wasn't for Cap'n Willie, I'd never have gotten this far."

Bull's good friend, Larry, would serve as mate aboard the 'Dr. Hook'. Larry and his brother were partners in a tackle shop at Whalebone Junction. Lately, though, he had felt like a fish out of water, itching to return to the ocean, as mating and fishing were his first loves.

At home that evening by nine o'clock, little Buddy was fast asleep and his sister, Di, was at her grandmother's. Kelly and Bull were cuddled in their bed, talking softly. Kelly said, "I feel bad about getting after Buddy the way I did today; but, honestly, that child has no fear; and lately, I've noticed a stubborn streak about him . . . I wonder which side of the family he gets it from."

"Well, he learned a good lesson today."

"I hope so, he nearly scared me to death . . . I couldn't live if something happened to one of my children," she said softer still.

Bull lifted her chin and tried to erase the sad thought with a tender kiss followed by a reassurance he would never let anything bad happen to their children. Then, optimistically, he said, "You know, we have a lot to be happy about. Two great kids and careers we love . . ."

Kelly broke in, "I still can't get over it was Captain Dan . . . Dan's prize money and Sid's idea that paid my tuition. Until then, my becoming a doctor was only a dream."

Bull affectionately drew closer to his wife, and just before their lips touched, he whispered, "My dream came true the day I married you." They made love and fell asleep with their bodies entwined.

38

The weather was ideal to enjoy a fun day of offshore fishing with family and friends aboard the 'Dr. Hook'. At seven o'clock, Little Buddy was eager to get going as soon as the party arrived at the boat. Everyone aboard enjoyed a light breakfast of coffee cake and fruit salad prepared by Kelly.

Running through the inlet, all the men were on the flying bridge with Bull. Grandpa Willie said, "Now you got me up here, I reckon this is where I'll stay all day. I don't think an old man like me should be getting up and down that ladder."

Brad said, "What are you talking about Cap'n Willie, you got lots of good fishing years left in you yet."

"Ha, I'm so old I don't even buy green bananas." They all laughed.

Bull said, "I know you didn't bring any bananas!"

Larry asked, "How does the boat handle, Bull?"

"Like a dream, very responsive."

As they left sight of land and the ocean water began to turn clear, Kelly thought how wonderful to finally be out here again. It was hard to believe, but this was her first trip to the Gulf Stream since Jimmy's accident almost ten years ago.

Cruising at thirty knots, 'Dr. Hook' was fast for a boat its size. Although they had left the dock almost an hour after most of the fleet, they started fishing about the same time as everyone else. In only four hours of trolling, the group saw lots of action. Six gaffer dolphin and three yellowfin tuna were boated. Bull was especially pleased to have seen several white marlin in the baits. Two of them were caught, tagged, and released. The highlight of the day was when little Buddy caught one. With his mother coaching, the eight-year-old dropped the bait back to the trailing marlin and hooked the fish like a pro. He was full of himself with pride.

It was a proud time for the captain. The new boat had performed well and amply proven its ability to raise marlin. With three marlin flags flying and meat in the fish box, the group decided to leave early enough to finish the day by tasting the fruits of their efforts--- fresh tuna steaks on the grill. The sleek craft raced across the gentle swells on its way back to Nags Head. After a busy day on the water, little Buddy was getting somewhat rambunctious, and his understanding mother knew he needed a nap. In anticipation of the fishing trip, the youngster could hardly sleep the night before. In fact, she was tired herself and wanted to rest during the trip home. She offered to lie down beside him, but typical for a boy his age, it took some persuading and compromising for him to agree. He wanted to remove his life jacket, which against her good judgement, she allowed.

Within minutes, she was fast asleep, yet Buddy remained wide awake. He slipped out of the stateroom, sneaked past Willie who was resting on the sofa, and did exactly what his mother had told him not to do the day before. The over zealous youth ran across the cockpit and leaned over the transom with his feet in the air. He stretched to get a better look, only this time, the child slipped and overboard he went! In the wink of an eye, he was swallowed by the churning wake!

Helplessly, the dazed eight-year-old sank deeper as breathless seconds ticked away before he somehow managed to swim to the surface. Gasping for air, the terrified child cried out for help, but his pleas went unheard. Everyone was up on the bridge with Bull, under the assumption the youth was asleep, safe and sound, in the cabin below.

Treading water, ten miles from shore and with no life jacket, the boy tried to be brave and remember the survival swimming technique his parents had taught him. It was hard to do while trying not to think about the hammerhead shark he had seen earlier in the day. His eyes were glued to the vanishing boat, hoping it would soon come back to rescue him, but the drone of the diesel engines continued to fade in the distance. Surrounded by vast ocean, the child desperately cried for his mother.

Asleep in the cabin, she was roused for some unexplained reason, by a voice calling her name. Faint at first, but becoming clearer, she soon recognized the voice from her past as someone dear. It was Jimmy! Her long lost first husband, pleading, "Kelly, Turn back! Save Buddy!"

The startled mother opened her eyes, realized her son was not there beside her, and feared the dream was true. She called his name, "Buddy!" A quick search determined he was nowhere in the cabin; his life jacket lay on the floor beside the bed. She shouted up to the bridge, "Bull, is Buddy up there?"

"No, isn't he with you?"

"Oh my God!"

"What's the matter?"

"Turn around!" she screamed. "I can't find Buddy. He must have fallen overboard!"

Those words made Bull's heart sink to his stomach. Immediately turning 180 degrees to retrace his path, he thought this can't be happening. Just when life seemed perfect, the sea was demanding another sacrifice from a woman who had already lost her father and Jimmy to a watery grave.

The sudden turn of events alarmed everyone on board. Brad thought maybe the boy was playing hide n' seek, and they all frantically searched the boat from stem to stern. Up on the bridge with her husband, Kelly looked through teary eyes, straining to see anything up ahead, knowing it would take a miracle for such a small boy to be found in this huge expanse of open ocean. Bull called the Coast Guard on the emergency channel and also called other boats to come quickly to help search for his missing son.

After many anxious minutes, Kelly shouted hopefully, "I see something! Over there!" She pointed to a flock of sea gulls circling about a mile off their starboard bow. Bull looked at his course plotter and said, "Honey, that's pretty far from our original path. It's probably just a bunch of birds over a school of mackerel. We'd better hold this course."

Kelly grabbed the binoculars and trained her eyes on the small patch of sea beneath the birds, but saw nothing. "Maybe you're right," she said. "No, wait!" Slowly a vague shape came into view. "I see something. Something's floating! We have to check it out!"

Bull altered his course and the object soon became clearer in the lenses of Kelly's binoculars. She said, "It looks like an oblong piece of wreckage . . . and!"

"And what? What do you see?"

It took several seconds to convince herself she was not imagining the tiny figure of her son clinging to the floating board and waving frantically. She burst into screams, "It's Buddy! It's Buddy!" Everyone joined with cheers of joy! "He sees us!" she said, "he's waving!"

All Bull could say was, "Thank God! Thank God!" He was still chanting "Thank God" as he carefully maneuvered the boat along side the old chunk of floating wood which had served as his son's life raft. Words could not describe how happy they felt as the shivering, dripping wet child was rescued. Wrapped in a blanket and appearing to be none the worst for his ordeal, Buddy looked back at the make-shift raft drifting away and said, "Dad, can we take it home with us?"

Puzzled, he asked, "Why, son? It's just an old piece of drift wood."

"But, it saved my life, Dad." The boy explained, "At first, I thought it was a shark coming after me! It just floated up out of nowhere, right beside me."

"But it's only a plank from an old boat. It probably weighs a couple of hundred pounds."

Brad sided with his young grandson, "Let's go back and get it, Bull. Besides, it's a hazard to navigation out here."

The barnacle-crusted piece of old wreckage was hauled onto the deck. Bull radioed the happy outcome to the Coast Guard and the other boats who were on their way. The relieved family and friends resumed their journey home.

A few minutes later, from the helm on the bridge, Bull noticed Cap'n Willie had taken a peculiar interest in the retrieved relic. The aging captain picked up a cleaning brush and started scrubbing the fouled plank. A trace of red paint emerged from behind the years of scum and marine build-up. Larry, too, was now interested, and obligingly took over the task. Kelly came from the cabin and stood beside her grandfather, not sure of what was going on. Together they observed the paint materialize . . . into a faded, but legible letter, "L." Further cleaning revealed an "a," followed by "d,' and finally, "y," *LADY*. Cap'n Willie uttered, "I don't believe it. After all these years."

Bull rose to his feet asking Brad to take over at the helm. He hurried down the ladder and stood by his wife and Willie. They were the only three who had made the connection. But, from the way they behaved in utter astonishment, the others knew there was something very special about that chunk of wood. Larry carefully scrubbed the boat's full name into view. . . "Lady-B", Manteo, North Carolina. The three awestruck family members cried and hugged. Their lives had come full circle. A section of the old workboat's transom had resurfaced after nearly thirty years beneath the sea.

Kelly was first to speak. Teary eyed and her heart overflowing with faith and happiness, she asked her husband, "Do you believe in guardian angels, now?"

EPILOGUE

Kids have a remarkable way of rebounding. An adult who suffered an ordeal like Buddy's would probably never leave sight of land, but the boy seemed eager to go fishing again. And that is just what he did . . . two days later. His father said, "It's like falling off a horse, you gotta get right back on!" Apparently the correct therapy, because after several fishing trips, Buddy seemed to have suffered no ill effects. He was not at all afraid of the water. Of course, he would never forget what happened, but he considered his near tragedy as a big adventure.

He behaved normally at home, still full of himself . . . one minute playing with his sister, the next, yelling and fussing. But Kelly did not mind hearing them argue. It reminded her she had two healthy children, and for that, she was thankful.

At last, Bull was living his dream . . . running his own charter boat, married to his true love, and they had two great kids. Dr. Kelly Sullivan quickly gained acceptance with the patients at the clinic. There was already talk of making her a full partner.

And, as for the recurring nightmare she had been plagued by over the years . . . it never returned. On the day Buddy was rescued, a wave of peaceful assurance had passed over her. She believed her son's life had been spared for some very special purpose.